"You have to get back to work. There's been a heinous murder, and there's a murder victim who no longer has a face. Spencer, there's a face wandering around out there. If you don't get back to work, there's no hope that the murder will be solved."

Spencer's color returned, and his smirk returned. "Pinkie, you complimented me," he said. "I might pass out from shock."

I squirmed in my seat. "I didn't compliment you. I merely pointed out that you are the least incompetent of your police force. That's not saying a lot."

"You complimented me. You said I could solve the No-Face Case."

"Shut up."

"You can't take it back now," he said, interlocking his fingers behind his head. "Okay, so I'm a great cop. Tell me how sexy I am. Tell me you want me."

"You are not sexy, and I don't want you," I lied.

"You're almost naked. When you bend down, I can see the whole triple play. It's only a hiccup to a grand-slam home run. Just say the word, and I'll come up to bat."

"You gross me out."

Spencer leaned forward, studied my face for a moment, read something there, and then popped a Dorito into his mouth. "You can't blame a guy for trying," he said.

"Focus on your work, dammit. The town is going to pieces, and there's a face out there. Why isn't anybody impressed by the face?"

By Elise Sax

An Affair to Dismember
Matchpoint

Matchpoint

THE MATCHMAKER SERIES

ELISE SAX

BALLANTINE BOOKS • NEW YORK

A Ballantine Books Mass Market Original

Copyright © 2013 by Elise Sax
Excerpt from Untitled Matchmaker series novel copyright © 2013 by Elise Sax

Published in the United States by Ballantine Books, an imprint of The Random House Publishing Group, a division of Random House, Inc., New York.

BALLANTINE and the HOUSE colophon are trademarks of Random House, Inc.

This book contains an excerpt from the forthcoming untitled Matchmaker series novel by Elise Sax. This excerpt has been set for this edition only and may not reflect the final content of the forthcoming edition.

ISBN 978-0-345-53224-4
eBook ISBN 978-0-345-53225-1

Cover design: Lynn Andreozzi
Cover photograph: © George Kerrigan

Printed in the United States of America

www.ballantinebooks.com

9 8 7 6 5 4 3 2 1

Ballantine mass market edition: August 2013

For my father

Chapter 1

✦ ♥ ✦

Love is pain. Don't let anyone tell you different. You may be surprised to learn that we're in the pain business. It's true. Love eats away at you like Murray's homemade horseradish eats away at your stomach. Eats away until you cry and wonder why you wanted to find love in the first place. Eats away until you beg for mercy. But there is no mercy where love is concerned. It does what it wants, and you are powerless to stop it. So, you may have a couple of miserable clients, bubeleh. A couple miserable clients, in pain. They may even complain to you. Remind them this: pleasure and pain, they're not so far apart. Like having your hair pulled. Sometimes, in the right context, having your hair pulled isn't all that bad. It may feel a little good, even. John Schlumberger pulled my hair once, and I kind of liked it. Get used to the pain and you can enjoy the love. Get used to the pain and soon it won't feel painful at all anymore.

Lesson 64,
Matchmaking Advice from Your Grandma Zelda

"NO!"

"Don't even think about going anywhere, Gladie. You can't get away. I've got you where I want you."

"Please. I'm scared," I whimpered. My ears grew hot, and I saw little silver spots in front of my eyes. Her voice came at me in a booming echo, as if in a cave. A cave with no exit. A cave with no exit and not enough air.

Great, now I was terrified, and I was claustrophobic. I made a play for her sympathy. "Please. Let me go. Please, I want to go home," I said.

"No way." She was tall and muscular, in much better shape than I was. I hadn't exercised in months, not since I worked at the juice bar at the Phoenix Women's Gym for ten days. What was wrong with me? Would it have killed me to hop on a treadmill or at least try yoga? Yoga. Who was I kidding? One Downward-Facing Dog, and I would dislocate something important, like my spine or gallbladder.

"Don't look at me like that, Gladie. There's no way you can take me."

I gulped air. "Don't hurt me. Don't hurt me," I said.

"Gladie, at worst it will sting a little. This is bigger than the both of us. There's no going back. Look at yourself."

She turned my chair to give me a good look in the mirror. I looked just like I always did. My hair stood up in frizzy spikes around my head, mimicking my panicked mood. I shut my eyes tight.

"Fine," I said. "Fine, Bird. Just do it."

My hairdresser, Bird Gonzalez, clapped her hands together and hopped on her heels. "Oh, Gladie. Thank you, thank you. You won't be sorry. I've been wanting to do this for ages. You're going to be so happy. The Ecuadoran Erect will change your life. Straight hair, Gladie. Straight hair. You'll be a new woman."

Being a new woman wasn't entirely a bad idea. After years of moving around from one temporary job to another in one city or another, I let my Grandma Zelda convince me to settle in with her in the small mountain town of Cannes, California, and work in her matchmaking business. I wasn't a great success in my new career. So far

I had made two matches, one on my own and the other with her help. Two matches in four months didn't set any records, but Grandma said I was cooking with gas.

My personal life was going at an even slower pace. There had been a burst of interest in me a few weeks ago. My first client thought I was Angelina Jolie on a Ritz cracker, and the womanizing chief of police, Spencer Bolton, flirted with me nonstop, but then I matched my client with a clumsy waitress, and Spencer moved on to dating half the town. My hunky new neighbor, Arthur Holden, took me out a couple times, even called me his girlfriend. Then he disappeared. Not totally disappeared, but he was busy every night and day and never offered one explanation to me. I didn't know where he was going, didn't even know what he did for a living. And I didn't think I had the right to ask him.

I knew one thing for certain. I was a woman with wild, out-of-control frizzy hair. Maybe change needed to start at the top—in my case, my head.

Bird squirted Ecuadoran Erect solution into a bowl, added water, and stirred. The salon was at once filled with a noxious smell.

"It doesn't cause cancer, does it?" I asked Bird.

"Gladie, you are going to look just like Kate Hudson with boobs."

"So it doesn't cause cancer?"

Bird painted the solution onto my hair. "I don't think that was proven," she said. I held my breath and thought healthy thoughts. It was too late to change my mind. Half my head was covered in stinky Ecuadoran Erect.

"It's starting to sting," I said.

"That's normal. It will go away in an hour or two."

Two hours later, my hair was straight as a board. Dark blond hair fell flat down past my shoulders. I was unrecognizable, unless I really was Kate Hudson with boobs. Bird was thrilled with her work.

"Uh," I said.

"You have twenty-year-old hair. You know what I mean?" she squealed. "It's soft and supple and luxurious, just like you're twenty years old again."

"When I was twenty, I was growing out a pixie cut. I looked like a cotton ball after it was plugged into a light socket."

"But it was soft, right?"

"I don't know. I was scared to touch it."

I ran my hand over my new hair. It *was* soft.

"You look bitchin'," Bird said. "Men are going to chase you down the street. Oh, speaking of that, I have something for you."

She handed me a box. "Chinese tea," she explained. "Special diet tea. Imported. Shh—don't tell anyone I gave it to you. I've got a waiting list."

"Diet tea?" I sucked in my stomach.

"Don't give me that face, Gladie. You told me you wanted to lose a couple pounds. I know what you're up against in that house with your grandma and her junk food habit. The tea works. Trust me."

She was right. I had turned mushy in the four months I had been living with my french-fry-loving grandma.

My hair swished against my shoulders as I stuffed the tea into my purse. I paid Bird, emptying my bank account with the one check. Ecuadoran Erect and Chinese diet tea did not come cheap. I would have to make another match, quickly. Luckily, I was on my way to see Belinda Womble. Belinda had curly hair and heaps of disposable income. And best of all, she wanted me to match her.

BLISS DENTAL was located in the old Cannes Small Animal Hospital building on Pear Lane, just outside the historic district. Dr. Simon Dulur bought the building about twenty years ago and transformed it into a cutting-edge dental practice.

I had a phobia of all things medical. I couldn't even watch medical shows, so I never set foot in the Bliss Dental building. The idea of X-rays raised my blood pressure. The idea of a routine teeth cleaning made my gums bleed. No way was I getting near any possible root canals. Now I had no choice. Belinda Womble, the receptionist at Bliss Dental, was my new client. A job was a job, and Belinda had requested me as her matchmaker. It was my first request. Normally, clients wanted my grandma, and why wouldn't they? *She* knew what she was doing.

I had to overcome my fears and the sympathy pains I experienced every time I was near suffering or disease. Successful matchmakers didn't think they had tuberculosis every time someone near them coughed. Successful matchmakers didn't imagine they had leprosy every time their foot fell asleep.

Sure enough, two blocks away from the Bliss Dental building, a searing pain shot from my upper right bicuspid through my nerve endings and into my brain. I grimaced in agony and gripped the wheel, swerving into traffic.

I narrowly missed a Toyota Camry and a Chevy Malibu, driving my ancient Oldsmobile Cutlass Supreme up onto the sidewalk. I came to a screeching stop inches away from a fire hydrant and a group of backpackers who were walking down the street wearing tin pyramid hats and T-shirts with ALIENS, TAKE ME FIRST! written in pink neon.

I stumbled out of my car and closed the rusty door with a creak. I gripped my face, willing the pain in my tooth to subside.

"You're breaking the chakras of the path."

The head backpacker tugged at my sleeve. He was tall

and good-looking, about fifty years old, and smelled of old money. His T-shirt was tucked into perfectly tailored slacks cuffed over Prada loafers. He wagged his finger at me, his wrist wrapped in a gold Rolex watch.

"Excuse me?" I asked. The pain in my mouth cooled to a throb. The backpackers gathered in a group around us, the better to hear what their leader was saying.

"The chakras of the path. You're in the way. You're blocking the chakras and putting the Arrival in jeopardy," he said.

"The Arrival," echoed several of the backpackers.

"I'm sorry?" I said. "Did I hit you with my car?" I looked over at my Cutlass. The front bumper hung at a weird angle. That didn't mean anything. My car was built during Clinton's first term. It was a miracle it still had a bumper. I would have sworn I hadn't hit anything. Besides, nobody was bleeding, as far as I could tell.

"The energies of tomorrow," shouted one of the backpackers.

"The Arrival," the others said.

"The arrival?" I asked.

The hair on the back of my neck tingled, and my palms got sweaty. I took stock of the situation. I was surrounded. Strangers speaking in unison had me cornered between the fire hydrant and Andy Gilmore's closed hardware store. Cannes was a very small town. The only strangers were tourists who came up the mountain to hunt for antiques, sit in tea shops, and eat apple pie in the fall. We didn't get a lot of strangers wearing pyramid hats, shouting about chakras of the path and the energies of tomorrow.

"Did you hear?" the leader demanded. "You're blocking the chakras. Chakras. It's simple."

"The Arrival!" the others announced a little more forcefully.

"Terribly sorry about your chakras," I said, sweeping

the ground with the bottom of my shoe to clear away any bad chakras. "I'll just be on my way."

I enunciated each word slowly. I took two steps backward and smiled. *No sudden movements*, I thought, easing into the car. I waved goodbye, bounced off the sidewalk, and made my way toward Bliss Dental. In the rearview mirror, the backpackers were studying the spot where the Cutlass ran off the road. From their expressions, I must have flattened the path's chakras, and tomorrow's energies would come at least a few hours late.

THE BLISS Dental waiting room smelled like Lysol, dental putty impressions, and fear. Two women sat on plaid upholstered chairs, busily texting on their phones. My new client manned the front desk, separated from the waiting room by a sliding window.

Belinda was busy reading through patient files. I caught her eye and gave her a wave. She scowled and stuck her index finger up in the air, the international symbol to wait, and then pointed toward one of the plaid chairs.

I checked the time. Ten o'clock. Right on time. I had two hours before I was supposed to bring Grandma back a bucket from Chik'n Lik'n for lunch. Grandma usually wanted fried chicken after her Tuesday morning Second Chancers singles meeting, which I was missing to meet with Belinda.

I picked up an old copy of *People* magazine. I was behind on reality shows. Matchmakers-in-training don't have a lot of downtime, and my grandma didn't have cable. I was reading about a real housewife's new breasts when one of the women in the waiting room screeched.

"What a jerk. I mean, what a total jerk."

She flashed her phone at the other woman, who grabbed

it to study it longer. Whatever was on the screen made the woman's eyes bug out.

"What a jerk," echoed the second woman.

"I have never seen anything like it. Not even at the zoo."

I craned my head, but I couldn't get a good look at the phone.

"Turns out he was screwing most of the town," the first woman said.

"And telling them all he was in love with them, no doubt."

"Well, obviously. Otherwise they wouldn't go around talking about him like they were getting married."

"Men are dogs," the second woman said. "He made eyes at me, too, you know."

The first woman looked doubtful. "Me too," she said after a moment. "But I saw through his charm and good looks right down to his little mercenary heart."

I craned my head a little more, but I was still getting nothing. I was about to move seats when Belinda opened the sliding window. "Do you have an appointment?" she asked in my direction.

"Yes, ten o'clock," I said.

"With who? Dr. Dulur or Holly?"

I broke out in a sweat. I stumbled over to the sliding window. "No, Belinda. I don't want to see the dentist. My teeth are fine. No dental work needed," I said, flashing her my toothy smile.

"That's what they all say. It's called denial. I see it all the time. Whatever. It's your mouth. But there's a fifty-dollar fee for cancellations on such short notice."

I didn't have fifty dollars. All I had in my purse was three dollars, a maxed-out Visa card, a Hershey bar, two lipsticks, and a mascara wand. Besides, I didn't have a dentist appointment. What was Belinda talking about?

"Belinda, what are you talking about?" I asked. "I

don't have a dentist appointment. Don't you remember? *We* have an appointment. You and me. You called me."

Belinda squinted and leaned forward. "Gladie? Is that you?"

"Of course it's me. Who did you think it was?"

"I didn't recognize you. You don't look like yourself." She pointed at me. "It's your head. Your head is different. How did you give yourself a different head?"

"I had my hair straightened. Do I look that different?"

"You look like you got a new head. Not a Gladie head at all."

I pictured someone taking my Gladie head off my shoulders and replacing it with a non-Gladie head. Maybe having a non-Gladie head would be an improvement. I flicked my soft hair back. It swished against my shoulder, falling in a cascade, before returning elegantly to its original position. Oh, nice. It was like a commercial for bouncing and behaving hair. My Gladie head would never have done that. It would have poofed out at some weird angle with renewed frizz, making me look like the Bride of Frankenstein.

"Come on back, Gladie. We'll chat." Belinda pushed a button, and the door to the back buzzed open. She sat behind an L-shaped desk that stretched along one wall. The other walls were lined from floor to ceiling with patient files.

It smelled wonderful, not like dentistry and torture at all, but like a botanical paradise. At least twenty flowerpots covered Belinda's desk.

"Beautiful," I said. "Someone must really like you."

"Oh, these weren't gifts. I grew them. I'm a flower enthusiast."

I was honestly impressed. "My grandmother is proud of her roses, but she's never grown anything this varied and exotic."

At the mention of my grandmother, Belinda flinched and took a step back. "I'm glad you took my case, Gladie," she said. "I saw what you did for Ruth's niece, and it gave me hope for, you know, me."

I had fixed up Ruth's danger-prone grandniece, Julie, with my client, a danger-prone police sergeant. It was my one real case and a resounding success, if the cooing I heard from them in the back of the dollar movie theater last Friday was any proof.

I took a long hard look at Belinda. She and Julie had nothing in common. Julie looked like a prepubescent boy in slouchy clothes with her hair perennially in her eyes. Belinda's hair was curly but tamed in a tight bun. Her clothes were ironed and starched. Her no-nonsense, size-eighteen tan slacks met her glittery gold-and-black sweater, which was emblazoned with a lavender appliqué flower that took up most of her ample abdomen and flat chest, at about mid-thigh. Two little gold flower earrings adorned her ears, and her face was painted with thick layers of foundation and blush, her eyes draped in lavender—to match her sweater, I guessed.

"Maybe you have a police sergeant for me, too," she said.

"At least a sergeant," I said, trying to sound positive.

"Do you have pictures to show me so, you know, I can choose?"

We took a seat at her desk. "I thought I would first get to know you better, see what you're interested in," I said, taking out a notepad and a pen.

"Well, I'm looking for a man. Someone who appreciates me. And I'm losing weight! I have been drinking Chinese diet tea, and I've lost four pounds. These pants were tight on me last week. Usually I have a metabolism like sludge."

I nodded. Maybe there was something to Bird's diet tea. I promised myself to brew a cup when I got home. I had gotten soft since I moved in with my grandma. A woman could refuse only so many chili cheese fries before she caved.

"Where the hell are the brownies? Did you eat all the brownies?"

Belinda's office was invaded by a woman in a tight miniskirt and camisole. There was something off about her face, as if I was seeing her through an altered Hollywood camera lens.

"I am on a diet, Holly. Of course I didn't eat the brownies," Belinda said, clearly upset by the woman.

"Yeah, right," she sneered. Her lips were curved up unnaturally like the Joker's, pulling at her taut skin. Everything about her was tight. Her body defied gravity like it was made of wax. I caught myself staring and looked away quickly, pretending to go over my notes about Belinda's desires in a mate.

"Here they are," Holly announced, pulling a Tupperware container filled with brownies from a drawer. She took a big bite of one and tossed the container on the desk, unconcerned about resealing it and unconcerned about apologizing to Belinda. I disliked her instantly.

"That was Holly the hygienist," Belinda told me the moment Holly left the room. "She had fat from her ass put into her boobs, and she had Phil the plumber stick her with industrial Botox so her face never changes expression."

I realized my mouth was open, and I snapped it closed. "Her face has been that way for four years," Belinda continued. "When she won Sunday night bingo, her face stayed the same. Ditto the day a patient had a heart attack and died in her chair when she was flossing him. She's a class A whore, too. I don't want to tell tales, but she likes them young."

She said "young" in a conspiratorial whisper that made me lean forward to hear more. But Belinda strayed from the topic. "She doesn't need Chinese tea, that's for sure. She's got a metabolism like a hummingbird. She must eat ten times her weight. Of course, that's only about ten pounds." She found this uproariously funny and burst into hysterics. I had to slap her on the back for her to catch her breath.

When she came around, she described what she was looking for in a man, which sounded eerily similar to George Clooney. "How long do you think it will take?" she asked.

"Well, we can't rush these things. Love, I mean." It was the wrong thing to say. Belinda looked at me like I had told her Santa Claus didn't exist. "Give me a week to look through my files," I amended. "I'm sure Mr. Right is in there."

What was I saying? I didn't have files. Grandma had stacks of index cards I could pilfer and look through, but otherwise, I had no clue who to fix Belinda up with.

"Now, who do we have here? Hey, pretty lady, here for a checkup?"

I jumped three feet in the air. Dr. Simon Dulur stood in the doorway, a shiny dental instrument in his hand, pointing at me with it. The instrument was metal and long with a sharp hooked end. My eyes swirled in their sockets, and I saw stars.

"Whoa, we got a fainter! We got a fainter! Code Six!" Dr. Dulur waved his hands around and moved his head from side to side as he shouted, like a quarterback at a football game, calling the plays before the snap. He was moving the dental instrument around pretty good now, and it caught a glint of sun and shined in my eyes.

I wonder what Codes One through Five are, I thought just before I lost consciousness.

· · ·

"**THERE SHE** is. She's coming around now."

"Where am I?" I asked, but I knew exactly where I was. My body hung almost upside down in a Bliss Dental chair, and a spit cloth was draped on my chest. Dr. Dulur hung over me, his polyester shirt unbuttoned halfway to reveal a tuft of curly gray chest hair and three gold chains that seemed to float in midair as he leaned perilously close to my head. A long white scar traced a path down his right cheek. His hands were in my mouth, the scary dental instrument between his fingers, busily inspecting my teeth and gums. "Where am I?" came out muffled because my mouth was open and full of Dr. Dulur.

"Uh-oh. This is what I feared," he said.

"What are you doing?" I tried to say.

"Dr. Dulur likes to take advantage of a fainter." The voice came from somewhere to my left. "That didn't come out right," the voice said, his head appearing behind Dr. Dulur. He was young, no more than twenty. I noticed he was prematurely balding and had perfectly straight white teeth. "What I meant to say is that he likes to do as much work on you as possible while you're unconscious so you're not scared," he explained.

"But I'm not here to see the dentist," I tried to say. Sweat had popped out on my forehead. I wanted to swat Dr. Dulur's hands from my mouth, but I was paralyzed with fear.

"That's what I tried to tell him." Belinda appeared above me, the third head to hang over my face. "He wouldn't listen."

"Well, I'm afraid the news isn't all that great, but it's fixable," said Dr. Dulur. "Lucky you came in when you did." He put the instrument down and smiled at me. "Seven cavities."

My hand flew to my mouth. "Seven what? No, I don't have cavities. I'm just neurotic. It's in my head."

"Yes, it's in your head, all right," he said, still smiling. "All seven cavities are right there in your head. Somebody hasn't been brushing regularly."

"But that can't be. I brush and floss religiously."

I wasn't lying. I was a big brusher, and I changed toothbrushes every month. I did what I had to so I wouldn't have to see a dentist.

"Oh, then it's probably age. We're not as young as we were, you know." Dr. Dulur was still smiling. He must not have realized how close my fist was to his face.

"Age?" I echoed. "Age?" I was carded at the 7-Eleven only last year. Was it the generic face cream I was using?

Dr. Dulur flinched. "Maybe not age. You probably just need to do a rinse before bed. Keep your mouth moist during the night. Dry mouth can cause cavities. You must have your mouth open at night when you snore."

"I don't snore!" I said a little too loudly.

"Should we fill up those little holes right away? How about I get you numbed up and start drilling?" Dr. Dulur asked.

And then I was running. I made it out of the chair, through the office, and out the front door in a matter of seconds.

Once outside, I gulped fresh air. Matchmaking wasn't easy.

I started counting my teeth to make sure they were all still there. That's why I didn't see him until it was too late, until his strong arm caught mine in a viselike grip and pulled me around the side of the building.

Chapter 2

✦ ♥ ✦

What's wrong with men? Oh, dolly, the list is so long I would have to alphabetize it and collate it and add roman numerals. Way too much work to write up that list. But up around the top of that list would be: Men never grow up. They are little boys in adult-sized pants. Pay attention! *Sometimes men don't do that. I make their match, they go out on a date, but they can't focus. They're sitting at a nice Italian restaurant with low lighting and soft music, and the potential love of their life right in front of them, but they're looking all over the place. They're looking at this waitress and that hostess, the other man's wife at the next table, even the grandma who walks by on her way to the bathroom. They're looking everyplace except where they should be looking. So, before a man takes that match you worked so hard on for their first date, make him understand his priorities. If necessary, slap him against the head to settle his eyeballs in his sockets so they don't roll around where they're not supposed to. Tell him to focus on what's important. Focus on the here and now. Focus on the what is, not the maybe, almost, and could be.*

Lesson 29,
Matchmaking Advice from Your Grandma Zelda

HE PULLED me so hard, my teeth rattled. I gathered air in my lungs to scream, but he stopped me, putting his hand over my mouth. He had me pinned against the wall of the building, and his body leaned into me. That's when I realized who he was.

"What the hell, Spencer, you scared the pants off me," I said, pushing away his hand. Spencer Bolton was the Cannes police chief and an unapologetic man-whore. He also made my body temperature rise to a nice rolling boil, but I didn't want him to know that. He was almost as new to the town as I, and we had run into each other last month when I stepped on his toes in the legal department.

He was tall and muscular, with dark blue eyes that could see right through a woman's Walmart skirt to her pink underpants. His thick, wavy dark hair was silky. I knew because I touched it once and I didn't want to let go. He was a metrosexual in the best sense of the word, and he usually had a supermodel attached to his body at some level—an arm, a leg, something.

He was infuriating.

"Pinkie, don't tease me, talking about your pants." He ran his fingers through my hair. "What the hell is this? I barely recognized you."

"It's the Ecuadoran Erect. It cost me a month's salary. You don't like it?"

"Since when do you get a salary?" He slid his hand down my smooth hair. "It's nice, but—"

"What do you mean, since when do I get a salary?" He was right. I didn't get a salary. Grandma said she would cover my expenses, but I wanted to pull my own weight and live off the matches I brought in. So far, those matches had bought me generic deodorant and Ecuadoran Erect. Warren Buffett, I wasn't.

Spencer had me pinned against the wall, and he was looking over his shoulder every couple of seconds. "What's going on, Spencer?" I asked. "Do you mind unlocking your hips from mine?"

"Oh, yeah, sure," he said, and took a step back. It

was unusual behavior, to say the least. Spencer would have normally taken a lot longer to unlock his hips. "Listen, can you do me a favor, Pinkie?"

"You want *me* to do you a favor?"

"I need a place to stay. Just for a little while."

"I don't have time for your pickup lines, Spencer. I have cavities. Real ones. Ones that need a drill."

Spencer looked around and ducked next to me, flattening his body against the building. "Sorry about your teeth, Pinkie. But I need to stay at your place. I'll take the couch. A couple nights, tops." He gave another look around. "Just until things blow over."

"Blow over?" I asked, but the door to Bliss Dental opened, and a woman came out. When I looked back over at Spencer, he was gone.

Like Batman.

I NEEDED coffee. I also needed a margarita, but I was going to start with coffee. I drove back to the historic district. Tea Time had the best coffee in town, despite its name and despite its crotchety old owner, Ruth Fletcher, an eighty-five-year-old woman who despised coffee drinkers.

I circled the block three times before I found a parking space. I had never seen so many cars on Main Street. I figured there must be some kind of event in town. The Cannes townsfolk were always putting together some kind of fair, festival, or rummage sale. Tourism was the number one moneymaker for the mountain village, and Cannes kept things popping with the apple-pie-eating, antique-buying set.

I looked forward to a tranquil moment in the tea shop. Sure, it used to be a saloon back when Cannes was a gold-rush town in the 1800s, but now it was all lace tablecloths, yellow painted daisies, porcelain teapots on every table, classical music piped in at a respectable level, and a rack of crocheted tea cozies for sale at ludicrous prices. I needed a moment of Zen, and Tea Time was the closest I would get today.

Out in front, a crowd had gathered. Two middle-aged women dressed in sheer white dresses with flowers in their hair argued with several shirtless men in bare feet and torn jeans. It wasn't Ruth's usual crowd, and a feeling of foreboding marched up my back like ants at a picnic.

I caught the words "the Arrival" as I made my way to the door.

Inside was bedlam. Every chair was occupied, and people huddled around the tables in thick groups, most in color-coded clothes, so that one part of the tea shop was blue, another was green, and so on. Piles of duffel bags and backpacks covered the empty places on the floor. I had to step over them on my way to the bar.

Normally I wouldn't have braved the crowds just for a latte, but the experience at the dentist's had left me unsettled. I needed coffee in a bad way, and I was relieved when I made it to the bar with Ruth behind it, a tea towel in her hand.

"Ruth, business sure is booming," I said, plopping my Visa down on the bar. "The usual, please."

Up close, Ruth didn't look so good. Despite her advanced age, she usually had more energy than I, and looked a good twenty years younger than she actually was, even without a smidge of makeup on her face and wearing a Katharine Hepburn–esque wardrobe of men's trousers and baggy shirts. But now she looked haggard and disoriented. It took a moment for her eyes to focus and recognize me.

"Booming?" she asked, her voice rising over the din. "Business? You call this business? The lunatic, sandal-wearing, mushroom-chewing, New Age loopdie-doos have come to roost in *my* tea shop. Who the hell are you?"

"What do you mean? It's me, Gladie."

Ruth blinked and scowled. "What the hell did you do to yourself, girl? Have you gone Hollywood? Cannes not good enough for you anymore?"

"I didn't go Hollywood." Whatever that meant. "I had my hair straightened. Why is that such a big deal to everyone?"

"You're a curly-headed girl, Gladie," Ruth said. "What would you think if a rat terrier tried to look like a poodle? I'll tell you what you'd say. You'd say it was unnatural, a freak of nature."

"Am I the rat terrier or the poodle?" I asked.

"Accept who you are, girl," she said. "It don't matter if you're not what you want to be. Nobody is."

"Ruth, you have a way of brightening a person's day," I said. I tapped on my Visa to remind her about my latte, but she was distracted by the surge in her clientele. "A new crowd?" I asked.

"End-of-world crackpots," she said. "But that's not the worst thing."

"Excuse me," a man in a Laura Ashley floral-print dress said, interrupting Ruth. I stumbled to the left as he crowded me with his elbow. "I have been waiting for my milk thistle tea for twenty minutes," he told her, patting down his ruffled bodice, which had gotten rolled up in his beard during his walk through the crowd.

"Hey, I was here first!" I shouted. I really needed coffee. Why couldn't we get a drive-through coffee place in this town?

"Hey, hottie, I was here first," he growled. "I have been waiting for twenty minutes. What do I have to do to get some milk thistle tea?"

"You think I'm a hottie?" I asked.

"Oh, Gladie, get over yourself," Ruth said. She grabbed

the guy by his bow neckline. "Listen, buddy, you can wait for milk thistle tea until there's bacon in the trees because pigs fly. Screw you with your milk thistle tea. I don't serve commie tea!"

"Ruth, remember you're a Democrat," I said, trying to calm her before she came to blows with the man.

"Wackadoo pot tea!" she screeched.

I had heard Ruth won Miss Congeniality in the Miss Cannes pageant of 1942, but I had my doubts.

I watched the guy's face transform as he debated with himself whether to deck the old lady or to hold back. I didn't know what milk thistle tea was, but it sure got people's hackles up. No one ever got violent over a mocha.

"Hey, Ruth," I said. "Is this a bad time to remind you about my latte?"

Ruth gripped the guy's dress tighter. "What do you say? Is this a good time?"

"Sure," he said, pulling back from Ruth's grip. "The aliens under the mountain aren't going to spirit *you* away," he told Ruth acidly. I didn't know how to take this statement, and neither did Ruth from the look of her. She stood stock-still, speechless. We watched the Laura Ashley guy walk back to a table of yellow-wearing, hairy people.

"The world is spinning backwards," Ruth said to me. "This whole damned mess is your grandmother's fault. Wackos attract wackos."

I wondered if that was true. Did like attract like? As a matchmaker in training, I should have been an expert on attraction. Grandma had made some peculiar matches. Vegan Josephine Fellows had found love with cattle rancher Philip Rojos. Baritone Joe Segelman was married very happily to Mary Smith, who had been deaf since birth. Grandma thought out of the box when it came to attraction, but she was different. She knew things that nobody could know. Maybe Ruth was right. Maybe Grandma was a wacko.

"Grandma is not a wacko," I said. "Ruth, take that back."

Ruth handed me a latte in a to-go cup. "The only thing I'll take back, Gladys Burger, is that latte if you give me an ounce of trouble. I've got enough trouble. These lunatics put my shop on the Internet as a beacon to all the other lunatics. I'll never get these freaks out of here. There's not enough DDT in the world."

"Julie's not around to help?" I asked. Julie was Ruth's grandniece and my first match.

"And pour kerosene on this fire? The damned girl is more trouble than she's worth. Besides, she got a job at the Christmas store. She's already broken half the ornaments stock, but Loretta won't fire her. Fool woman."

It was a much more congenial visit with Ruth than I was used to. Normally she harangued me about my coffee habit, which she considered only slightly better than sniffing glue, but now she was too distracted by the wackos to give me grief over drinking a latte.

"What the hell do you think you are doing with that teapot?" Ruth yelled at a group on the other side of the shop. "That's a genuine Harrods special from Prince Charles's wedding. The first wedding!" She stomped out from behind the bar, wielding the tea towel like a weapon, and headed toward a group of shirtless men with THEY COME written in black on their bare chests.

Ruth was right. The lunatic, sandal-wearing, mushroom-chewing, New Age loopdie-doos had come to roost in her tea shop.

It was a good time to leave.

A COUPLE blocks away, cars filled Grandma's driveway, and I had to find a parking space down the street.

People were filing into her house as I walked up to the door. For the life of me, I couldn't recall any big events set for the afternoon, but Grandma's was a hub of life in Cannes. Since she never left her house, Cannes had to come to her.

I had driven the short distance to my grandmother's house, thrilled to be away from dentists and lunatics and on my way to Grandma, who was warm and loving and probably had a stash of Pop-Tarts somewhere that she would gladly share with me.

But as I stood in the entranceway, I could see that her front parlor was crammed with lunatics of a different sort. Sweater-set-wearing lunatics. Dockers-wearing lunatics. In other words, Cannes's movers and shakers.

Mayor Robinson stood in the middle, surrounded by the town's gentry—the leaders of the Historical Preservation Society, the Neighborhood Watch, and the Craft Show, just to name a few—all gesturing at him and foaming at the mouth as they tried to get their points across. It was a houseful of power.

I had a feeling it would be awhile before I got my Pop-Tarts.

Luckily, my best friend, Bridget, came out of the kitchen right toward me carrying a platter of ham-and-cheese hoagies from Herbie's Hoagies and Pies. I spotted Herbie himself yelling at the mayor while clutching one of the sandwiches in his hand. As he gestured wildly, bits of lettuce and pepperoncini flew and landed on the mayor's Ralph Lauren custom-fit shirt with French cuffs. Damn, that sandwich looked good.

Bridget got close enough for me to grab one. "Just in time," I said. "I'm starving. I guess my diet can wait until tomorrow."

"Sorry, miss," she said, pushing her big hoot-owl glasses up on her nose. "Those are for the concerned citizens."

"Get outta here," I said, lunging for a sandwich. "I'm a concerned citizen for my blood sugar level. You won't believe my day. Wait until I tell you about the wackos at Tea Time."

Bridget leaned forward. Her large eyes were swathed in blue eye shadow and studied me with an interest she usually reserved for ACLU rallies. "Have we met?"

"What? Bridget, are you high?"

"Gladie, is that you?"

"Come on, not you, too."

"Dang, I would never have recognized you in a million years," she said. "Did you have plastic surgery? Don't tell me you have fallen victim to society's misogynistic dictates."

"Uh," I said. I wondered if Bridget would think Ecuadoran Erect was a misogynistic dictate. Probably. So far my new head was not paying off. I was more anonymous than fabulous.

We were interrupted by a cloud of White Diamonds perfume followed by my grandmother, bulging out of her finest Valentino-knockoff black-and-white sheath dress.

"Bridget, get those hoagies into the parlor," she ordered. "We have to do something to calm the folks. One more minute and they'll be bringing out the torches and pitchforks."

Bridget skipped into the parlor, and Grandma turned to me. "Hmm . . . ," she said, giving me her all-seeing look. Grandma had a way of knowing things that couldn't be known. "You've got trouble," she said. "Oral trouble."

"I'm sure it's nothing," I said. "I'll brush twice tonight."

"That's up to you, dolly. But Frances Farian brought over her coconut sour cream fudge bars, and one bite is going to give you a pain in your upper right bicuspid that'll shoot up through the nerve endings to your brain."

My hand flew to my mouth. "I'm on a diet, anyway,"

I said, but I had my doubts about saying no to coconut sour cream fudge bars.

"You're forgiven about forgetting the chicken."

"Oh, Chik'n Lik'n! I'm sorry." My teeth had distracted me.

"Have you ever seen the like?" Grandma asked, the subjects of my teeth and fried chicken forgotten. Half the town was gathered in her parlor. The noise was deafening as they shrieked and hollered. I caught bits and pieces of conversations. "Crazies" and "pagans" seemed to be the most common words thrown around.

"No Second Chancers meeting?" I asked.

"The town is up in arms about the invasion of the pagans. They called an emergency gathering."

I followed Grandma into the parlor, and the crowd parted like the Red Sea to let her pass. Bridget had saved two places for us on one of the sofas, and as soon as Grandma took a seat, the room quieted. The mayor stood across from us, facing the crowd. After waiting a couple of beats, he cleared his throat.

He was a good-looking man, around fifty years old, clean-cut, well dressed, with perfect, deep-mocha skin and a commanding voice. Single. I wondered why Grandma had never matched Mayor Robinson. It was unlike her to let a single, middle-aged man with money go matchless for long.

"What are you going to do about the wackos, Robinson?" shouted a man to my left.

"I heard you gave those pagans permits to camp out all over town. What do you have to say about that, Wayne?" a lady in a green sweater set said.

"They're putting up a yurt camp in the playground in the Main Street park," Bridget whispered to me. "They say the chakras of the path are really strong there."

"Who are they?" I whispered back. "Where did they come from?"

"They say aliens are living under this mountain and are coming out to take those nutcases away with them when the end of the world happens," Herbie announced. "Do you have any idea what that's going to do to my pie business? Pie season is coming, Wayne. What are you going to do about it?"

The mayor scratched his nose and seemed to think about Herbie's pie problem. The room erupted into murmurs, everyone worrying about how aliens would hurt their businesses.

"They call Cannes 'the Sacred Mountain,'" Bridget whispered to me. "They say we've been living on a whole passel of Martians."

A movement in the entranceway caught my eye. Spencer Bolton, dressed in black sweatpants and a large black hoodie, skulked past and tiptoed up the stairs, like a burglar. I rubbed my eyes to make sure I was seeing what I thought I was seeing. Nobody else in the parlor noticed him. They were caught up in their worries about aliens and yurts.

"I don't believe it," I said, watching him climb the stairs.

"Me either," Bridget said. "Aliens and the end of the world. Cannes used to be a sleepy town."

The mayor cleared his throat, and the room was dead silent, waiting for his response.

"Barbra Streisand," he said, his big voice resonating in the room. "She said it best in *Funny Girl*."

I heard the pipes rumble, the sound of my toilet flushing. When I got my hands on Spencer, I was going to wring his *GQ* neck and punch him in his metrosexual face. What was he playing at?

"'People who need people are the luckiest people in the world'!" Mayor Robinson shouted, making me jump in my seat. "Would Barbra be happy?"

I didn't know if this was a rhetorical question or not.

Nobody moved in their seats. Herbie's mouth was open, a half-eaten bit of sandwich out for everyone to see.

"I hate when people say 'Hello, everyone,'" the mayor continued. "Who's 'everyone'? Everyone is not people. I'm not everyone. Barbra is not everyone."

Grandma leaned over to me. "No dumber man ever walked the earth on two legs," she muttered in my ear.

Out the window, I saw Holden's truck drive by. My heart skipped a beat, and my stomach fluttered. The last time we went out, we got to second base and were sliding into third when he got a phone call and rushed away into the night. He sent me flowers to apologize, but I hadn't seen him in nearly two weeks, and I was jonesing for the tall, hot man of mystery. And his hands. He had great hands. Especially when they were on my breasts.

I leaned forward and, before I realized what I was doing, grabbed one of Frances Farian's coconut sour cream fudge bars off the coffee table and shoved it in my mouth. I had a moment of pure sensual pleasure as the fudge bar settled onto my taste buds, but it was quickly followed by a searing hot pain that shot through my teeth and into my brain. I clutched Grandma's knee for support, my eyes squeezed shut against the agony. I heard her *tsk-tsk*.

"I'm not saying a word," she said diplomatically.

The mayor finished his crazy speech, and the meeting dissolved into chaos, with people forming into groups. Grandma was right. It was just a matter of time before they got out the torches and pitchforks.

"Grandma, what does this all mean?" I asked her.

"Dolly, this means war, and in war someone is going to get hurt."

Chapter 3

Boo! Were you scared? Sometimes we don't know we're scared of something until we're scared by it. We can go our whole life thinking we're not scared of clowns and then one day we go to the circus and BOOM! a man in face paint and floppy shoes hands us a balloon animal, and we're running for our lives. The same thing happens now and then to a man. He doesn't think he's afraid of women. Then BOOM! One gets under his skin, and he's running for his life. This is a touchy situation for a matchmaker. The man is not ready for commitment. But we're in the love business! We don't care about being scared. We don't care about balloon animals. Slap him silly and get him back on the treasure path of love. No one is allowed to be afraid of love. Send him to the circus. Let him see what real fear is all about.

Lesson 58,
Matchmaking Advice from Your Grandma Zelda

GRANDMA'S HOUSE cleared out quickly. The movers and shakers stormed out like angry villagers on a mission, shouting about pagans and wackos and aliens. I might have also heard something about yurts and kerosene, but it could have been the dental pain distorting my hearing.

Bridget stuck around to help me clean up the paper cups and hoagie wrappers. Grandma was napping in her room after refusing Jocelyn Porkish's request to be set up with the mayor. "I just couldn't do it to Jocelyn," Grandma explained to me. Saying no to a potential client was more than Grandma could bear, and it sent her straight to bed.

The front door opened, and my other best friend, Lucy Smythe, stomped in in a swirl of peach organza. "Did I miss it? Did I miss it? Oh, please tell me I didn't miss the alien apocalypse meeting!" she drawled, her accent dripping with Mississippi Delta.

She spun around in the entranceway, her dress billowing up in a feminine wave, just like Scarlett O'Hara. I popped my head out of the parlor, a trash bag in my hand.

"You missed it," I said. "But Bridget and I are in here. We can give you the recap."

Lucy stared at me. "Is that you under all that va-va-voom?" she asked.

"I didn't recognize her, either," Bridget said.

"I only straightened my hair," I moaned. If I wanted to become a superhero, my disguise was set. I didn't even need a cape.

"It's lovely, darlin'," Lucy said. "Very straight."

Lucy sat on a couch and crossed her legs. "Damn," she said. "I wanted to make this meeting, but business held me up. I drove up from L.A. as fast as I could." Lucy was in marketing, whatever that was.

"The mayor even spoke," Bridget said.

"I missed that?" Lucy asked. "Drat. What did he say? Did he talk about his hemorrhoids again?"

"I remember something about Barbra Streisand," I said.

"Shoot! That's better than hemorrhoids." Lucy picked up one of Frances Farian's fudge bars and took a big bite.

"They filed out of here on the warpath. It's the Episcopalians against the vegan, end-of-worlder, New Agey alien worshippers. I think this is how the Crusades started," Bridget said, stuffing cups into a garbage bag.

"That's it?" Lucy asked with a mouthful of fudge bar. "You got nothing more? You said more last week when I said 'God bless you' after you sneezed." Bridget was not a fan of religion, and her rants against the "sexist, paternalistic, religious dictatorship" were legendary, though recently we discovered she was a closet Catholic.

"I'm still battling self-doubt," she said. "I can't take sides yet."

"Well, you're the only one," Lucy said. "On the way here, I saw a group of barefoot hippies with 'The Arrival' signs blocking traffic on Main Street, and the Cannes Ladies' Saturday Sewing Circle was facing them off, shouting 'God hates aliens.' I almost crashed my Mercedes."

"I wonder where all this came from," I said. "Aliens sleeping under the mountain, waiting to take away the worthy when the end of the world comes? It's so out of the blue, like they came out of nowhere."

Lucy pointed at me. "I'll tell you what else came out of nowhere, what else I saw on my drive over here. Mr. Tall Drink of Water, your mysterious boyfriend-neighbor."

"Holden's not really my boyfriend," I said, turning red. I wanted him to be my boyfriend. He could be a really good boyfriend if he would stick around and take me out and do boyfriend things consistently. "What was he doing?" I asked, trying not to sound desperate.

"He was skulking. I think he was talking to one of the wackos, one of the khaki-colored ones."

"Oh," I said.

"Not a khaki woman, darlin'," she said. "A khaki man. Don't worry."

We were quiet for a moment as unspoken questions and comments flooded the room. Should I be worried that Holden was seeing another woman? Why didn't I know what he was doing with his days? Why wasn't he communicating with me, and should I break off whatever relationship I had with him? His hot quotient was pretty high, but would a self-respecting woman let herself be strung along like this? Bridget and Lucy waited for me to broach the subject, remaining quiet like only good friends could.

I remained quiet also, too chicken to talk about Holden. I grabbed a fudge bar to hide my embarrassment, but one bite made me yelp in pain. I tried to downplay it, but in the end, I had to fess up about my appointment with Belinda and the discovery of my seven cavities.

"Dr. Dulur is gentle as a baby, Gladie," said Lucy. "He gave me a crown. Put me to sleep, and when I woke up, my mouth was fixed, my teeth whitened, and I could swear that my hands were newly moisturized."

I looked at my hands. They could use moisturizing.

"I think my teeth can wait. I don't think it's urgent," I said, but my teeth disagreed. The pain was getting worse. I grimaced in discomfort and moaned.

"Oh, you've got it bad, Gladie," Lucy said.

"Let's call for an emergency appointment," said Bridget. "I bet Belinda will make sure you get in."

I whimpered and instantly hated myself for it. I am a terrible coward. "I should have been born brave," I said.

Bridget put her hand on mine. "Dr. Dulur is known for being very good with children. All the moms bring their kids to him. He gives out toys and lollipops."

My bottom lip jutted out. "Yeah," I said. "But the lollipops are probably sugar-free."

"Yeah, they probably are," Bridget said, looking down at the floor.

Lucy stood up and took her cellphone out of her purse. "I'm making the appointment right now, and I'm going to add in a whitening treatment, on me. No charge for you. There, doesn't that make you feel better, Gladie? You are going to have blinding pearly whites. You're going to be a new person. You won't need a smidge of makeup with your new teeth."

I was doubtful. "Without mascara, my eyes look like two holes burned in a blanket," I said. But Lucy wasn't listening. She got me an appointment for after office hours and threatened to give my cellphone number to Visa's collection agency if I didn't show up to have my teeth filled and whitened. Ha-ha on her. I hadn't paid my cellphone bill in three months, and it was due to be shut off any second now. The collection agency would never find me. As soon as I got Spencer out of the house, I would pick up Orajel at the pharmacy and then never eat sugar again. No sugar, no pain. It was a plan.

By the time we got the house cleaned up, the sun was getting ready to set, and Bridget and Lucy went out to have dinner in town, where they could have a front-row seat for the war between the townspeople and the end-of-worlders. I was tempted to join them, but Spencer was still upstairs in my bedroom, and I wanted to see why he felt the need to hide there, make sure he was all right, and kick him out.

But out the window, I could see Holden's truck still in his driveway, and I realized Spencer would have to wait, as well. Before I could get him out of my underwear drawer, I had some pressing spying to do.

SPENCER WASN'T the only one who knew how to skulk. I did a pretty good job at it, skulking across Grandma's lawn on tiptoe, careful not to draw Holden's attention, whenever he was next door.

I was congratulating myself on my athletic grace and spylike reflexes when I thought I saw Holden's shadow hovering close by. I jumped to the side, trampling through

Grandma's prized roses and snagging my cotton sweater. I pulled it free and stumbled backward into the bushes that separated her property from Holden's, landing flat on my back. I lay there dazed for a minute before rolling into a sitting position.

Now I was sure I heard Holden. I squatted on all fours and made a little peephole through the bushes with my hands. Holden was in his side yard, sitting on an old metal chair, sipping iced tea and reading a letter. It was a perfect vantage point to spy on him. He was wearing a plaid shirt, jeans, and work boots. His sleeves were rolled up to his elbows, even though it was a chilly day. His forearms were thick with corded muscles.

I felt spittle gather at the corners of my mouth. He was a beautiful man, tall and composed. He was entirely focused on the contents of his letter, and that's probably why he didn't hear my heart beat, which would have given the Marine Marching Band a run for its money. I leaned forward, trying to read the letter, but I was too far away.

"What's this? Spying on the neighbor?" Spencer came out of nowhere and scared the daylights out of me.

I yelped. Fortunately, Holden's phone rang at the same time, camouflaging my shriek. He went inside to answer it, oblivious to my spying.

I clutched at my heart and fell back onto my butt. Spencer was leaning down, his face inches from mine, his annoying little smirk planted on his face. He was still wearing his sweats and hoodie, a strange look for the usually dapper police chief.

"I was not spying," I replied. Holden's side door opened with a creak, and I pulled Spencer down on top of me by the front of his hoodie so Holden wouldn't see him.

"Shh," I urged. We lay quiet for a moment while I listened for Holden's approach. What would he think if he saw me spying on him? Would he shout at me about his personal space and tell me he never really liked my thighs? I should have known that was a line when he said it. No man in his right mind would like my thighs. I had very unlikable thighs.

"He probably hates my thighs," I muttered.

"Really? They feel pretty good to me," Spencer said. He was lying directly on top of me in a pelvis lock. His breath smelled of coffee and oatmeal. Funny, I figured him for a no-carb kind of guy.

"Did he hear us?" I whispered. "What's he doing?"

"I don't know," Spencer whispered back. "He's out of my line of sight, but I bet whatever he's doing, it's less interesting than what I'm doing."

My eyes narrowed. Spencer's smirk was growing. I hoped it was the only thing growing. "If you are enjoying this, stop," I said. "You should get off me, *now*."

"Too risky. What if Holden hears me rolling off you? It wouldn't look good."

He had a point. What would Holden think if he saw Spencer with me? My breasts would never feel his big warm hands on them again.

"Why were you spying on Mr. Lumberjack, anyway?" Spencer asked.

"He's not a lumberjack. He's . . ."

Spencer smirked again. "You don't even know what he is, do you?"

"No, do you?" It dawned on me that as police chief and not Holden's number one fan, he had the resources and wherewithal to do a background check and might have looked into Holden's past.

"No. I mind my business, unlike you, Ms. Perez Hilton."

"You're awfully heavy," I said, but he wasn't. He was supporting most of his weight on his forearms. He was warm, and there was an energy building between us, which was making me melt like ice cream on a summer's day. Spencer's eyes were huge, and his focus sharp and directed at me.

"Uh," I said.

"We haven't gotten to spend a lot of time together lately," he said, his voice low in his throat.

"Uh," I repeated.

"I forgot how good you smell," he said, breathing me in.

"That's Herbie's Hoagies. I ate two. They stick with a person."

"I don't think that's Herbie's Hoagies," he said. His face was closer. I could taste his breath. Testosterone. His lips were so close. If I moved my head just a little, I would be kissing him. I thought about moving my head. I thought about moving my head a lot.

Spencer was a good kisser. I had kissed him once before, and it was like kissing flame. He nearly blistered my lips. It might be good to test that out again, see if he still was a good kisser.

What was wrong with me? Of course he was a good kisser. The man got more practice time kissing than Michael Phelps got for swimming. His lips had been on huge numbers of women.

"What the hell were you doing in my bedroom?" I asked.

"Unpacking. I told you I had to lie low for a while."

"In my bedroom?"

"They wouldn't think to look for me there."

"Are you hiding?" I asked. He wasn't the hiding type. He was the storming-the-castle type. "From who? Mobsters? Terrorists?"

"What does it matter? I just need a place to stay for a while."

I smelled a rat. "Spencer Bolton, fess up or I'll tell Bridget you're a Republican."

He pulled back. "You wouldn't dare. That would be cruel. She would hound me."

"Oh, wouldn't I?"

Holden's side door creaked again, and the sound of his work boots receding into his house reached us on the lawn.

Spencer rolled off me. Lying on his side next to me, he leaned up on his elbow, rested his head in his hand, and took a big breath. "I have Facebook problems."

"Excuse me?"

"Facebook. A Facebook status problem. Several women said they were involved with me at the same time. It caused a stir."

"You're hiding from—no, it can't be." But Spencer's face was dead serious. Even his smirk was gone. "You're hiding from Facebook friends?"

He jumped up and put out his hand to help me up and walked me toward the house. "These women are persistent. And angry." Spencer looked around before opening Grandma's door.

"How many women are we talking about, Spencer?" I asked.

"Several."

"Several? More than two?"

"Yes."

"More than five?"

"Yes."

"You're disgusting," I said. "Foul. You make my flesh crawl with your stereotypical womanizing, reprehensible, male behavior."

"And people say you're introverted," he said, his smirk reappearing on his face.

"Remember, Spencer, herpes is forever."

"Ouch. You went right to STDs."

"Tough love, Spencer," I said.

"Love? Are you trying to tell me something?"

I punched him in the arm. He was solid, more muscular than Holden but a couple inches shorter. I figured he was a notch above Vin Diesel but a hair less than The Rock. He took one more look around to make sure the coast was clear and closed the door behind us.

"What's for dinner?" he asked.

"Are you kidding me?"

"Do you cook?"

"Of course I cook," I said. I made a mean macaroni and cheese out of a box, and I could open a can of ravioli better than Paula Deen. "But I'm not cooking for *you*. You are going home and facing the music."

"What side of the bed do you sleep on? I sleep more diagonally, but I can stick to a side if forced."

I threw up my arms in defeat. "I'm leaving."

"Where? Obviously, you don't have a date with Neighbor Boy. That whole thing smells done to me."

"It's not done," I said, my voice coming out an octave higher than normal.

Spencer counted on his fingers. "You don't know what he does for a living, you don't know where he goes, you have to spy on him instead of just asking him—"

"I don't have time for this. I have to go."

Spencer stood with his arms crossed and his feet apart like he was bracing for impact. "Where? Where do you have to go? You're trying to hide from me."

"I don't need to hide. I have an appointment. I have cavities to fill."

Spencer laughed. "Right. You'll never keep that appointment. You're a class A chicken when it comes to medical stuff. Your grandmother told me about the checkup incident."

"Hey, I was much younger."

"Five years ago?" He smirked his annoying smirk.

"That story is way exaggerated!" I shouted, stomping my feet.

"She showed me photographs." The doctor had come at me with his stethoscope, and I bit him. Hard. I don't know what came over me. Fight or flight, I guess. I drew blood, and then I passed out from the sight of blood.

Spencer raised an eyebrow. I was speechless and embarrassed. I tried to say something, but it all came out like *buh-buh-buh-buh*.

I grabbed my purse from the table in the entranceway. "Feed yourself. I'm going to get my teeth filled and whitened. I won't need to wear makeup anymore."

"Huh?" Spencer asked. But I was halfway out the door. That's why I actually made it to my dentist appointment. I wanted to show Spencer what's what. Otherwise, I would have rather have had my teeth rot out, infect my jaw, bleed into my heart, and kill me before I let a drill get near my face. It was all Spencer's fault.

IT WAS hard to turn the car's steering wheel with sweaty palms, and I was drenched from head to toe. Nerves. But it was too late to turn back. Spencer would never let me live it down if I chickened out. He wouldn't be quiet until I returned with swollen cheeks, drooling from my numb mouth. I tried to concentrate on the sugar-free lollipops I was going to get, but it was hard to get past the vision of me screaming in agony as the drill went through my molar.

Otherwise, it was a beautiful evening. The sun was setting, leaving the sky a warm pink. The weather was turning chilly. Soon, Ruth would be serving hot cider with cinnamon sticks. Autumn was the time of year Cannes did best.

About halfway to Bliss Dental, caught up in the reverie of cinnamon cider, I didn't see the traffic stopped in the street and almost crashed my car. Cannes's idea of a traffic jam is three cars and an electric mobility scooter.

But now Pear Lane was bumper to bumper with cars idling, their drivers standing outside on the street, trying to figure out what was going on.

At the front of the quagmire, cop cars blocked the traffic. The crowd migrated forward toward the police. Lights flashed, and someone practiced on a megaphone.

"What the hell? How do I get this to work?" it blared. I recognized the voice. Officer James was nice enough but slightly incompetent. I had met him a month ago.

"Citizens of Cannes, please stand back from the penis! I repeat, stand back from the penis!" he yelled through the megaphone.

With this warning, the crowd surged forward in earnest. I joined them.

I hopped in place to see past the people. Up ahead, several officers stood around a man, staring down at him and shaking their heads. The man was a stranger, average height and build, around forty years old with dark curly hair, and clean shaven. He wore a white T-shirt and a tight leather jacket. He had worn jeans, but they were now pooled at his ankles. He was a boxers man, but those were hovering just over the jeans. He had a hairy butt, and when he turned I saw that he had the world's longest penis.

And it was silver.

"Holy cow, have you ever seen the like?" Meryl, the town's blue-haired librarian, said next to me. She whistled long and slow in appreciation. "How does he walk?"

A couple of the police officers were curious, too. They took out their nightsticks and tapped the man's penis, making the man scream in pain and making a strange clanging noise.

"Have you ever?" Meryl repeated. She pushed forward, shoving aside the man in front of her.

"Meryl, get back here. Be careful," I called after her.

I don't know why I feared for her safety, but enormous, clanging penises spelled danger to me.

"Hey, is that you, Underwear Girl? I barely recognized you. Hey, guys, it's Underwear Girl. Hi, Underwear Girl!" Officer James waved at me. He couldn't have been more than eighteen years old. He still had teenage acne. He, like most of the Cannes police force, knew me as Underwear Girl because of an unfortunate experience that had resulted in a giant-sized photo of me hanging upside down in my underpants, which they had plastered on the wall in the police station's processing room.

I ducked behind Meryl, hoping Officer James would forget about me, but he turned the megaphone back on. "Underwear Girl! Over here. You gotta see this." His voice echoed off the buildings. Meryl turned around to me, a question on her face.

"It's not what you think," I said. And then Officer James was there, urging me to follow him all the way to the penis man.

Up close, I could see why his penis was silver. It wasn't his penis. It was a pipe. The man had gotten his penis stuck in a pipe, and it was causing him obvious agony. He clutched his head and jutted out his pelvis, all the while biting his lip.

"He won't say how it got in there," Officer James explained. "But it swelled up inside, and it's wedged pretty good."

"I have a dentist appointment," I said.

The man in the pipe noticed me. "I'm Tim," he said. "I'm new in town."

"Nice to meet you. I'm actually running late. I have cavities."

"Oh, I hate the dentist's office. I had a root canal. Worst pain I ever had, you know, until now." He pointed at his pipe, and we all looked down at it.

"Are you going to leave him like this?" I asked Officer James.

The sound of sirens answered my question. A fire truck and an ambulance came careening around the corner and stopped short of the man. The police changed their focus to managing traffic and rerouting cars while the firefighters pulled out a large power tool.

"What's that?" Tim asked, more than a tinge of panic in his voice.

"An industrial grinder," a fireman said.

"What's that for?" Tim asked.

"I have a dentist appointment," I said, and took a step back.

"It wasn't my fault," Tim yelled as the fireman approached his pipe with the grinder. "It was the pagans. They lured me."

The fireman started the grinder, and it made a horrible noise. I trotted back to my car without looking back, trying to blot the sound out of my mind. Meryl intercepted me as I opened the car door. She put her hand on my shoulder. "Did you hear that?" she asked me, serious like it was Banned Books Week. "The pagans lured him. If they can lure a man to stick his penis into a pipe, what else can they do? I'll tell you, this is Jim Jones all over again."

I nodded, waved goodbye, and started my car as the sound of the grinder's blades hitting metal pipe cut through the evening. I burned rubber getting out of there. It was a blessing in disguise. Tim's unfortunate circumstance had changed my perspective. I wanted to be anywhere away from his penis and the industrial grinder. I had never been so happy to go to the dentist.

THE WAITING room was empty, but Bliss Dental still smelled of fear. With Tim and the industrial grinder still on my mind, I figured fear was relative, and suddenly a drill didn't seem so bad.

The door dinged when I entered, and Belinda came out to the waiting room to greet me. "Any news?" she asked me. "Did you find anybody in those records of yours? I forgot to tell you I like muscles. I don't want a pudgy man."

People sure are hard to please. What could I tell her? I hadn't begun to think about her match, and I didn't have any records.

"I did meet with someone today," I fibbed. "He's new in town. His name's Tim. He's in good shape." At least he was when I last saw him. Hopefully, the fireman had a steady hand. "But I'm not sure he's perfect for you," I said. "I want you to have the perfect guy."

Belinda's eyes twinkled. "I knew you were the right matchmaker for me. I don't need a witch to fix me up. Are you ready? I'm heading home, but Dr. Dulur stayed late for you."

Belinda walked me back, and my fear returned with a vengeance. I wanted to cry and run away, but I thought that might jeopardize my business relationship with Belinda. I needed to match her to have any hope of paying off my Visa. So I stayed strong and followed her to chair number three and only slightly hyperventilated.

Bliss Dental was laid out in a mostly open floor plan. Behind Belinda's desk, there was a short hallway with Dr. Dulur's office on one side. I got a quick glimpse of it as I walked back. It was littered with files and old takeout boxes. Eighties-style car posters covered the walls, and Dr. Dulur's desk was oriented away from a floor-to-ceiling window that overlooked the parking lot.

The main part of the practice was a more or less open area, only separated into small examination rooms by low walls. Each room had a chair, a television, and various dental instruments, which I didn't look at too closely because they made me dizzy. On the other side of the large room were three smaller rooms: a bathroom, a lab/workroom, and a lunchroom/locker room.

The young man whose head I'd seen when I was in the chair that morning came out of nowhere and gave me a big smile. "Hi, Gladie. I'm so glad you made it back," he said. He looked familiar, like I had met him somewhere else, but I couldn't place him. He was about my height of five foot seven. Not much to look at except for big brown eyes with long eyelashes. Why did men always get the best eyelashes? What a waste.

"I'm Nathan. I'm the dental assistant," he said. "You'll be fine. Dr. Dulur is known for zero pain. It's almost a spa experience."

"I worked at a spa once," I said, trying to stay clear of any dental conversation. "I was the towel girl at the Purple Door in Fresno for two weeks." I saw a lot during those two weeks. Rich people like to be naked. "You look awfully familiar," I told Nathan. "Have we met before?"

"I don't think so," he said. "Except for today. I moved into town a couple months ago."

"Maybe one of your family members? My grandmother's house is Grand Central here. Maybe I met your parents or your grandparents?"

Nathan steered me to chair number three and had me sit. He draped a spit cloth around my neck. "Nope. Sorry. I'm an orphan, born and raised. I don't have any family."

"This is freaking ridiculous." Holly, the surgically altered hygienist, stormed into the cubicle with her hands on her nonexistent hips and hovered over me. She shot daggers out her eyes at poor Nathan, who flinched and took a step back. "I am not staying after hours for a lousy teeth whitening. Where the hell is that loser Simon? Off reading his magazines again?"

Holly was yelling pretty loudly, but her face didn't move. I was transfixed, watching her inflated lips pucker and recede, pucker and recede, leaving the rest of her face completely immobile. She caught me staring, and I looked away, making a point of rearranging my bib.

"I could have worked in Beverly Hills, you know, making three times the money, but I'm doing Simon a favor," she spat out.

"I know, Holly," Nathan said. "But I think Dr. Dulur is going to do the whitening himself?" he said like a question. Nathan was shrinking by the second, his posture becoming more and more submissive to the overly aggressive Holly. Her boobs alone would have scared an average man.

"Taking business away from me? Whitening is my bailiwick." She stomped her foot and stormed out. I didn't know what impressed me more, her use of the word "bailiwick," or the fact that when she stomped her foot, her boobs stayed in place like they were suspended in air. They were *Matrix* boobs.

Nathan busied himself with dental instruments. He opened and closed drawers more often than what I suspected was necessary. My fear started to bubble up again in the quiet, but it was interrupted by Holly's and Dr. Dulur's voices, arguing in another room.

Holly was yelling about deals and how much she was worth, but Dr. Dulur was not as passive as Nathan. "Listen, bitch, I don't owe you anything," Dr. Dulur said. His voice was chilling, like he didn't mess around, like you wouldn't want to meet him in a dark alley. Gone was the folksy, happy dentist of the people and giver of sugar-free lollipops and toys to the young.

"Maybe this is a bad time," I said to Nathan. But Nathan was ignoring me. The conversation in the other room had all his attention.

"Nobody asked you to stay tonight," Dr. Dulur told

Holly. "I got this. Listen, I'm tired of your shit. You're more trouble than you're worth."

Holly replied with a string of obscenities I hadn't heard since I worked eight days on the docks in New Jersey.

"You're harshing my vibe, Holly," he said in response.

And then he was there in Examination Room 3, a wide smile on his face, the scar on his cheek pulled at a weird angle. He was still dressed as a middle-aged *Saturday Night Fever* stand-in. He looked thrilled to see me, and maybe he was.

"If this is a bad time, I could come back later, say in a couple weeks," I said.

Dr. Dulur guffawed. "Oh, that's a good one. This will just take a minute." He sat behind me. My chair leaned back automatically with a soft *wrr*ing noise. It was all going too fast. Fear overtook me.

"Are you going to use a drill?" I sniffed.

"Yep."

"Oh," I said, sniffing again. "Do you have to?"

"Nathan, the gas," he said, and Nathan put a mask on my nose. The world spun around, and then the world was no more.

I'VE NEVER had surgery. Not one operation. I still have my tonsils, my appendix, and my gallbladder. I had had cavities filled in my life before ever walking into Bliss Dental, but I had never had anesthesia. So, lying on the Examination Room 3 chair, sucking the gas, I had nothing to compare the experience to. I thought it was perfectly normal to be flying in the clouds, and I thought it was perfectly normal to hear screams and the sounds of fighting.

But when I woke up alone on the floor of Examination Room 3, the gas mask hanging off me, I knew something was wrong. I was woozy and nauseated. The only pain I felt was from my left knee, which must have hit wrong when I fell off the chair. My mouth was untouched. For some reason, Dr. Dulur hadn't done any dental work on me, and for some reason, he and Nathan had left me there to fall off the chair.

It took me awhile to orient myself and wake up. I struggled to a sitting position and looked around. Everything looked normal. The lights were on, and it looked like business as usual. But Bliss Dental was quiet. It was a quiet that told me I was alone. There wasn't a movement anywhere.

The hair on the back of my neck stood up. I was worried that I was having a bad trip, that I was hallucinating, that I was on an episode of *The Twilight Zone,* or that I had died and was damned to live an eternity in a dental office.

I found my purse and got up, took off the spit bib, and adjusted my sweater. I started to panic; I wanted to run out of there, but I was scared. I only managed a few small steps. Foreboding overtook me, and it didn't take long to figure out why.

I got as far as Examination Room 2, and that's when I realized I wasn't alone, after all. Dr. Simon Dulur hadn't left me. He was still there, but he was lying on a dental chair, and he wasn't breathing. At least I didn't think he could be breathing, not without a face. And Dr. Dulur didn't have a face.

Chapter 4

✦ ♥ ✦

Is there a sign on my head? Do I walk around with a neon sign telling you I like french fries dipped in chocolate shakes? Do I have a billboard on my chest saying I can't stand men who pick their teeth after dinner? No! So you don't know me. I don't have a label. You know what I mean, dolly? People don't have labels. They don't have signs over their heads. Nobody comes with a set of instructions or an owner's manual. You can't figure out a person just by looking at him. Or her. Throw away the stereotypes. If you think you see a label, remember it's only a mirage, like an oasis in the desert. It ain't there, bubeleh. Nobody is going to help you out, either. You got to go with your gut when it comes to matches, when it comes to understanding who people really are and who would be their love match. A gut is a wonderful thing. But sometimes your gut lets you down, and in those cases, don't panic. If your gut isn't helping, be patient and study your matches awhile. They're not going anywhere. Go ahead and study them.

Lesson 3,
Matchmaking Advice from Your Grandma Zelda

I RECOGNIZED him by his polyester shirt, gold chains, and chest hair. The world spun around, and I saw black. I was on the verge of passing out. I never could stand the sight of blood, and here I was face to face—excuse the expression—with a lot of blood. Dr.

Dulur was in there somewhere, underneath the gore, and the thought of what happened to him made me retreat toward unconsciousness.

But my skin prickled. A new sense took over that woke me up. I became at once aware of my surroundings. It occurred to me that I was in danger, that a sadistic murderer was around, and that my face could be the next to go.

With a shaky hand, I rummaged in my purse for my cellphone. I had Spencer's number on speed dial. He had inputted the number into my phone, saying something about Danger-Prone Daphne and succumbing to the inevitable.

I stared at Dr. Dulur's bloody head while my hand fished around in my enormous bag. I should have gone with a small clutch like Lucy. She managed to be very organized with a tiny purse. She even had a little pocket just for her phone. Why couldn't I be more like Lucy? She didn't have cavities. Her life wasn't in danger. She wasn't staring at a man with no face.

My hand blindly reached my wallet, my brush, and my Chinese diet tea. I threw them out of my bag, trying to clear the way to find my cellphone. By the time I got to it, I had a pile of items at my feet. Dr. Dulur hadn't moved. The only sound had been the gentle thud of my purse's contents hitting the plush carpeting.

I pushed buttons on my phone, careful not to take my eyes off Dr. Dulur, but the phone wasn't working. I frantically pushed more buttons. I had just charged the phone that morning before meeting Belinda, but now it was dead. A whimper escaped from my throat. I realized the cellphone company had chosen that moment to cut off my phone. I wanted to kick myself for getting the Ecuadoran Erect. I should have paid my cellphone bill instead. Now I was alone with only Dr. Dulur's corpse and possibly a maniacal killer to keep me company.

I dropped my purse to the ground and slowly turned around, scanning my surroundings. Fluorescent lights illuminated every corner of the dental office. The large space filled with examination rooms was empty. I could easily see over the low walls to tell that Dr. Dulur and I were the only ones there. The two side room doors were open, and from what I could tell, they were empty, too.

With no immediate threat, I took a deep breath and approached Dr. Dulur. I gingerly checked for a pulse, holding two fingers against his neck. As I already knew, he was dead. My fingers trembled and slipped in the blood on his neck, covering my hand with it.

That's when I threw up, and that's when I heard the sound.

I stood, doubled over, and listened. It was a low guttural noise, a man. The sound repeated, getting louder and stronger. It sounded just like the movies when Jason or Freddy Krueger was getting ready to hack some unsuspecting female to death. My fight-or-flight response kicked in. I turned on my heel sharply, ready to run out of there as fast as I could. I was betting I could run pretty fast.

But I turned too sharply, and my heel got caught on the carpeting, and I was sent careening forward. I fell toward Dr. Dulur, flinging my arms around in a wild attempt to defy gravity, anything not to land on him. Like a slapstick comedy routine, my limbs took on a life of their own, swaying and circling through the air, trying to alter the inevitable. And it worked. I narrowly missed Dr. Dulur by inches, falling on all fours to the sticky, blood-soaked floor with a thud and hurting my knee again. Trying to alleviate the pain and get out of the bloody puddle, I quickly changed positions, attempting to hop up, not knowing how close my shoulder was to the dentist chair.

I knocked it with force, making it sway. My hand flew

to my shoulder, which was probably bruised, and I felt
another hand clap on top of mine. I froze. I'm sure my
heart stopped. I gasped for air and thought of my face—
not bad, some would even say pretty, and I didn't want
to lose it. Then I heard a thud. I turned to see Dr. Dulur's leg had fallen off the chair, and I realized it was his
hand on top of mine. I swallowed a scream, and tears
filled my eyes. As if in slow motion, although really fast
for a dead guy, Dr. Dulur rolled off the chair, landing
directly on top of me.

I probably turned green, because suddenly I was im-
bued with Incredible Hulk strength. Pushing Dr. Dulur
off me, I scattered to my feet and ran for the exit. I got all
the way to Bliss Dental's front door, but Nathan Smith,
the dental assistant, was blocking the exit. He was lying
slumped in the doorway. I recognized his moaning as the
sound I heard earlier. I wanted to jump over him and run
for my life, but the Good Samaritan part of me inter-
fered, and I knelt down to see how he was.

The back of his head was bleeding, and he was going
in and out of consciousness.

"Nathan?" I asked. "Are you all right? What happened here?"

"I tried to get away," he said. "But he hit me from
behind."

"You saw the person who did this?"

"A shadow. A large shadow."

I USED the Bliss Dental phone and got through to the
police after trying Spencer, whose phone was off. I
stayed with Nathan and urged him to stay awake until
help arrived. I was covered in my own vomit and Dr.
Dulur's blood. I had witnessed something gruesome,
and according to every medical show on TV, my shiver-
ing meant that shock was setting in. Nathan gave no

more information. He was holding on through his own shock and pain. I sat by him in the doorway for no more than ten minutes before what looked like Cannes's entire police force and fire department arrived.

Paramedics whisked Nathan off to the hospital, and after ascertaining that none of the blood that covered me from head to toe was my own, they handcuffed me, read me my rights, and shoved me in the back of a police car.

Despite knowing most of the police force, despite the fact that my photo was hanging in their processing room and they affectionately called me Underwear Girl, I was practically bathed in Dr. Simon Dulur's blood, my belongings were found next to his corpse, and my fingerprints had to be all over him. There was the pesky problem of not finding the dentist's missing face, but otherwise, they thought they had a pretty airtight case against me.

They looked at me differently. I thought I detected fear, but I wasn't in my right mind, and it could have been anything: fear, fatigue, indigestion.

I forgot to tell them I was under the gas when Dr. Dulur was murdered. Frankly, I was tired, and I thought the truth would come out soon enough. Besides, I was covered in blood, and I was beyond caring about mundane problems like jail time.

I had been booked and handcuffed to a desk and left to sit, the blood drying sticky on my body and clothes, when the need to see my grandmother gripped me. I was panicked with it.

I wanted my grandma. Others would want their mother, but it was just as likely that my mother was also handcuffed to a desk in some other police station as anywhere else. And it would take more than her granddaughter being arrested for murder to get my grandmother out of her house. She hadn't left voluntarily since my father died years before. So I was alone.

My body trembled, on the verge of a monumental freak-out. Where was Spencer? He hadn't come to the crime scene, and he wasn't at the station. He was the chief of police, for crying out loud. What kind of work ethic was that?

If Spencer were around, he would make certain I was all right. Sure, he would yell at me and tell me how much trouble I was, but he would take the handcuffs off me, and he would know I had been under the gas, and he would get me back to my grandma.

I worried that I would start crying the ugly cry where my nose ran and my face contorted. The ugly cry was building in my chest. I could feel it rising, and it was only a matter of seconds until I would completely humiliate myself.

"Who did this to you?"

Holden knelt in front of me, his strong, tall body crouching easily, and looked into my eyes. He wore a leather jacket over his plaid shirt. I was dimly aware that I was surprised to see him, but he immediately calmed me, and I felt slightly warmer.

"I was under the gas," I said. "And the dentist had no face." I sniffed and hiccupped.

"I will be right back," he said. He laid his hand on my arm and squeezed gently. "I mean *right* back. Only a moment. Will you be all right?"

I didn't know how to answer that. I probably wouldn't ever be all right again. "He had no face," I said.

I hiccupped once more and closed my eyes. When I opened them again, Holden was gone, but I could hear him behind me, talking to the police sergeant I'd just met. *He must work the night shift,* I thought. Otherwise, I would have seen him before. It was getting pretty late. I must have been under the gas a long time.

Holden's voice was scary, like a high school principal's voice with a Mr. T edge to it. He was telling the police sergeant to take my clothes for evidence. He was threatening legal action if they didn't release me.

Maybe he's a lawyer, I thought, but threw that idea out of my head. He was nothing like a lawyer. Lawyers wore suits.

The police sergeant uncuffed me. "Sorry about that, miss," he said. "Mr. Smith at the hospital told us you were under the gas, and it was some big guy who offed the dentist."

"He had no face," I told him, like I was telling him that ground beef was on sale at Pete's Market.

Cannes didn't have a detective or a female police officer. So I was in charge of undressing myself and placing the clothes in an evidence bag. Holden insisted that I be allowed to use their shower and get some clean clothes.

I dressed in a towel, and he guided me to the shower with a gentle yet firm hand. He turned on the water and handed me the soap and put a clean towel and clothes on a hook.

"Take as long as you need," he said. "I'm not leaving you. I will be here. Do you understand?"

I nodded, not really understanding anything but feeling the need to make him feel better about my state.

After he turned his back and started walking out of the bathroom, I dropped the towel and let the hot water pour over me. My chills grew worse, as if they were battling the warmth of the water. I hoped the water would win. I was tired of being cold.

It took a long time. I stood maybe ten or fifteen minutes before I was warm enough to start with the soap. Was it only that morning that I'd had my hair straightened and styled? Now it was sticky and matted, and I did what I could do to get it clean. Luckily, besides my face and hands, the rest of me was clean, protected by my clothes. Still, I scrubbed, trying to clean the memory off me, I supposed. Logically, I knew that was impossible, but emotionally it was the only thing that was keeping me from screaming.

How many minutes passed, I didn't know, but finally I turned off the shower and put on the sweats and tank top that Holden left for me. The clothes smelled familiar, like coffee and oatmeal. I called Holden in and worried for a moment that I wasn't wearing a bra and then felt relief that I still worried about such things.

Holden took off his jacket and wrapped it around me. "Home?" he asked.

"You know what?" I said. "I want a hamburger."

"Really?"

"Let's not analyze it. That's what I want, and I want tequila shots to wash it down."

Holden drove me to a dive just outside the historic district; it was dark and warm and served drinks and pub food until two in the morning. When faced with the hamburger, I couldn't eat, but I did manage to get three tequila shots down.

Holden was careful not to broach the subject of what happened at Bliss Dental, allowing me to determine the extent of the conversation. I was tempted to ask him all about himself, every intimate detail, but I knew in my compromised state that he would tell me everything just to make me feel better, and I didn't want to take advantage of him that way.

He drank a hot chocolate, and when I said it looked good, he ordered me one. It turned out it was the perfect drink. I was feeling warm and cared for.

"I'm ready to go home now," I said.

Wordlessly he paid the tab and led me out of the bar, his arm wrapped around my waist. As he drove, I laid my head on his shoulder and managed to doze. He wanted to come in the house with me, to watch over me during the night, but I saw Spencer's head, spying on us through the window, and told Holden I wanted to be alone. It was a lie. I never wanted to be alone again.

"I didn't get my teeth fixed," I told him. "I still have my cavities."

"Don't worry about that now, Gladie," he said. "These are the wounds that are easy to heal."

He kissed me good night lightly on the lips, and I noticed he smelled like meat. "No carbs," I muttered, and opened the front door.

The light was on inside Grandma's entranceway, giving off a warm glow. Spencer stood waiting for me.

"I just found out," he said. "Just now. I didn't know before."

I walked toward him, and he took me into his arms. He squeezed me, and for the first time that night I felt whole, as if he was squeezing my pieces back together.

"I just found out," he said again.

And finally, I cried. I wailed the pain and shock right out of me and into Spencer's arms. And he took it all from me. And he squeezed tighter.

Chapter 5

✦ ♥ ✦

I'm sure you remember the story of Myron Schonbein, my most dismal match failure. We don't have to go over the details, but yes, there was a fire involved, and match-induced colitis. The part about the palm tree was mostly made up. Anyway, the Myron failure happened when I was young, just starting out in the matchmaking business. Not only did I think I was through with matchmaking, I never wanted to show my face again. I was in a dark place. I stopped putting on eyeliner. I threw all my Estée Lauder in a drawer. I started wearing jeans. It was bad. Then one day a mousy little girl about your age came knocking on my door. I didn't want to answer because I was feeling low, and I hadn't hairsprayed my hair in days. But that little thing was persistent. She wanted a match, quick, and she knew I was the person to make it happen. I knew in my heart she was right. Instantly, I felt she would find happiness with Florida Farangano. They were my first lesbian couple. They're still together to this day. The moral of this story is (1) lesbian couples generally have amazing staying power, and (2) answer the door even when you feel like you can't go on. You don't have a choice but to put one foot in front of the other and do what you're supposed to do. Heed the call. You have to keep living, dolly. It sure beats the alternative.

Lesson 99,
Matchmaking Advice from Your Grandma Zelda

. . .

MY TEARS dried up just as suddenly as they began.
I pulled back out of Spencer's embrace and punched
him in the arm.

"Where were you?" I demanded. "You didn't answer
your phone. You didn't come with the cops. You weren't
at the police station."

Spencer ran his hand through his thick, dark hair. "I
told you, I'm lying low. I'm on a leave of absence. They
know not to disturb me, no matter what."

"Is this about your penis?" I asked, pointing at his
crotch. "Your out-of-control, roving, happy-pants penis?"

"Gladie, you make it sound like you've given a lot of
thought to my happy-pants penis."

"Only enough to stay clear of it," I said. "Besides, it
probably has spots on it, or worse."

"Would you like to check it to make sure?"

"You are five years old," I said.

Spencer smirked his annoying little smirk. "You're
wearing my workout clothes. My wifebeater shirt has
never looked better."

I looked down at my braless chest and covered myself
with one arm. "I didn't know they were your clothes," I
said. "What do you mean, don't bother you no matter
what? You're not going to get involved with this murder
case?"

Spencer looked down at his feet. "I'll keep tabs on it
from afar, but I'm not going out there."

"You mean out there where your Facebook friends
are? Spencer, aren't you taking this a little far?"

"Trust me, Pinkie, hell hath no fury."

My body sagged. I closed my eyes and swayed in
place. "I'm tired," I said, more to myself than to Spencer.

Without hesitating, he swept me up in his arms, and I

laid my head on his shoulder. "Then rest, Pinkie. Rest," he said.

Spencer took the stairs two at a time. He laid me down gently on my bed and closed my bedroom door. Turning out the light, he settled in next to me and drew the covers up over us.

"Stick to your side, Spencer. I don't want Mr. Happy Pants near me. I haven't forgotten what a disgusting player you are."

"Don't worry, Gladys, I'll stick to my side," he said.

"Don't call me Gladys," I said, but I was already half asleep. Spencer gathered me to him, spoonlike, and draped his arm around me. Lying in his warmth, I fell asleep.

THANKFULLY, I didn't dream. I slept as if in a coma and woke up fourteen hours later. Spencer was sitting up in bed, watching TV.

"What is that?" I asked.

"I don't know," Spencer said. "It's some show about how we're all going to die young if we don't drink kale juice. It was either this or four women talking about Botox. Daytime TV is crap. Why do people watch this stuff?"

"No," I said. "I mean what is that? I don't have a TV in my room."

Spencer flipped through a few channels, settling on an infomercial with a muscly man talking about working out ten minutes a day for bodybuilder results. "I brought it in. I figured I would need it if I'm going to hide out here for a while."

"What on earth did you do to those Facebook women?"

"Whatever I did, it didn't deserve the response I got," he said.

"What response? What did they do?"

"I'm not going to get into it with you, Pinkie. Let's just say I have my reasons for hiding out in your bedroom."

"How are you going to eat?" I asked. "Don't expect me to wait on you. If you do, you are sadly mistaken."

"You grandma is waiting on me. She likes me being here. I guess she's not keen on Neighbor Boy."

"She's keen enough," I said. "Why wouldn't she be? He's perfect."

"How do you know? You don't know anything about him."

Spencer knew how to stop a conversation cold.

"Your grandmother is keeping my whereabouts secret, and I expect the same from you, Pinkie," he said. "She's got so many people coming and going that I'll have to be up here most of the time."

"This is a cosmic joke," I said. "How long do I have to suffer through this?"

"Not long. I have a plan."

"Says the man watching teen reality shows."

"I'm glad your hair is back to normal," he said. "You're not the sleek and styled type."

My hands flew to my head. "What?"

I ran to the bathroom and looked in the mirror. It was like the Ecuadoran Erect never happened. My hair was a giant frizzball.

I stood at the foot of my bed. "It was supposed to last four months," I whined. "I spent my last dollar on it."

"You must have superhuman hair," Spencer said, never taking his eyes off the television.

"It was the blood," I said with sudden realization. "Dr. Dulur's blood did something to the Ecuadoran Erect."

"Don't blame Dr. Dulur," Spencer said. "He's had a bad week."

. . .

AFTER SHUTTING Spencer in my room with a ten-year-old baseball game on one of the sports channels, I stood at the top of the stairs and listened. Quiet. Grandma's house was usually busy in the afternoon, but she must have shooed everyone away. She could be very thoughtful. Obviously, she wanted to give me time to heal after last night's ordeal without the spotlight of the entire town on me.

It was good to be in the sanctuary of my grandmother's house. I felt safe. And hungry. There were toaster waffles in the freezer calling my name. I bet there was also chocolate milk in the fridge. The perfect late-lunch meal, as far as I was concerned.

When I got to the bottom of the stairs, Grandma was waiting for me. She wore her favorite Jean Paul Gaultier–knockoff cocktail dress and Louis Vuitton shoes. My antenna shot up. She only wore that outfit when company was coming.

She took my hand and pulled me toward her. She looked up into my eyes and studied me for a moment. "You're fine," she said like she was telling me the weather. "You'll have nightmares, mostly next week, and again in two months—those will be the worst—but you're fine. You're healing. It didn't get you inside where it counts."

I realized I was holding my breath and exhaled. It was good to know I was all right.

"Everyone's on their way. They'll be here in a couple minutes," she said.

"Who's everyone?"

Everyone meant everyone.

Within minutes, Grandma's house was invaded by at least thirty people, most bearing foil pans filled with food. I scooped up some mashed potatoes and a burrito and fielded questions about Dr. Dulur.

"Yes, I'm sure he was dead," I answered. Lucy, Bridget, and three of Grandma's friends sat with me at the kitchen table. The rest stood around us, holding plates of food. The police had released precious few details of what happened the night before, and so they were trying to suck the nitty-gritty out of me. I wasn't ready to give them all the details. I wasn't ready to relive it all.

"Oh, honey, you are a magnet for death," Lucy declared. "Like you're the Pied Piper of corpses. Last month and now this." The month before, I had seen some dead people, but they all had faces.

"What are the odds that the moment you work up the courage to see a dentist, he gets murdered?" Bridget asked.

"Has to be astronomical," said Lou the mechanic. "Gladie's seen more dead people than me." Lou was rumored to have a checkered past as a member of a notorious gang in L.A. The room started chewing furiously, probably thinking about me being a badass gangbanger.

"Did you see the killer?" Meryl the librarian asked. She leaned forward, her mouth open. I hadn't seen her this excited since the library almost booked Janet Evanovich for an author reading.

"I was under the gas, asleep," I said. "I didn't see anything until it was over."

Meryl whistled. "I bet it was the pagans. I bet those freaks did it."

The chewing stopped. It was as if the room's atoms rearranged themselves.

Meryl took a breath to say something more but was interrupted by the slamming of the front door.

"Zelda! Zelda Burger, don't worry. I'm here," Mayor Robinson announced. He made quite an entrance, pausing at the kitchen doorway, his arms outstretched like he was doing a benediction, dressed in a black suit with a silk scarf around his neck. His shoes were polished to a brilliant shine. He took in the crowd in Grandma's kitchen and seemed to gain energy from it. Smiling wide, he focused in on me. "Gladie, my darling," he said, edging Bridget out of her chair and taking the seat next to me.

"You have my word that we will find the perpetrator of this heinous act," he said, patting my hand. "You can call me anytime." He handed me his business card. COMMUNICATOR IN CHIEF was written in raised gold lettering with a cellphone number.

"Wayne, what are you doing about those murderous pagans?" Meryl asked.

"Now, Meryl, we don't know for sure the alien worshippers killed Simon Dulur," he said.

He turned to me. "Does my breath smell?" he asked, exhaling sharply in my face.

Bird Gonzalez, the hairdresser, appeared suddenly in the kitchen with her hair unusually messed. "You have to roust the bastards," she said, out of breath. "The heathens vandalized my shop. I don't care if it's the end of the world or not, we need to pack up their yurts and get them the hell out of town. Gladie, what on earth happened to your hair?"

IT TOOK two gin and tonics to calm Bird down and to get her to tell us exactly what the end-of-worlders did to her shop. In the end, it wasn't really vandalism, just a lot of flowers thrown around and what could be described as an incense bomb by a group claiming that all those with permanents had to make way for the Arrival. Obviously, they weren't aware that permanents were not in style.

It was a toss-up which made Bird more upset: the so-called vandalism or my hair. The failure of her Ecuadoran Erect was more than she could bear at the moment. "The world is all topsy-turvy," she said, her lower lip quivering. Evidently, I was the first human to defy the straightening effects of the Ecuadoran Erect. She offered to try it again, but the consensus at the table was I was more like me, albeit less attractive, with curly hair and should stay like I am. Bird kindly refunded my money.

I almost wept seeing the cash in my hand. I could now pay my cellphone bill and the minimum on my Visa, and have enough left over to buy lattes for the week. I was thankful for my superhuman hair that defied styling. Now I was almost flush.

Despite having no evidence of the pagan cult's guilt in Dr. Dulur's murder and despite Bird's rather weak charge of vandalism against them, the group in Grandma's house was up in arms. With murmurings about the Manson Family, they decided to make a show about the town's pious nature and intimidate the end-of-worlders into leaving. After a cursory meeting in Grandma's parlor, they went out to implement their plan with the mayor's blessing.

Grandma, Bridget, Lucy, and I were left alone at the kitchen table. I took second helpings. Grandma was sipping a Coke. She had been uncharacteristically quiet during the whole meeting.

"It's never what you think in this town," Lucy said. "It all looks like pretty antique shops and pie houses, and then a war starts with alien lovers. You couldn't get me to move out of Cannes with a crowbar."

"I think I know who killed Dr. Dulur," Bridget said, making us jump. The conversation had steered so far away from the murder that I almost forgot it had happened.

"All this talk of murder and violence," Grandma said. "It's not good for the love business. I only know love, and murders just mess with my sight." She meant her third eye, which was great for love and daily activities but seemed to be myopic when it came to murder and mayhem.

"This is right up your alley, then, Zelda," Bridget said. "I think the police chief's girlfriends murdered Dr. Dulur."

The mashed potatoes went down the wrong way, and I choked. I hacked and sputtered, trying to breathe. Grandma handed me a glass of water, and I took a sip.

"Why do you think that, dear?" she asked Bridget.

"You haven't heard?" Bridget's eyes grew enormous, and her glasses slid down her nose. "Chief Bolton has disappeared. At least a half dozen women in this town are looking for him in order to skin him alive. Some say they've already done it, and he's lying dead somewhere in the apple orchards." Bridget looked at me for confirmation.

"I don't know about every death," I said, affronted. Sheesh, a woman sees a few dead bodies, and suddenly she's the go-to person for finding corpses.

"Why do they want to skin him alive?" I asked. Spencer had given me the general idea, but I was betting Bridget had all the juicy details. She did half the books in town and got the lowdown sometimes even before Grandma.

"Where have you been?" Lucy chimed in. "Rosalie Rodriguez changed her Facebook status to 'involved with Spencer Bolton.'"

"That can't be," I said. "Spencer is fifteen years younger than Rosalie."

"Spencer likes them older. Didn't you know that?" Bridget asked.

I didn't. I only saw him with supermodels, and they were all young.

"I think you're mistaken," I said. I turned to Grandma to see what she thought, but she was busy slicing a piece of monkey bread to go with her coffee.

"Spencer has had a whole slew of older women," Lucy explained. "Not me, though. That bee hasn't buzzed anywhere near this honeypot."

I tried to imagine Spencer with a slew of older women. I don't know why the thought made me so upset. Maybe because I had always imagined him with young women, prettier than me.

"I'm prettier than Rosalie Rodriguez," I said, aloud. I clamped down on my lip. It was too late. They looked at me, each with one eyebrow raised. "I didn't mean that," I said.

"You are *much* prettier than Rosalie," Grandma said.

"Holden thinks you're prettier," Bridget said. "And he's the best-looking man in town. Maybe the best-looking man in Southern California, if you don't count Los Angeles."

Holden was good-looking, but I didn't know if he thought I was prettier than Rosalie. I didn't know what he thought about anything. Our relationship was in a low-lying trough.

"What happened when Rosalie changed her status?" I asked Bridget, steering her back to the original path of our conversation.

"The other five women he was involved with on Facebook saw red. They all discovered each other when they wrote horrible things on Rosalie's page," Lucy said. "It was the catfight to end all catfights."

" 'Catfight' is a sexist term," Bridget said.

"Fine," Lucy said to Bridget. "It was a bitchfest. Is that better?" She turned to me. "Half of the women are married, too. Did you know that, Gladie? They didn't care. They made a real show of it. They didn't want to lose Spencer, and they didn't care if they lost their husbands while trying to get him back."

I felt dirty. Spencer was upstairs in my bed, watching

reality TV and baseball reruns. Meanwhile, middle-aged women were hunting him down on the streets.

"What kind of show did they make?" I asked.

"Well, they set his car on fire for one," Bridget said.

"And they ransacked his house and cut up all his Armani into handkerchief-sized swatches," said Lucy.

I found it hard to believe that they could commit crimes against the police chief and face no repercussions, but maybe Spencer thought he could handle it on his own. That would be typical for his ego.

"And they called his brother in the middle of the night and threatened him when they couldn't find Spencer," Grandma said.

"Spencer has a brother?" I asked.

"I heard Rosalie was found outside his apartment in the middle of the night, crying and begging him to make love to her right there on the street," Bridget said.

"Yikes," I said.

"Men are worthless souls who suck the dignity out of women," Bridget said. "I brought her a box of chocolates this morning to make her feel better, but her sister told me she had gone out."

"At least she's going out again," I said.

"She went out with her entire set of Rachael Ray knives," Bridget explained, taking a piece of monkey bread. "See where I'm going with this?" she asked with her mouth full.

"The dentist," Lucy said, her voice low and thick with awe. "Gladie, was the dentist stabbed?"

"Well . . . ," I started. I still wasn't sure I wanted to discuss Dr. Dulur's face. "I think there was a knife involved."

"Gladie, do you want to go out with Bridget and me to the lake?" Lucy asked. The subject of Rosalie's knives and Spencer's misadventures seemed to have run its course. "They say the cult is meeting there this afternoon to do some kind of salutation ritual to their aliens, and the Cannes Astronomy Club is going to protest. It should be a hoot."

"It might do you good to get out," Bridget said.

"Maybe I could manage seeing a few aliens," I said. The fresh air would be nice, I figured. Besides, I could use a break from Spencer.

"Good, come with us," Bridget said.

"Not a good day for the lake," Grandma said, startling us. "After sunset, it should be okay. But wear a rain hat."

"It's not supposed to rain, Zelda," Bridget said.

"I didn't say it would rain," Grandma said.

Grandma shooed Bridget and Lucy away while I cleaned up the foil pans. I told them I would come along in a little while after I got things taken care of at the house. Grudgingly, I made a plate for Spencer. It occurred to me that I could starve him out of my room, but no matter how much I hated him, I didn't want him to meet up with Rosalie's set of Rachael Ray knives.

Upstairs, Spencer was lying in my bed, hugging a family-sized bag of chips and watching *Family Guy* on TV. He pointed at the screen and laughed out loud. "Vagina boob," he squealed. "Vagina boob!"

I handed him the plate of food. "You are regressing, Spencer."

"This show is hysterical," he said, accepting the plate.

"Regressing when you were already five to begin with. You are amazing."

Spencer inspected the food. "I didn't think you were going to wait on me."

"I'm not," I said. "I just brought you food."

He shoveled a fork into his mouth. "Delish. You're a woman after my own heart."

"No, I'm not. I'm at least twenty years too young for that."

"Meow," he said with his mouth full.

"No. No, meow. There's no meowing. I'm not meowing. I'm stating a fact."

"Sounded like meowing."

"You're not going to put this on me, Mrs. Robinson. You're the one in hiding."

"Mrs. Robinson was the old one," he said with a smirk. "I'm the young one. The Dustin Hoffman character." He squirmed, his smirk gone. "Why are you looking at me like that, Pinkie? You're making me nervous."

Grandma walked into my room, behind me. "Dolly," she said, "this arrived for you. It's short notice, but you can't get out of it."

She handed me a fancy linen envelope. "You can't get out of it. I made the match, and she wants to thank me by making you one of her bridesmaids."

"Bridesmaid?" I asked.

"You can't get out of it," she repeated. She turned her attention to Spencer. "Don't incite Gladie. She's easily excitable."

"That's what I was hoping for," he said, his smirk back.

"I've got business," Grandma said to me. "I'll see you when you get back. Take a pen."

Grandma left, and Spencer got out of bed. He pulled off his sweatshirt, and my eyes bugged out, traveling from his wide, muscular chest down to his chiseled abs and the line of dark hair that started at his belly button and went down to below his sweatpants, which now hung loosely at a precariously low level on his hips.

"I'm going to hop in the shower," he said, turning and giving me an eyeful of the top of his firm butt. I was pretty sure my heart stopped, and I really hated Spencer for that. "See ya later," he said, and went into my bathroom.

I got my purse and searched for a pen next to my bed.

"The bed is filled with crumbs!" I shouted. "Were you rolling around in the chips or something?" I heard the shower start. I dusted off the sheets, but I couldn't make any headway and gave up. That's when I noticed Spencer liked to shower with the door open. "The door! The door!" I yelled, and slammed it shut. I rubbed my eyes. Nope, I couldn't get the vision out. Now I wouldn't be able to focus all day. Maybe not for the next year.

"Hey, Miss Burger, is this a bad time?"

I screamed and jumped back. Sergeant Brody was at my threshold in full police regalia.

"What are you doing here?" I asked, out of breath.

"We need you to come with us, Miss Burger. We need you to walk us through the scene of the crime."

The pain in my tooth suddenly came roaring back.

Chapter 6

✦ ♥ ✦

*H*air! *That was a great musical, dolly. Good music, dancing, naked tushies. My kind of musical. But the sixties are over, bubeleh. The LSD is gone, and the hippies have moved on to drive BMWs and worry about their 401(k)s. The bras are back on, and now it's time to cut the fringe off the suede jackets. You hear what I'm saying? I'm talking hair. I'm talking personal grooming. (That's what they call it these days.) More than cutting a few inches off the top. More than nose hair. I'm talking about the down under. The south of the border. The Tropic of Capricorn. The below the Bible Belt. Dolly, you just never know what you're going to find down there these days. I've seen matches go south and then go bad after the discovery that their potential mate for life is growing the Bridge over the River Kwai. I know these are embarrassing topics. That's why I haven't used the words "pubic hair" once. But you are going to have to get beyond your shyness, your squeamishness. You have to ask them straight out if they have tamed the lion's mane, if they are presentable. Get right in there where it's none of your business and make it your business. The future happiness of your matches is dependent on it. Be a yenta. Be a busybody. It's your genetic heritage.*

Lesson 31,
Matchmaking Advice from Your Grandma Zelda

. . .

SERGEANT BRODY put me in the back of the police car and turned it in the direction of Bliss Dental. "Easy listening or top forty?" he asked me, turning on the radio.

"Don't you have to listen to the police radio?" I asked.

"I need a break," he said. "It's been crazy in town since the wackos showed up."

"The townspeople seem to be up in arms," I said.

"I don't know what they want from us. It's not like we can do anything about it. The cult members have all the right permits."

"So you turned off the police radio?"

"The town's gone berserk," he explained. "The police radio doesn't make sense anymore."

To illustrate, he turned it on. Screams blared from the speakers. "Nutcases in the trees by the lake!" one man yelled. "Sex! Sex Sex!" yelled another until he was interrupted by "For the love of God, use a porta-potty, you freaks!" Then, several shouts of "Aliens in Sector Three!" And finally came one desperate cry from a man, obviously in tears, "The horror! The horror!"

"Okay, easy listening," I said.

Sergeant Brody flipped a switch, and Neil Diamond replaced the mayhem. "I can't wait until the aliens show themselves so these wackjobs will leave," Brody said.

"Are the aliens going to fly out of the mountain to take the end-of-worlders to other worlds anytime soon?" It was a question I never thought I would ask.

"The sooner the better," he said. "I don't care if a killer virus takes all of us unworthies, or if we are lasered to ashes by Martians, like the culters say, depending which group you talk to."

"It makes eating organic redundant," I said.

"I'm glad I won the coin toss. I'd much prefer to handle the No-Face Case instead of the cult."

"Do you have any leads on the No-Face Case?" I asked. Another question I never thought I would ask.

"A couple guys in the station think coyotes did it. I'd say that's a long shot."

"Uh," I said. I couldn't believe Spencer took that moment to go AWOL. It looked like poor Dr. Dulur's murder would never get solved.

"The walk-through shouldn't take too long," he said. "Just point out all the highlights, and I'll take notes."

The throbbing in my tooth came back with a vengeance. My hand flew to my face, and I scrunched my eyes against the pain. It was agony. That's how I knew we had arrived.

The exterior of the Bliss Dental building showed no evidence that a grisly murder had happened inside only a few hours before. It looked like business as usual with three cars in the parking lot. I recognized Belinda's Toyota. It comforted me for whatever reason.

Belinda, along with the other Bliss Dental employees—Nathan and Holly—sat in the waiting room. Holly flipped through a *Cosmo* while Belinda inspected flowerpots and Nathan stared out into space.

"Sorry to keep you waiting," Brody told them when we entered. "This shouldn't take too long."

"When can we open up again?" asked Holly.

"Dr. Dulur isn't even cold," Nathan said, clearly annoyed at her.

"He's cold enough," said Holly. "I have my own clients, you know. I have fifteen cleaning appointments this week." She seemed to notice me for the first time. "You want me to handle that whitening for you? I can get it done today."

"I'm good," I said.

"The office is closed until further notice," Brody said. "I don't know who the heir is."

"The doctor didn't own the practice," Belinda explained. "It's owned by a group of dentists out of L.A. Dr. Dulur was just an employee."

That was news to me, and by the looks of them, news to Nathan and Brody, too. It was impossible to tell if Holly was surprised. With her face frozen in one expression, I thought she needed a sign to hold up to announce her emotions. MAD. HAPPY. SURPRISED. It would be a big help.

"I've been in contact with them," Belinda continued. "They said to open up just as soon as the police allowed, and they're sending a replacement dentist."

Belinda continued to inspect the waiting-room plants. Brody stared at her, the little cogs in his brain turning loudly, cranking his brain cells into activity, and I knew what he was thinking. He was thinking that Belinda had gotten right back to business, seemingly unfazed in the wake of her boss's gory murder.

Brody took out a notepad and scribbled something. "All right, folks," he said. "Let's get to it. I'm on overtime as it is, and it's mac-n-cheese night at home. Walk me through the events."

Again, Belinda took charge. "Gladie came in at six-thirty. She was the last patient of the night. I left after I checked her in."

"Where did you go?" Brody asked.

Belinda flinched and took a step back. "What do you mean?" she asked.

"Where did you go after you left? It's a pretty simple question."

"I don't remember," she said. Brody stopped scribbling and looked up.

"You don't remember? It was last night."

"I don't remember," she repeated.

Brody scribbled in his notebook. "Then what happened?" he asked.

"Then I left," Holly said. "You want to know where I went? Bar None. I had three whiskey sours and went home with Gianni Marchi."

"You're at Bar None every Tuesday night. Everyone knows that," Brody said. "That leaves you, Mr. Smith."

Nathan stood. He had a small shaved patch on the back of his head and a bunch of stitches. I swayed in place and took a seat.

"I prepped Miss Burger for her dental work. Seven fillings and a whitening treatment."

"Where was that?" Brody asked.

"Examination Room Three."

"Let's go back there."

I dragged my feet on the carpet behind the others as we filed past the yellow police tape that blocked off the back office. It occurred to me that they might be curious to see the actual scene of the crime. I was trying to block it out of my mind, like Sarah Palin's bus tour. I had almost convinced myself that what I had seen the night before wasn't all that bad. I was pretty neurotic, and I had probably blown the whole scene way out of proportion.

"I prepped Miss Burger," Nathan explained at Examination Room 3. "Everything happened so fast." His voice hitched, and he closed his eyes. I patted his back to steady him, but I was picturing myself lying on the chair, unconscious and helpless.

He turned to me. "Thank you. I'm all right," he said, and took a deep breath. "Then the lights went out. Dr. Dulur said something. A bad word. I got up to check the breakers. I could barely see, and I was wondering how I was going to make it through the office like that, when Dr. Dulur cried out."

"Cried out how?" asked Brody.

"Like a scream that was cut off, and he fell to the floor."

"Did you get a look at the guy?" Brody asked.

"It was dark. I felt his presence, and I ran. I heard him running after me, like he was heavy. He made noise, you know what I mean? I got to the waiting room, and I turned and saw him by the glow of the Exit sign. He was big, really big, and dressed all in black. I couldn't make out his face. I made it to the door when he hit me over the back of the head. The next thing I knew, Miss Burger was standing over me."

Brody whistled. "Eighteen stitches, right? That bastard."

Nathan absentmindedly touched his head, like the act of telling his story made the injury hurt all the more. I could relate. My tooth felt like it was on fire, and a couple others were starting to throb, too.

"Okay, Underwear Girl, it's your turn," Brody said.

"I w-w-woke up here on the floor," I said. "But the lights were on. I don't know what time it was."

Brody flipped through his notebook. "You called the police at 11:53."

"I was under the gas for almost five and a half hours," I said to no one in particular.

Unconscious at the mercy of a killer.

I struggled to steady my quivering lower lip. If I let it go, there would be no turning back. I would need a Xanax drip.

"Where did you find him?" Brody asked.

I pointed to Examination Room 2. "Over there."

It had been cleaned up. The chair was gone, as well as a swath of carpet, which had been cut out, leaving a large rectangular hole in the floor, showing the concrete below. It was a relief. It didn't look anything like *Saw III* anymore. It was more like Costco.

"How did his blood get all over you?" Brody asked.

Nathan, Holly, and Belinda turned in unison and stared at me.

"It sort of happened in stages. I checked his pulse, and then, you know."

"No, what?" Belinda asked.

"It happened," I said.

"What happened?" Belinda asked.

"He fell on me."

"A dead guy fell on you?" Holly asked. I could have sworn her eyebrows twitched.

"Yes," I said.

"I've seen that before," Brody said. "Happens all the time."

I let that hang in the air for a moment. "Did you find his, you know?" I asked.

"His face?" Brody asked. "Not yet."

"He didn't have a face?" Holly asked. "I didn't know he didn't have a face."

"What do you mean, he didn't have a face?" Belinda asked.

"What kind of sick fuck takes a man's face?" Nathan chimed in. I was wondering the same thing.

With the walk-through finished, Brody locked up Bliss Dental, and we walked toward the cars. Belinda pulled me aside.

"Any luck with a match?" she asked me.

"Belinda, a dead guy with no face fell on me," I said.

She smacked the side of her head. "Oh, of course. What was I thinking? You think you'll have something for me by tomorrow?"

Belinda was more focused than most. "Tomorrow? Sure, why not? You'll have a name by then," I promised.

"So, I'll have a date Saturday night?"

"Sure." My shirt was stuck to my back. Flop sweat. Matchmaking gave me stage fright. I wasn't what you would call a natural.

Nathan hopped into his Geo, and Holly into her truck, and they peeled out of the parking lot. Sergeant Brody was having a heated conversation with a couple who had wandered into the lot and removed half of their clothing. "The Arrival!" they called to the sky, flapping their arms like wings. They broke out in dance, and Brody chased them around, trying to get them to put their clothes back on.

"Is it a full moon?" I asked Belinda.

"How would I know?" she said. "Listen, Gladie, there's something else I want to talk to you about."

Beating all odds, Brody captured the couple and shoved them into the back of the squad car. He stood doubled over with his hands on his thighs and tried to catch his breath.

"Gladie, they found something fishy about the books," Belinda said quietly.

"What books?"

"The Bliss Dental books. A financial discrepancy."

"Who found it?" I asked.

"The police, and they're looking at me. They asked me questions, and they want to ask more questions. They told me to get a lawyer."

I was going to hell because all I could think of was that my first real client was going to go to prison and with her my Visa card. "That's terrible, Belinda."

Her eyes filled with tears. "Holly said it's a perfect motive for murder."

"What motive?"

"If I was stealing money and Dr. Dulur found out."

"Are you saying—?"

"I'm innocent, Gladie. Do you believe me?" She put her hand on my arm. She was wearing another large sweater, this time with a giant yellow daisy embroidered in glittery thread on her chest. The daisy matched her yellow knit pants, which were a size too small and outlined her ample thighs. She wasn't the stereotype of a crazed killer who butchered her victims.

"Of course I believe you, Belinda," I said.

"So, will you help me?"

"I'm going to match you right up."

"No, I meant with the murder. Will you help me prove my innocence?"

The month before, I had been peripherally involved in solving a murder. I guess the news had gotten around. "Belinda, I really want to help, but I think you need a professional."

Belinda fished her keys out of her purse and unlocked her car with a beep. "No, I want you, Gladie. We can talk more tomorrow when we meet about my match."

I was seriously sweating now. It was getting dark. Tomorrow was only hours away, and I didn't have a match for Belinda. I had to find someone quick.

I watched Belinda drive out of the parking lot and then I approached the squad car. The windows were fogged, and the car was rocking in a familiar rhythm. Brody put his hands up to the window to look inside and then jumped back.

"Stop!" he yelled. "Stop it now!" He pounded on the window. "Stop defiling the police car! This is government property."

The car bounced in earnest. Either the police department didn't splurge for decent shocks, or the couple was unusually energetic.

Brody threw up his hands. "I'll never get my mac-n-cheese now," he moaned.

"They'll have to finish sometime," I pointed out. But I wasn't eager to ride in that backseat anytime soon. I started to call Bridget to pick me up, but I hadn't paid my cellphone bill yet, and it was still dead.

"Stop!" Brody yelled again, and pounded on the windows. I sighed. It occurred to me that just about everybody was having more sex than me. It also occurred to me that I was hungry.

"Need a ride, pretty lady?" As if by magic, Holden came up behind me and slid his arm around my waist. He nuzzled my neck, and my skin burst into flame, instantly drying my back.

"I was just thinking about you," I croaked. "Where did you come from?"

"I was driving by and saw you standing there." He pointed to the squad car in disbelief. "Are they—?"

"Yeah, and Sergeant Brody isn't going to get his macaroni and cheese."

Holden raised an eyebrow. "Okay."

"So the answer is yes," I said.

"To what?"

"I want a ride."

THE LAKE was at the southwesternmost corner of Cannes, way out of the historic district, past the orchards. It was mostly used by rich tourists who came up during the summer to get drunk while boating. But it was past the boating season, and the lake was usually deserted this time of year.

We drove into the sunset. The sky was painted with brilliant pinks and blues. I had lived in a lot of places, but I had to admit Cannes was one of the most beautiful. Unfortunately, it also seemed to attract every escaped lunatic west of the Mississippi.

End-of-worlders, alien worshippers, and murderers aside, the women were bonkers. I mean, no less than six older women were gunning for Spencer? What were they thinking? Didn't they have any self-respect?

"What do you think about Facebook?" I asked Holden.

"I'm not much for the computer," he said. "I like to maintain a low profile."

He wasn't kidding. But it did give me an idea. I wondered how much I could find out about Holden online. Maybe a little snooping would uncover just what he was hiding from me and why he wanted to keep a low profile.

The parking lot at the lake's activity center near its main dock was filled with RVs and cars. Music blared and people milled about, with bonfires dotting the shore. It was just like Burning Man.

Holden helped me out of the truck. He took off his leather jacket and wrapped it around my shoulders. "It's a little chilly," he said.

It was all I could do not to wrap my legs around his waist and beg him to impregnate me right there between the Airstream travel trailer and the impromptu garbage dump.

The glow of the last vestiges of the day outlined his tall, strong body, and a sigh escaped my lips. "Should we find Bridget and Lucy?" he asked me.

"Who?" I asked. But Lucy was walking straight for me, still in her signature heels and flowy dress, even out in the wilds.

"Gladie Burger, is that you?" Her heels clacked against the blacktop. "Bridget, I found her! And she brought the tall drink of water. It's safe. Come on out."

Lucy sidled up next to me, and I noticed her hair was askew and her lipstick had smeared off her lips onto her left cheek. "It's been hell, Gladie," she said. "Poor Bridget."

I smelled Bridget before I saw her. At first I thought I was smelling barbecue, but it was Bridget.

I gasped. "Bridget, your hair."

"It's still smoking," Bridget said, hobbling toward us

with one shoe off and one shoe on. "But as far as I can tell, the fire is out."

Half her hair was singed off, and smoke billowed off her head. "Are you sure you're not on fire?" I asked.

"No, she's out," Lucy said. "I made sure. I don't know why it keeps smoking."

"The pagans did this to you?" I asked.

"The pagans? No, it was the PTA."

"The PTA set your head on fire?" Holden asked.

"Not quite," Lucy explained. "It was a candlelight vigil. They were carrying the candles to protest the pagans, and Bridget got too close."

"I was discussing free speech with them."

"It got heated, excuse the word," Lucy said. "They were waving their candles around, gesturing wildly while telling Bridget she was a bleeding-heart pagan lover."

"I've been called worse," Bridget said, pushing her glasses up on her nose.

"She didn't know she was on fire for a good minute, minute and a half," Lucy explained. "She kept arguing, and the flames kept growing around her head. It was a biblical sight, excuse the expression, Bridget."

"That's when the screaming started," Bridget said. "Not mine, theirs. I didn't know I was on fire yet. I just thought they were making s'mores nearby."

"Sixty-five stampeding PTA moms," Lucy said. "It was a fearsome sight, worse than Bridget on fire."

"Holy crap, it's a miracle you're not hurt," I said.

"I tried to get close to her to put her out, but the stampeding school moms got in the way," Lucy said.

"That was the terrible part," Bridget said, staring far off as she relived the memory. "Wave after wave of yoga pants, running toward me without pity. And they're in shape, Gladie. Solid. I was no match for them. I went down fast and then it was me dodging sixty-five pairs of merciless platform shoes."

"That's what put the fire out," Lucy explained.

"Holy crap," Holden said.

"We've been wandering around for an hour, looking for you," Lucy said. "I've got to get Bridget home."

"Why didn't you drive?" I asked.

"Oh, Lucy's Mercedes is in the lake," Bridget said.

I gasped. "The PTA moms pushed your car into the lake?"

"Oh, no. That happened hours before the PTA showed up," Lucy explained.

It took some convincing, but Holden left me at the lake while he drove Bridget and Lucy home, since there was only enough room in the truck's cab for three. I assured him I would be fine by myself, which, in light of Bridget's smoking hair, was difficult to say in the least. In the end, though, his chivalry made him side with Bridget and Lucy, who were truly damsels in distress. If only there hadn't been an invasion of a thousand lunatics, we could have called a taxi, but the town's two taxis had more business than they could handle right now.

Holden's jacket was good protection against the night chill, and I didn't need a hat like Grandma had suggested. The evening had taken on a nice party atmosphere, with bonfires and music and the smell of steaks in the air. I stood back under a tree and enjoyed the solitude.

It had been an intense couple of days, and I had a lot to think about. But the most pressing was Belinda's match. She expected at least a name by tomorrow and a real date by Saturday. And I had no ideas. Nothing. Bubkes. Even Penis Pipe Tim was nowhere to be seen. Good idea! I would look at the hospital the first thing in the morning. There had to be single men at the hospital, I reasoned, and they probably couldn't get away, which would improve Belinda's odds.

It was a clear night, and the stars were putting on a

breathtaking light show, but it wasn't a full moon like I had suspected. It was such a clear night that I was shocked when I felt droplets on my head. Drip, drop, they landed on my head and dripped down my face.

I could have sworn I heard whispers of "The Arrival, the Arrival" above me, along with a few giggles, and then the stream fell on me like a waterfall. The giggles intensified.

And then it got weird.

Holly from Bliss Dental dropped down from a nearby Winnebago, spotted me, and walked over. "You're being peed on," she said.

"I'm what?" I asked.

"You're being peed on. The cult kids are in the trees. They're peeing on you."

I jumped forward out of the line of fire. My hair was dripping pee down Holden's jacket.

"At least it isn't a dead guy on you," Holly said, no hint of humor in her voice.

"I can't believe they peed on me," I said.

"They've been doing it all day," she said. "Or so they tell me."

I shook out my hair. "Thank you for warning me," I said.

"No problem. Quite a week, huh?" she said. "Not all bad. At least the dentist is finally dead, right?"

Chapter 7

+ ♥ +

Like the commercial says, "Ask your doctor if your heart is healthy enough for sex." Not a bad idea at all. I also say, ask yourself if your heart is healthy enough for sex, and you should ask your matches the same thing. Because let me tell you something: your heart will be in it, even if you don't think it will be. We all partake in a casual dalliance from time to time. I know that. I'm not a prude, you know. But we need to be honest with ourselves: what happens in Vegas doesn't always stay in Vegas. It can follow you in your heart, in your soul. So tell your matches to take a deep breath and think before they act. Don't shtup unless you know you can handle it.

Lesson 80,
Matchmaking Advice from Your Grandma Zelda

MY BODY shot straight up, flinging my hair back and throwing a stream of urine behind me, making an impressive *thwack* noise as it hit the tree.

"What did you say?" I asked.

"Simon, the asshole," she said. "The dentist. No tears shed for that lowlife, am I right?"

"Uh," I said.

Holly pulled a pack of cigarettes from her back pocket. She lit one up, took a drag, and let out a long line of smoke. "Do you mind if I smoke?" she asked.

"Yes," I said.

She took another drag. "So, what's your story?" she asked.

"My story?"

"What was your relationship with Simon? You ballin' him?"

"He was dead most of the time I knew him," I said.

"Yeah? How could you tell?"

"Well, he had no face."

"Serves him right," she said.

"Holly, you are creeping me out," I said. "See the lines on my forehead? They are indicative of being creeped out. You probably don't recognize facial expressions anymore, being out of practice yourself."

"Meow," Holly said.

I stomped my foot. "What's with all the meow talk all of a sudden? I don't meow."

"Whatever. I say the jerk got what was coming to him."

"He had no face." Was I the only one impressed by that detail?

"Okay, fine, don't believe me. I'm just saying he wasn't all that nice."

"Thanks for the info." I couldn't warm up to Holly. She wasn't a nice person and wasn't really all human anymore. More plastic than anything else. But maybe I was allergic to silicone. "I have pee in my hair," I told her by way of an apology.

"You have pee all over you," she said. "You smell like the men's bathroom at a football game."

Suddenly we were lit up in the lights of Holden's truck as he stopped at the curb and cut the engine. His door opened, and his work boots hit the pavement.

"Holy God," Holly said. "Who the hell is that?"

"That's my boyfriend." *Eat your heart out, Wax Woman.*

"How did you swing that?" she asked.

"I held him off as long as I could, but he wore me down," I lied. I was so going to hell.

Holden put his arms around me and kissed me lightly on the lips. "Sorry I took so long," he said. He looked at his hand. "You're wet."

"She was peed on," Holly explained.

"She was what?"

"Holden, this is Holly. She's the hygienist at Bliss Dental," I said.

Holden put out his hand, but then changed his mind, probably because his hand was covered in pee. "Nice to meet you," he said.

"Not as nice as it is to meet *you*," she said, shaking her hips. "You can find me most nights at the Bar None. I'm what you'd call a good time." She traced her finger down the buttons of his shirt.

His expression was unreadable, a lot like Holly's. I had less success hiding my feelings. I wanted to do the ladylike thing and scratch out her eyes. *How's that for* meow, *beotch?*

Holly got the picture and stepped back, and Holden guided me to the truck, opened my door for me, then closed me in. "Do you mind if I open the window a crack?" he asked me as he drove out of the parking lot.

"I smell like the men's room at a football game, right?" I said.

"After halftime, when the toilets back up," he said.

"I'm sorry about your jacket."

"I wanted to get a new one anyway." Holden was understanding and protective and pretty much perfect. He even smelled good, although it was hard to catch his scent through the cloud of urine stench.

"I hope you don't mind, but I've made dinner plans for us," he said.

"Good, I'm starved," I said. "But I should get cleaned up first."

"The place I have in mind has a bathroom. You can get cleaned up there. I'm talking about my house."

"Your house?" I asked, as surprised as if he'd told me boys in trees peed on me. "I've never been in your house."

"Really?" he asked, turning the corner to our street. "That's strange."

I had been trying to get into his house for nearly a month. Holden was still much of a mystery to me, and now he was inviting me into his fortress of solitude, his bat cave, his Holly Hobbie Dream Dollhouse.

I caught myself rubbing my hands together in anticipation.

"Do you like duck?" he asked.

"Daffy or Donald?"

WE PASSED Grandma's house and parked in Holden's driveway. Grandma's house was lit up. It was time for the Wednesday night Single No More class. The week before, I co-hosted it with Grandma. But when she got Janet Schwartz and Tiffany Jenkins to practice their sexy walks in the participation part of the class, I unintentionally guffawed, and they got offended and ran out. Since then, I was banned from the class. "Just until I get Janet and Tiffany matched off," Grandma assured me.

Holden unlocked his front door and waited for me to enter first. I had imagined the inside of his house on more than one occasion. In my fantasies, it was alternately a one-room log cabin with a ratty couch, a large bed in the corner, and a bear rug on the floor in front of a roaring fire, or a stone keep with medieval tapestries on the walls and Holden's shiny suit of armor in the corner.

The reality was somewhere between the two. I entered right into a large, open great room, the living room, dining room, and kitchen all in one. There was a lot of wood, and it was tidy. Oriental rugs covered the wood floors, and overstuffed, comfy-looking furniture faced the large fireplace. The kitchen looked original—not as old as Grandma's, but predating Pearl Harbor. Not a drop of stainless steel anywhere.

"You can use my bathroom," he said. "Down the hall, the last room on the right. There's a clean robe on the hook on the back of the door. I'll start dinner." He walked to the kitchen and opened the refrigerator.

I stared at him with pity. Poor man, he really shouldn't leave me alone in his house to wander wherever I pleased. Didn't he know I was a no-good busybody? Who would stop me from rooting around in his underwear drawer and his night table? Who would stop me from hacking his computer?

Who was I kidding? I didn't know how to hack a computer. I hadn't even checked my email in weeks.

The hallway was lined with paintings of what I recognized to be Indian mythological figures. I had worked in the gift shop at an ashram in Cincinnati for two weeks. I had thought the job would help with my chi, but the politics of the place was dog-eat-dog. I had to move on quick, and luckily, I fell right into a job at the local methadone clinic, where the atmosphere was much more laid back.

Holden's paintings looked more expensive than the Xeroxed pictures we sold at the ashram. Hoity-toity.

I sneaked a peak at Holden's bedroom as I reached the bathroom. It was clean and spartan. There was a homemade quilt on his bed. I pushed back the desire to sniff his pillow.

My skin was starting to sting. The cult boys must have had very acidic pee. Probably too much junk food.

I turned the light on in the bathroom and closed the

door. The bathrobe was hanging there, as promised. It was plaid, just like most of Holden's wardrobe. The bathroom was clean and tidy and very small. No dried toothpaste in the sink, no splatter behind the toilet. Holden was like a Greek god. I was the dirtiest thing in his house.

I bundled his jacket and my clothes in the sink and turned on the shower. It was no-nonsense, no massage jets or anything. Holden used all-natural shampoo-and-soap-in-one, but it was the expensive kind, the brand they sold at the snooty organic store in San Diego.

When I was done, I didn't smell a bit like pee, but my hair was mad. It didn't appreciate all-natural shampoo. I searched through his medicine cabinet for hair products. All I found was aspirin and a small jar of Vaseline. Holden was old school and obviously looked gorgeous without the benefit of men's beauty products. I, on the other hand, needed all the help I could get.

Taking a deep breath, I put on the robe and stepped out of the bathroom. The house was filled with delicious smells and jazz music. The living room was lit only by the light of the fire in the fireplace and the lights coming from the kitchen. Holden's back was toward me as he stood at the stove. Lucy was right. He was a tall drink of water. I watched his muscular shoulders move as he cooked.

"Smells good," I said.

Holden turned, surprised. His eyes traveled up my body from my bare feet to my quickly frizzing hair. I looked down to see if the robe had melted off my body. Nope, it was still on. Damn that expensive material.

"Dinner is almost ready," he said. "Would you mind eating by the fire?"

"Yes. I hate warmth, soft lighting, and comfortable furniture."

My spying had netted nothing so far except now I

knew he was clean and spent too much money on organic shampoo. Where were the photos? Not one family pic or vacation souvenir, nothing to give me much-needed information about Holden.

I stood by the fire and scanned the room. The hair on the back of my neck stood up as I realized something was terribly wrong with the house.

"Holden," I said, alarmed. "Where's the TV?"

"No TV. I'm a reader."

He gestured behind me. The length of one wall was covered in bookshelves. I scanned them.

"I don't understand. Where's the remote control?"

"Find anything you like?" he asked.

"Your collection is sadly lacking in Nora Roberts."

"An oversight," he said.

"No Clancy, no Grisham. Obviously, you're not an intellectual."

"I'm a simple man," he said. The shelves were filled with reference materials. Atlases, encyclopedias, and history, history, history were next to books on every culture on the planet.

"Oh, thank God," I said. "You have the complete Virgil collection. I was looking for a copy. And it's next to Sartre in the original French. You disgust me with your simple mind."

Holden came up behind me, fitting his body against mine. His hands slipped around my waist, coming to rest on my belly, his fingers splayed. He bent down and nuzzled my ear. I felt my triglycerides shoot up and my toenails grow.

"Holy Christ," I said.

"You're Jewish," he whispered in my ear.

"Who cares? I'll be whatever you want."

"You are what I want."

I wanted to get naked, and it occurred to me that a

little slip of the robe's belt would accomplish that feat. But Virgil or no, Holden wasn't that bright.

"Dinner is served," he said.

"Are you sure?"

"Come on, let's eat."

He took my hand and pulled me toward the couch. The music changed from jazz to classical. Two plates were set on the coffee table. I didn't recognize the food, but it looked French, with some sort of sauce. He had gone to a lot of effort, not realizing I would have been his for a burrito and a box of stale Milk Duds.

We sat close on the couch, holding our plates in our laps, our legs touching, our feet propped up on the table. I watched the fire dance in the fireplace, throwing shadows over us. It was perfect, and I was scared to move for fear that something would change, the atoms would rearrange themselves, Holden would no longer want me, and this moment of pure pleasure would disappear.

"I forgot the wine," Holden said, and moved to get up, but I put my hand on his leg to stop him. We sat in silence, eating. It was delicious, and I couldn't help imagining what it would be like to be involved with a man who could cook.

When we finished, Holden took the plates to the kitchen and returned with coffee and chocolate. "Coffee? I'll be up all night," I said.

"Good." He sat back down, his body even closer to mine. "How are you doing? You seem to be holding together all right after last night."

"I'm pretending it didn't happen." I flinched as my tooth pain returned. "Most of the time it works."

"Do they have any leads on the murder?"

I thought about the suspicions against Belinda. "Not really. The police department seems to be distracted by the aliens."

Holden shifted in his seat. "The cult."

"Yes, the end-of-worlders. The town is up in arms about them."

Holden took my hand and rubbed my palm with his thumb. "I'm glad you're here," he said.

I tried to speak, but I could only suck air.

The music changed again, back to jazz. "I love this song," Holden said. "Would you dance with me?"

He gathered me to him, my head resting on his chest, and we swayed to the music. "Did I tell you how beautiful you look tonight in my robe?"

"No." With no moisturizer, mascara, or hair gel, I figured he was a liar.

"You are radiant," he said.

"That might just be leftover duck sauce."

"Are you nervous?" he asked.

"Yes." I was nervous he wasn't going to stick his tongue in my mouth. I was nervous that I was going to keep the robe on all night. I was nervous that I had forgotten to shave my legs. Holden stopped dancing. He put his finger under my chin and raised my face toward his.

"I'm nervous, too," he said, and kissed me. He was a terrible liar, but he was a damned good kisser. His lips were warm, his mouth firm, and my lips parted for him. I felt my skin grow hot, my face must have been beet red, and my hair was curling way beyond normal.

He deepened the kiss, tugging me closer to him. When my legs gave way, he swept me up in his arms and deposited me gently on the couch. And then he was on top of me.

Finally I was well on my way to third base and then most likely a home run with Arthur Holden. It had been a long road to this place on his couch. He had blown hot and cold since he had moved to town. When he was with me, he acted like I was the woman of his dreams, but he wasn't with me that often. I thought he was living a secret life, but maybe he was just in a quiet corner somewhere, reading.

Holden lay half on me, one hand underneath me, cupping my buttock and pulling me closer to him. I was reasonably sure he didn't have a pistol in his pocket. No, he was definitely happy to see me. Our tongues darted against each other, making my head swim. My fingers traveled through his hair and then cupped his face, bringing him closer. I was drowning in his kiss.

I was half aware of him undoing his belt buckle and kicking off his shoes. I squirmed against him, unwilling to let him get distracted from our kiss. Our Olympic gold medal kiss.

He groaned against my lips, which drove me on. I let my hands wander down his chest and around his back. He was hard all over, hairless and strong. I felt an insane need to cover him in oil and make him sit there naked while I just sat and stared. And while I probably ate peanut M&M's or something. It was something to think about and do. Right after we sealed the deal. And the deal was coming pretty fast and furious now.

Holden broke off the kiss and sat up, peeling the shirt off his body at the same time. He looked down at me, and I followed his gaze to my chest. My robe had come slightly undone, baring my cleavage. I have good cleavage, if I do say so myself, and I was happy to show it off for a moment. It seemed to produce the desired effect.

Holden slipped a finger under my belt and slowly lifted up, undoing the belt as he did. Then, with a slow hand, he opened the top of my robe. He looked down at my torso with real desire, so much desire that my breath hitched, and I was aware of a growing need that had to be sated soon or I would explode. I touched his shoulders and tried to pull him back down on me, but he resisted. Instead, he tentatively touched my abdomen, allowing his hand to travel up until he cupped my breast, kneading it gently. My insides melted, and if I wasn't mistaken, the throbbing in my tooth moved down lower. Much lower.

Holden was a good kisser, but he was even better at the whole boob thing. I wondered what else he was good at, and then his mouth was on my breast, and my eyes rolled back in my head.

We stayed like that for a while, him tasting my breast, and me writhing under him. I might have begged him to move on, but Holden was a man who took his time. And what's more, he was possessive. For the moment, at least, I was his, and he made that fact perfectly clear. He had a plan where my body was concerned, and he seemed to be goal-oriented and not at all a quitter.

There on that couch, being made love to by the sexiest man on the planet, I had to forgive him for his secret life, for not telling me about his past, for hiding the daily details of his existence. Maybe he was shy. After all, he finally allowed me into his house, let me shower in his bathroom, for goodness' sake. Perhaps he just took things slow.

And who was I to point a finger? Wasn't I hiding Spencer in my bed? Wasn't I keeping that secret from Holden? And wasn't I the one keeping Belinda's request secret from him? Why hadn't I told Holden about Belinda when he asked who the police suspected? What kind of girlfriend was I?

"I didn't tell you everything about the murder," I said.

Holden stopped and looked up. His face was flushed, and his normally light blue eyes were dark and enormous. He looked feral, on the prowl. I bit my lip.

"Did you want to say something?" he asked, out of breath. His chest was slightly heaving as he took deep breaths, trying to steady himself, I imagined.

"My client, Belinda Womble, the receptionist. She might be a suspect."

Holden looked like he might not care about Belinda Womble or the dentist's murder at that moment, but he rubbed his eyes and changed his position, adjusting his pants and sitting next to me.

"She is?" he asked.

"Maybe not officially, yet. But she asked me to help prove her innocence. They think she stole money from the business and maybe Dr. Dulur found out, and she killed him. There, now I've told you everything. Let's get back to it." *Told you everything except for the fact that Spencer is sleeping in my bed.*

"And she took his face? That sounds like a stretch."

Holden stared out into space, as if he was visualizing Belinda murdering Dr. Dulur. I had gotten Holden thinking now. What was wrong with me? My boobs had had his undivided attention, and then I threw Belinda Womble into his brain. Maybe I needed therapy.

"Yeah, it's far-fetched," I agreed. "So, she wants me to help her prove her innocence. It won't take much to prove that, probably less work than to find her a match. And once I do that, I can get on with my life." *And pay my Visa. And have Holden's children.*

"Are you sure she's innocent?" he asked, concern growing on his face. "If she is capable of that kind of murder once, she can do it a second time."

"I'm sure she's innocent," I said. "She likes flowers and big sweaters. Does that sound like a grisly murderer to you?"

"I think that people are good at keeping secrets." It was the perfect moment to ask him about his secrets, but I was a chicken. Chicken McChickster from Chickenland. Besides, there was that pesky secret I had, who was at that moment eating chips on my Martha Stewart sheets.

I touched Holden's chest. I was ready for round two, and I was pleased to see that so was he. He moved fast now, probably to make up for lost time. He bent down and kissed me hard. My breasts flattened against the weight of his chest on mine. I lifted my knees and wrapped my legs around him.

Happiness isn't complicated, if you are truly honest with yourself. All it really took for me was a perfectly gorgeous, rich man grinding his pelvis into me with his tongue down my throat. Easy peasy.

Then the phone rang. I thought it was my cellphone until I remembered mine had been cut off. Holden let the phone ring until it stopped, and meanwhile his hand traveled down my body, fully opening my robe. He fumbled with his pants with one hand, and then the phone started ringing again. He stopped what he was doing and exhaled, loudly.

"I probably need to get that," he said. "Don't move. Don't move an inch. I will be right back."

He jumped up off the couch and grabbed the phone. I lay there for a moment, my legs separated and my body bare to the world, before I became self-conscious and closed my robe again. I caught snippets of his conversation, mostly "yeah"s and "are you sure"s. I was a little piqued. I grabbed some chocolate off the coffee table and took a big bite, sending shock waves of pain through my mouth.

After about five minutes, Holden returned to the couch. "Where were we?" he asked.

"Who was that?"

"Business." He started to undo my belt again. I put my hand on his, stopping him.

"What business is that?" I asked.

"Just business. Nothing exciting."

I tried to be understanding and not the whiny, demanding girlfriend that I truly wanted to be, but it was stronger than my will.

I took a deep breath to prepare myself to finally give him the ultimatum: either he would tell me about his life, really share it with me, or there would be no more hanky-panky.

Luckily, the phone rang again. "One more second," he said, holding his finger up in the air. "I promise. It's the last time."

He answered the phone, and his face got serious. "I understand," he said into the phone. "Yes, I'll let her know. Is it serious? Yes, I'll tell her."

He clicked off the phone and held my hand. "You need to get back home," he said. "It's about your grandmother. It's urgent. You need to go back there before it's too late."

Chapter 8

◆ ♥ ◆

My grandmother used to say, "Timing is everything." I think she was talking about running away from the Cossacks, but we can use that lesson in our work as matchmakers. Sometimes you have to sit back and ruminate. Don't jump to conclusions about a match; let it settle in your mind for a while before sending someone out on dates. Even if they are impatient, watch them for a while. But when you are sure, bubeleh, strike like a cobra . . . fast and deadly.

Lesson 77,
Matchmaking Advice from Your Grandma Zelda

I CLOSED my robe and bolted upright. "What's the matter?" I asked. "Is she all right?"

Holden sat down next to me and put his hand on my thigh. "She's fine. That was a man from her Single No More class, saying you're late."

"But I've been banned," I said. "I'm not supposed to be there, and besides, the class was over two hours ago."

"I don't know. It sounded serious, like it was a major faux pas, you not going."

His eyes were dreamy, much dreamier than George Clooney's eyes, I was sure.

"It was probably a mistake," I said. I was about to grab him by the front of his shirt and pull him to me for another kiss and to get on with the show when his phone rang again.

"Really, I'm so sorry," he said. "I'll get rid of them and then I'll be all yours."

I was losing patience, but I was slightly mollified by the idea of being all his. He picked up the phone, and this time it sounded more serious. He took the conversation into another room, leaving me naked under his robe, watching the fire in his fireplace.

My feelings were hurt. I didn't expect to be the most important person in his life, but I expected him not to run away from my nakedness to take what sounded like a business call. I was important, too. I had matches to make, one match I had to make by the next day, and I hadn't a clue who I was going to match her with. Perhaps the Single No More class ran long, I thought. Maybe Grandma really did need me to help. Maybe I would find a match for Belinda at the class. Maybe Grandma was serving cupcakes.

I wrote Holden a note, saying I was tired, and tiptoed out of the house, dressed only in his robe. It was like the walk of shame without the fun part beforehand.

Halfway across Grandma's lawn, I remembered that there were no men in the Single No More class. So who was the man who called Holden? I opened the door, and Spencer was there, waiting for me. I should have known.

"I better be completely wrong," I said to him, closing the door.

Spencer was wearing cutoff sweats and a wifebeater shirt. The shirt was pulled tight over his chest and abs. I tried not to look at his arms.

"That's not what you were wearing the last time I saw you," he said.

I clutched the robe against me. "It's none of your business what I wear or don't wear. Tell me I'm wrong.

Tell me you didn't make the call that sabotaged my evening."

Spencer stared me down for a moment, and then his eyes slipped to my right.

"You did! You did!" I yelled, hitting his shoulder. "You called. You were my coitus interruptus. You bastard."

I hit him two more times before he caught my arm midair and held it there. "Coitus interruptus," he repeated. "Aren't you going a little fast with a man you don't even know?"

I felt my face turn red and hated myself for it. "Maybe not coitus," I corrected. "But definitely kiss interruptus."

"Are you naked under that robe?" he asked, his voice rising. "Are you naked under that masculine robe? That *man's* robe?"

I stepped back. "Where's Grandma? I'm assuming the line about the class was a complete fabrication."

"Cops are good liars," he said. "She went up to bed. It's just you and me, Pinkie."

"Let me make this clear. There isn't a you and me." I pulled at my arm. "Give it back," I said. "I'm going to get something to eat."

I was starving. I'd eaten a date dinner, which meant that I hadn't eaten much. I didn't want Holden to know what a pig I really was. Spencer let go of me and followed me into the kitchen, and I made us both turkey sandwiches with cranberry sauce. He took out a bag of Doritos from what had to be his never-ending supply of chips, and I popped open two cans of root beer.

"He didn't feed you?" Spencer asked with a mouthful of sandwich. "I would have fed you."

"He fed me duck and something vegetable. It was very good."

"Uh-huh," he said, handing me the bag of chips.

"How long am I going to suffer with you? Do I have

to deal with you until your Facebook friends come to their senses?"

"Hey, I rinsed out the shower after I used it," he pointed out. He got up and made himself another sandwich. I was still working on the first half of mine. "My Facebook friends are picketing the police station," he said. "It's better to lie low for a while."

"I might join them," I said. "Or better yet, I might tell them where you are hiding in order to finish with this once and for all."

Spencer noticeably blanched. He was completely drained of color. I handed him his can of root beer.

"Geez, Spencer, I was just kidding. Drink. You look terrified."

"I'm not terrified. I'm just careful."

"You have to get back to work. There's been a heinous murder, and there's a face wandering around out there. If you don't get back to work, there's no hope that the murder will be solved."

Spencer's color returned, and his smirk returned. "Pinkie, you complimented me," he said. "I might pass out from shock."

I squirmed in my seat. "I didn't compliment you. I merely pointed out that you are the least incompetent of your police force. That's not saying a lot."

"You complimented me. You said I could solve the No-Face Case."

"Shut up."

"You can't take it back now," he said, interlocking his fingers behind his head. "Okay, so I'm a great cop. Tell me how sexy I am. Tell me you want me."

"You are not sexy, and I don't want you," I lied.

"You're almost naked. When you bend down, I can see the whole triple play. It's only a hiccup to a grand-slam home run. Just say the word, and I'll come up to bat."

"You gross me out."

Spencer leaned forward, studied my face for a moment, read something there, and then popped a Dorito into his mouth. "You can't blame a guy for trying," he said.

"Focus on your work, dammit. The town is going to pieces, and there's a face out there. Why isn't anybody impressed by the face?"

"I'm impressed by the face," Spencer said. "I'm in touch with the station now. I'm calling the shots, so don't worry about that. As for the town, it's always going to pieces. It's the freakiest town out there. I don't think a cult and some aliens are going to do much to change that."

I didn't agree with him. I thought there was an all-out war going on, and if he didn't intervene soon, all hell would break loose, along with possible plagues, fire, and maybe a hurricane or two. But I was relieved he was on top of the murder case. He was the only chance of seeing justice for Dr. Dulur and for making sure that a psychotic killer would be found.

I caught Spencer trying to look down the gap of my robe. I ate a Dorito and tried to ignore him, but it wasn't easy. After we finished, we went up to bed. Spencer climbed the stairs behind me, bumping into me several times on purpose.

"You are five," I said. "Stop trying to cop a feel."

We brushed our teeth together over the bathroom sink, and then I kicked him out of my bathroom while I changed. When I finished, he was already in my bed with the lights off. I slipped under the covers, being careful to stay clear of him. I was still slightly aroused from my evening with Holden.

"You are so bad for my sex life," I told Spencer.

"Pinkie, I could be so good for your sex life if you would just let me."

"I can't even be my own best friend," I said. "I can't

even be self-sufficient, if you know what I mean, because you're here."

"I can fulfill all your needs," he said.

I turned over and tucked the blankets under my chin.
"How far are you going with the beard thing?" I asked.
"You ever going to shave again?"

"I was thinking of turning it into a goatee tomorrow," he said.

I fluffed my pillow. "If you do, you will have eaten
your last chip in my bed."

"Fine. No goatee."

It occurred to me that I should talk to Spencer about
Belinda. I needed to convince him that she couldn't possibly be the killer, and if I couldn't convince him, I could
at least squeeze him for the information he had so that
I could help her. But Spencer hated when I got involved
with police business, and if he suspected Belinda of killing the dentist and chopping off his face, I was reasonably sure he wouldn't let me hang around her and match
her up.

I was determined that nothing was going to get in between me and matching Belinda. She was the first client
to request me personally instead of my competent grandmother. She was the leaf I needed to turn over to go from
broke matchmaker-in-training to fabulous professional
with a Gold Card.

THE NEXT morning, I called Bridget and let her
know I was coming over to cheer her up after her hair
disaster, and I was bringing coffee and scones.

I took my car and drove the few blocks to Tea Time.
Ruth's coffee was calling to me, and I was betting things
had died down since the last time I was there. Ruth
wouldn't stand for wackos in her store for too long. She
only marginally tolerated me and my coffee habit.

It turned out I was right about the wackos being gone. Main Street was all but deserted. I had no trouble finding a parking place right in front of Tea Time. There were no more cultists blocking the door. In fact, you could hear a pin drop right there in the historic district.

On closer examination, I realized why. Most of the stores were closed, some of them even boarded up. No movement on the street. Everything looked abandoned. It was like the apocalypse, like a Stephen King novel or a teen book about a dystopian future. For a moment, I worried that the end-of-worlders were right. Maybe the end of the world already happened, and I was just late to the party.

I gave Tea Time's door handle a test push, and it swung freely. Phew. Luckily, the shop was open. Coffee was only seconds away, and I needed my caffeine fix. Lately, I had seen a dead person, gotten peed on, suffered coitus interruptus, and slept with Spencer. I might even need two coffees.

Inside, the shop was as quiet as outside, but it wasn't empty. It was packed wall-to-wall with people, but they were all lying on the floor on their backs.

My heart stopped for a moment before I realized they were alive. In fact, they breathed almost in unison, their chests rising and descending together like a choir.

Ruth stood behind the bar. Her hair looked like it had been teased for a good forty-five minutes. It swirled around her head like a hornet's nest. Her eyes were so bloodshot, I could see the redness from across the store.

I tiptoed over the bodies, trying not to step on anyone.

I will go through a lot for a latte.

"What on earth is going on here?" I asked Ruth when I finally made it through.

"The nutjobbers of the planet have landed in my shop," she said. "*My* shop!"

"I need three lattes to go and a box of assorted scones," I said. Ruth didn't swear at me for ordering coffee. So I knew she was out of sorts. "Why are they lying on the floor?" I asked.

"Why are they lying on the floor?" she repeated, loudly. "Because the aliens can commune better with their souls if they're horizontal, of course."

"Ruth, when did you sleep last?" I asked. "You look a little tired."

She looked like she'd flipped her lid and some of her screws had come loose. She looked like she had been writing letters to Jodie Foster. She leaned over the bar and stared me in the eye.

"I'm not closing Tea Time," she said. "I'm not giving them the satisfaction. The other business owners cut and ran, closing down until the wackos leave, but I'm not closing for anybody."

Ruth pointed at my chest. "I haven't closed this shop during normal business hours since 1954. If I didn't close when Kennedy was shot, I'm not closing for religious freaks." She handed me the lattes and the box of scones.

"Do they drink tea?" I asked.

"Gallons of it. Aliens like tea drinkers. Go figure."

BRIDGET LIVED in a townhouse just west of the historic district. She made a good living as an accountant for the locals, much better than I did as a matchmaker, obviously, but not nearly as good a living as Lucy made.

The townhouse was stuccoed in brown and had a tiny front yard. It was one of those tall townhouses that made use of a small area of land by building up. Her place was about one thousand square feet but laid out on three floors. I rang her doorbell, and she buzzed me in. I walked up to the second floor, where she sat at her kitchen table. I almost didn't recognize her.

Her once-long hair was now cropped in a pixie cut, I guess the aftermath of the whole fire scene from the night before.

"Do you hate it? Do I look butch?" she asked me. I could tell she was on the verge of tears. Hair is complicated. A little fire goes a long way.

"You look so cute!" I said with maybe too much enthusiasm, because Bridget wasn't mollified. "I mean it," I added. "You look like a French actress from the twenties. Very chic. Very cute."

"Like Claudette Colbert?" she asked, perking up a bit.

"I was just going to say Claudette Colbert," I lied. "You could be twins."

Bridget took a big breath. "Thanks. Lucy called Bird for me when I got home last night, and she fit me in for an emergency cut. It took five minutes with her hose to get my hair to stop smoking. She almost called the fire department," she said seriously.

"Holy crap," I said.

"This is what she had to do to repair the damage," she said, waving her hand at her head. "I told her I loved it, but I didn't know if I was lying. I think I was in shock, and I didn't want to hurt Bird's feelings. She's kind of having a nervous breakdown."

"She is?" I asked, surprised. Bird had always been a rock, heading her salon with nerves of steel. Managing the hair of most of Cannes's women was not for the faint of heart.

"She's taking the invasion of the cult people really hard," Bridget explained. "It's upset her balance, she said. She's blaming them for your Ecuadoran Erect.

You're her first failure. She fears she's lost her mojo. Oh, I almost forgot." Bridget pulled a box of Chinese diet tea from her purse. "She told me to give this to you to apologize for the hair."

I had left my box of tea at Bliss Dental. I didn't think it was worth it with the blood on it.

"Good," I said, taking the tea. "Let's finish the lattes and scones before I start the diet."

"Did you get chocolate chip?" Bridget asked.

We got through half our lattes and about three scones each before we relaxed. Bridget was getting back to her normal self, talking about the assault on women's rights in this country and saying that if it weren't for religion, she would still have her hair.

"Speaking of religion, Belinda is on her way over," she said. "She tried to reach you on your cell, and when she couldn't, she called me."

My stomach lurched. "She wants me to match her. I have no idea who to match her with," I said, my voice hitching up an octave. "What do you mean, speaking of religion? Is Belinda religious?"

"Oh, yeah," Bridget said. "Belinda has gone through at least a half dozen religions. She's a seeker. I told her that religion was the scourge of civilization, but she didn't believe me."

I wondered why Belinda didn't mention religion to me when she spoke of her dream man. More often than not, religion was a deal breaker.

"What religion is she now?" I asked.

"I lost count at Methodist. No, that's not right. I think she's full-on Southern Baptist now."

I thought of escaping before Belinda arrived. I didn't have anybody in mind for her, not a Southern Baptist or Methodist or even an Episcopalian. The pressure was intense.

"I wish she had warned me she would be here," I said. "Why didn't she call me at Grandma's?"

"She wouldn't say, but I get the impression she's scared of Zelda."

The door buzzed, and I jumped. My flop sweat was out in force again, but it turned out it wasn't Belinda.

"Lord have mercy, I am so glad to be somewhere safe!" Lucy floated up the stairs in a lavender-colored Donna Karan dress and heels.

"Take me into your bosoms, my darling friends. I have gone to hell and back," she said, plopping down on one of the kitchen chairs. She picked up a scone. "Yes, I would love a cup of coffee, Bridget darlin'."

Bridget jumped up and started making a pot.

"I don't know how you do it, investigating murders like you do," Lucy said to me.

"It was just that one time," I insisted.

Lucy stared at me like I had three heads. "What are you talking about? You're not investigating this case? But you saw the dead dentist yourself. Honey, you are involved, do you hear me? You need to hop to it and start investigating. I can't do it alone, you know."

"What have you been doing?" Bridget asked. "Have you figured out who the killer is?"

"Well, I can't swear in a court of law, but I would say I have narrowed the field," Lucy said, out of breath. She punctuated her words with her scone, swinging it around like a conductor's baton.

"Did you find his face?" I asked.

"His what?" Lucy asked.

"Never mind."

"I'll tell you what I've been doing," Lucy said. "I've been tracking down the crazy women in Police Chief Spencer Bolton's life, that's what I've been doing. It's a miracle I'm still alive."

Bridget handed Lucy a cup of coffee. "What did you find out?"

Lucy leaned forward. "Well, I found out that Spencer has a magic penis."

I choked. "A magic penis?" I asked.

"Yes, one poke with his magic penis, and women go completely crazy," she said, like having a poke from a magic penis was a bad thing.

"Why is it magic? Does it do tricks or something?" Bridget asked seriously.

"I couldn't get specifics," Lucy said. "But it changes women into blathering idiots and psychotic loony bins. Rosalie's bin is the looniest of them all. With my informant's help, I found Rosalie by the police station clutching her set of knives to her chest."

"Yikes," I said.

"Men are pigs," said Bridget.

Lucy took a sip of coffee. "Rosalie isn't too much better, darlin'. She came after me with one of the knives, and all I was doing was telling her that Spencer wasn't worth her sorrow."

"I need a drink," I said.

Lucy raised an eyebrow. "I keep a flask in my purse, but I partook after the Rosalie incident and now it's empty. I ran all the way here in my three-inch mules. I needed a couple hairs of the dog."

Bridget shrugged. "Don't look at me. My house is dry, but I heard there will be a margarita bar at the parade this morning."

"Margarita bar at nine in the morning? This town is getting better all the time," Lucy said. "Just give me a moment to freshen up."

She sauntered off to Bridget's guest bathroom. "What parade?" I asked Bridget.

"The Christmas pageant."

"But it's September."

"The Christians are trying to one-up the pagans. Everyone is going. Normally I picket with my sandwich board, but I think I'll hold off until the December Christmas pageant and just be a spectator for the September one. I could go for a margarita."

"Isn't it a little weird to have a Christmas pageant in September?" I asked.

"Well, it's a cover."

"A cover?"

"For the showdown. Christians versus pagans. Townsfolk against end-of-worlder alien worshippers. I wonder if they'll have tortilla chips."

Chips and margaritas sounded good, but nothing could drag me out to the showdown Christmas pageant. I had to get far away before Belinda arrived, looking for her George Clooney. My hospital idea was a good one. Maybe I could find Belinda a male nurse before lunch.

I downed the last of my second latte and hugged Bridget goodbye just as her doorbell rang, effectively thwarting my escape.

"Caught like a rat on a ship," I muttered.

Belinda walked up the stairs. She had dressed up in a black velour tracksuit with a purple violet bedazzled on the front of her hoodie. "Thank you so much for meeting with me, Gladie," she said, even though I didn't know she was coming until a few minutes before.

"I've been working on your match," I lied.

"And the other thing?" she asked.

The other thing was Dr. Dulur's murder and the police's conviction that Belinda was guilty. I hadn't done a thing about the other thing. Nothing. Instead of fixing up Belinda and proving her innocence, I had gone to second base with Holden and binged on Doritos with Spencer.

"Uh," I said.

Lucy returned from the bathroom, her makeup fresh,

her hair tamed, and her dress flouncing like it had been steam cleaned.

"Belinda Womble! So pleased to see you, darlin'," she said. "Just visiting? I suppose the dental office is closed after you know what happened. Did Gladie tell you about my morning?"

We sat back at the table as Lucy regaled us in detail about Spencer's besotted older lady Facebook friends. Six different levels of crazy. All certifiable.

"They all yelled at me like I was the one with the magic penis," she said. "The nerve of those women."

"Magic penis?" Belinda asked. She was sweating hope out of her pores.

"Men are pigs," Bridget said. "Did they admit to hacking him up in the groves?"

"Bridget honey," Lucy said, "these women are off their rockers. I didn't want to incite them by accusing them of hacking up the police chief. Just mentioning Spencer's name set their eyes rolling around their sockets like they had mad cow disease."

"I think they hacked him up," said Bridget, holding her finger up in the air as if she was testing which way the wind was blowing. "I heard a fresh mound of dirt appeared from one day to the next deep in the pears. It has to be a Spencer mound. Don't you see? There's a Spencer mound beneath the pear trees."

"A Spencer mound," Belinda echoed in a whisper.

I looked down at my cuticles. I was sure they could tell by my face that the only Spencer mound there was was lounging in my bed watching daytime TV. I hated lying to my best friends.

Lucy shook her head. "I don't think they hacked him up," she said. "They're looking for him. They want him back."

Belinda gasped. "They want the magic penis," she said.

"They want the magic penis and the whole package. They're looking for him," Lucy said.

"So Spencer is single?" Belinda asked in my direction.

BELINDA AND I joined Lucy and Bridget to watch the parade. I had told Belinda that a potential match was going to be there. It wasn't a total lie. The whole town was going to be there, and someone there had to be a potential match for Belinda, right?

We parked two blocks away from Main Street and followed the crowd to the parade. The September Christmas pageant drew as many people as the December Christmas pageant, but the atmosphere was different. There was a palpable anxiety in the air.

Dread.

The Christmas pageant walked westward toward the yurt camp, which was full of cultists who were waiting for the aliens to come out of the Sacred Mountain to take them away to another planet. The townspeople wanted to show them what's what, that this was a Christmas town, not an alien town.

When Bridget and Lucy wandered off to find the margarita bar, Belinda grabbed my arm and pulled me close. "The police were at my apartment this morning, Gladie. They wanted to know about the books. There's almost two hundred thousand dollars missing."

I whistled in appreciation. "And they think you took it?" I asked.

"Gladie, I wrote some checks for bills, but I didn't handle the books. At least not that often."

I sighed. It wasn't much of a defense. "So, who stole the money? You worked there. Who do you think is responsible?"

"I don't know. I thought about it all night. The only signers were me, Dr. Dulur, and the accountant."

"Who's the accountant?"

"Torrin McNally. He used to be in the FBI."

"So?" I said. "He still could have been stealing."

"That's what I said!" Belinda yelled out.

"Just because he was in law enforcement doesn't mean he can't be a criminal," I said.

"Exactly! But, they're accusing me. I've never even had a parking ticket, Gladie."

"Unreal."

"They won't leave me alone. It's blah, blah, blah, what did you do with the money . . . blah, blah, blah, how much did that sweater cost . . . blah, blah, blah, McNally died six months ago."

"Hold on. What was the third blah, blah, blah?"

"The accountant died in March. Oh, Gladie." Belinda put her face in her hands and wept. I rubbed her back and told her everything would be all right.

I felt useless. With the accountant dead, Belinda was the only suspect in Bliss Dental's embezzlement—and Dr. Dulur's murder. Belinda could have been the large figure Nathan described as the killer. But I couldn't imagine Belinda as a murderer. She was looking for love, and she liked flowers. I couldn't picture her cutting off Dr. Dulur's face.

"Belinda, Holly told me something ridiculous about Dr. Dulur. She said he wasn't nice. Like maybe he deserved to die. Is that true?"

Belinda sniffed and took out a portable Kleenex packet. "I never believed those rumors about child abuse. I think those kids had bruises before they came into the office."

"Child abuse? Where did you hear those rumors?"

"Rosalie Rodriguez. For years, she's been talking about Dr. Dulur breaking her son's arm. She tells that story to anybody who'll listen."

The pageant started with the sound of trumpets. The crowd lined Main Street, and we pushed forward to get a good vantage point. They had gone all out with costumes. Mary Ferguson played Mary and held a Cabbage Patch doll Jesus in her arms. Mayor Robinson was Joseph, and he waved to his constituents, seemingly having the time of his life, all the while pulling a donkey by a rope tether.

In unison, as if watching a tennis game, the crowd turned their attention to the other end of the street. The residents of the yurt camp stood there, their arms crossed, as if they were waiting for the Christmas pageant players to arrive. Within moments, they were joined by other cult members. At first they seemed dumbstruck, their mouths hanging open in surprise, but quickly they grew agitated.

The pageant actors broke out in song and the crowd turned their heads back toward them. The singers were in the moment, euphoric in their conviction, sure that they would shoo off the cult with their Christmas spirit.

But the moment was short-lived. The end-of-worlders began to bellow about *the Arrival*, making the pageant parade stumble and stop singing. Then the cultists unrolled a long banner that said YOU WILL ALL DIE WHEN THE ARRIVAL COMES.

The air grew even thicker with tension, and time stood still. The expectation was that something would happen, but we were unsure just how horrible that something would be.

Despite the end-of-worlders' banner, the pageant resumed, but quietly now, as they made their way more slowly down Main Street. Belinda's tears dried up, and she wiped the mascara from under her eyes.

"So, where's the guy you had in mind for me?" she asked me.

"Excuse me?"

"Is he in the pageant, or is he one of the spectators?"

"He's . . . ," I started, waving my hand around as if he

was close by. Belinda looked at me expectantly. My flop sweat returned. "I'll get him," I said.

I stepped off the curb onto the street, and I walked blindly, the sweat rolling off my forehead into my eyes. What was I doing? Was I going to pick a man at random and force him back to Belinda? What kind of matchmaker was I? Had I gone off my rocker like most of the town?

I scanned the crowd, looking for someone. Anyone. I wandered aimlessly. The pageant players were almost to me, the mayor heading the troupe, pulling the donkey, waving like he was campaigning, and probably he was.

And then it hit me, and I knew just what to do. It wasn't totally ethical, according to Grandma, but beggars can't be choosers, and I could always match Belinda up with someone better afterward. Besides, Mayor Robinson smelled good, and he looked great on paper.

I marched up to him, trying to be as inconspicuous as possible. "Yoo-hoo, Mr. Mayor," I called. "It's me, Gladie Burger."

The mayor waved at the crowd. "Lovely to see you," he told me. "I'm playing Joseph at present, though. Can't stop now."

"Maybe we could take a short break," Mary said, eyeing the cultists at the end of the street.

"I have a manicure at ten," the mayor explained.

"I have someone for you to meet," I told him, walking backward.

"A voter?"

"You might have to take her to dinner first," I muttered. "Right this way." I was being far more assertive than normal, but I had a now-or-never feeling.

"May I bring my donkey?" he asked.

"Sure."

But the donkey had other ideas. Because of the change

of route, the cult bellowing about the Arrival, or my perfume, the donkey wouldn't budge.

"Perhaps I could meet the voter some other time," the mayor said. But unwilling to let the opportunity slip away from me, I panicked and slapped the donkey on his rump to get him moving.

Karma is a bitch.

The slapped donkey went berserk, rising on his back legs and whinnying. He snapped at the mayor and the rest of the Christmas pageant players and then went on a rampage through the crowd.

Townsfolk went running, screaming through the street. The end-of-worlders' bellows changed to blood-curdling screams as the donkey changed direction and went right for them. I stood in the middle of the street with people coming and going wildly, throwing up their hands as if *everyone* believed the world was coming to an end, not just the pagans.

I spotted Lucy and Bridget clutching margaritas while pressed up against the pharmacy's front window, but Belinda was nowhere to be found. I hoped the donkey hadn't gotten her. The pageant actors had scattered like shrapnel, and I could make out turbans and veils sprinkled through the stampeding crowd.

It took forever, but it finally started to die down after a few minutes, and I had just turned to join Lucy and Bridget when a glint of metal caught my eye. Down the alley, across from me, Rosalie Rodriguez was running straight out, a Rachael Ray cleaver in one hand, heading right for me.

Chapter 9

✦ ♥ ✦

The world is full of stress, and there are more than a couple fakakta jobs out there that would make a person go crazy. The president, he has a stressful job. Charlie Sheen's probation officer, probably not too relaxed, either. But our business, dolly, that's got to be one of the most stressful jobs there is. Sometimes we get overwhelmed. Sometimes we get lost. You ever feel that way? Like you don't know which way is up? Left feels like right, and right feels like left? If you feel lost, you probably are. Just like the Boy Scouts say, if you're lost, stay in one place so we can find you. Hear that? Don't run around like a chicken trying to find your way. Stand still. Don't move. And, oh yeah, remember to breathe.

Lesson 15,
Matchmaking Advice from Your Grandma Zelda

SHE CAME at me, fast, like Flo-Jo at the Olympics, without the nails but with a Birkin bag and crazy psycho-killer eyes.

I saw it all in slow motion, giving me a flashback of the time when I was a kid at a baseball game and a foul ball flew into the stands directly at my head. That broken nose hurt for weeks. And now I was frozen in place, watching a middle-aged woman come at me with a cleaver in her hand and a determined expression on her face.

"Run, Gladie, run," I muttered, trying to will myself to move, to flee from Rosalie. Finally my feet complied. I turned on my heel and ran for everything I was worth, which wasn't much because I hadn't exercised since I moved to Cannes. What was wrong with me? I really needed to change my daily habits. I needed to try Ruth's Chinese tea. My priorities were all skewed. I had to think of my health.

I could hear Rosalie catching up to me. She was obviously in better shape than I was. She was barely breathing hard, whereas I sounded like a freight train.

I made a sharp left into an alley. If I couldn't outrun her, I thought, maybe I could outsmart her, confuse her. Lose her. But as crazy as she seemed to be, Rosalie was a woman with focus. She never let me out of her sight, and we wound up at the back of the alley in a dead end, my back up against a tall fence in between a couple dumpsters.

"Hey, Rosalie, how's it going?" I asked. Her eyes and mouth were wide open, like she was trying to suck up all the crazy in the world for herself.

I noticed that her face was perfectly done, and not a hair was out of place. She was also well dressed. Some people are like that. Even when they are on a murderous rampage through town, they take the time to care about their appearance. Meanwhile, my hair was a rat's nest, and I was wearing jeans, a Disneyland sweatshirt, and sneakers. No wonder Holden blew hot and cold. I don't wear enough eyeliner.

Rosalie grunted and raised the cleaver over her head.

"Love that outfit," I said truthfully. "You get that at Macy's?" I tried to think of an escape plan, but all I could think of was I should have had ice cream for breakfast.

Rosalie blinked twice. "No, Bloomingdale's," she said. "Calvin Klein."

"Love Calvin Klein," I said. "But I'm more of a Walmart-special girl these days. You know, not a lot of money."

Rosalie visibly relaxed and lowered the cleaver halfway to shoulder level. I took a deep breath, realizing that I had been holding it all this time. I eyed the dumpsters. If I could get on top of one, I might be able to climb the fence to safety. But on second thought, if I could climb the fence, Rosalie could do it in half the time. She looked like she did a lot of power yoga.

"I thought you Burgers were rich," Rosalie said.

"Rich?" Was that true? Were we Burgers rich? I wondered how much money Grandma made. She had a steady stream of clients, and not much in the way of expenses.

"I'm still in training," I explained. "Not much work yet. Hey, I have an idea. Why don't I fix you up?"

It was a stroke of genius. Rosalie perked up. "Really? That would be great. I could use your help."

"Sure, you're a real find, Rosalie. Any man would be thrilled to date you. You don't want Spencer, anyway. He's such a jerk." He was a jerk, but I wasn't sure who else I could get to date a woman who runs through town with a cleaver. "Maybe Joe the butcher," I said, a spark of an idea coming to me.

Rosalie's smile crashed. "I want Spencer!" she yelled. She raised the cleaver again. "He loves me, do you hear me? He just forgot that he loved me. Those other women confused him. He'll come around."

"Oh, Rosalie, you're better than he is," I said, although at that point, I believed that she was only marginally better than he was. "He doesn't deserve you."

She raised one eyebrow and cocked her head to the side, making the hair on the back of my neck stand up. She was only a few chromosomes away from being Jack Nicholson in *The Shining*. It occurred to me that I might get murdered because Spencer was a man-whore, and that pissed me off.

"What are you doing?" she asked me. "Are you trying to get in between us? Spencer and I belong together. I don't think I like you."

She took a couple steps toward me. I could see the crow's-feet around her eyes more clearly. I noticed that the skin on her face had started to sag a little. It was still a surprise to me that Spencer dated older women.

"I know you belong with him," I amended, trying to get her to like me. "I haven't been myself lately, don't know what I'm saying. The whole dentist situation has me turned around."

Rosalie's eyes grew enormous, and her attention shifted from her cleaver and her dislike of me. "You got a problem with your teeth? Don't go to that sadist Dulur," she said.

"I heard you had a story about him hurting children. Is that true?"

"Is that true? Of course it's true. Nobody listens to me. He broke my son's arm. My son was scared, and Dulur was impatient and wrenched his arm. I couldn't prove it in court, but he hurt my baby when he was twelve years old."

"Is that why you murdered him?" I asked like an idiot.

"Why? Is he dead?" she asked, surprised.

"He was murdered two nights ago."

"That's the best news I've heard in a long time," she said. "Somebody popped the jerk. Fabulous." Rosalie lowered the cleaver and fluffed her hair with her other hand. She seemed to notice the knife for the first time and then looked at me pointedly. "You think I killed him? If I wanted to kill him, I would have done it years ago when he hurt my boy. Listen, Gladie, a lot of people wanted that dentist dead. A lot of people."

"Why did they want him dead?"

"I told you! He was a sadist. He was mean, especially to children, to those weaker than him. He loved his position of power, and he abused it."

"Can you help me find the others who wanted him dead?" I asked, and instantly regretted it. I didn't need Rosalie Rodriguez as my companion in clearing Belinda's name.

"Sure, I guess," she said, looking over my shoulder. "Do you smell that?"

"What? The trash?"

She sniffed the air. "No, Spencer. I smell Spencer."

I turned back to what she was smelling but only saw the fence. "I don't smell anything," I said.

"I know Spencer when I smell him. It's coming from your direction." I tried to remember if I had put on his cologne this morning by mistake. If he was going to get me killed, I was going to wring his neck.

"It must be coming from behind me," I said. "From the next street."

And then she was gone, running around the block, searching for Spencer's scent. I hightailed it, too, before she realized his smell was coming from me.

I half-skipped back to Main Street, looking over my shoulder every couple steps for Rosalie, but she must have lost the scent and gone in another direction. I quickly patted my body parts to make sure I was in one piece and she hadn't stabbed me without me noticing.

It was starting to become clear why Spencer was in hiding. These women were crazy and determined. Not me. No matter how secretive and hard to get Holden was, I was not going to go berserk. I wasn't going to let a man get between me and my sanity. There were no Rachael Ray knives in my future.

. . .

MAIN STREET was a shambles, mostly abandoned except for a few stragglers, some wandering in shock, some looking for loved ones, I imagined. It was like the second half of a Godzilla movie, after the monsters got through with Tokyo.

Lucy and Bridget stood in the middle of the street, holding their empty margarita glasses as if they were waiting for someone to come and fill them up again.

"I'm so glad to see you," I said, hugging them. I was happy to be alive. It's not every day that a person is chased through the streets by a cleaver-wielding psychopath. I gave them the rundown about Rosalie. They were sympathetic but not totally surprised.

"Oh, honey, you have to be careful. Rachael Ray makes some sharp knives," Lucy said.

"Men make women go crazy," Bridget explained. "Rosalie was sane before she met Spencer's magic penis."

"I think it's the Food Network that makes women go crazy. This is just one more reason not to cook," said Lucy.

I thought they were both right. Who needed men and cooking when there was takeout?

It was the perfect time for a drink, and we spent ten minutes looking for the remnants of the margarita stand before we remembered about Belinda. There was no sign of her.

"Do you think she went back to your place to get her car?" I asked Bridget.

"I saw her run after the donkey," Bridget said. "Like she got confused and ran toward the stampede instead of away."

"What direction was that?" I asked. Bridget and Lucy pointed toward the yurt camp. "I guess we have to find her," I said. No way was I going by myself. I had had enough adventures for the day, and I would need backup if I saw Rosalie again.

"Hallelujah," Lucy said. "I have wanted an excuse to root around in that alien worshippers' den. How do I look?" Lucy fluffed her hair and reapplied her lipstick.

IT WAS only a couple blocks to the yurt camp, which had taken over the small park in the historic district. Two short blocks, but it seemed to take us forever to get there, because we had to navigate the debris left in the street by the fleeing spectators, and because we started dragging our feet after we heard residual screams ahead of us.

Despite our reluctance, and despite the many obstacles in our path, we did arrive at the yurt camp after a few minutes. It was more or less abandoned, like the rest of Main Street. I was surprised to see that the cult had set up about twenty very large yurts in the small park. Each circular yurt was covered in some kind of tarp and looked like it could house about ten people. Against my better judgment, we decided to spread out, to better search for Belinda.

Bridget walked further down the street, calling out Belinda's name, while Lucy and I divvied up the yurts.

There were so many reasons why I shouldn't have gone looking in the end-of-worlders' yurts. I could think of fifteen reasons just off the top of my head. But I was concerned about Belinda, not only because she had enlisted my help to find love and to clear her name, but because Main Street looked like a war zone, and with all the crazies running around, including Rosalie, it wasn't safe for Belinda to be on her own.

I opened a nylon flap and walked into a yurt. Inside, it looked like a big tent with sleeping bags littering the ground. In the center was a small kerosene heater, and I noticed a strong smell of pot. No sign of Belinda or the Arrival.

I stuck my head out to see if the coast was clear and then hopped into the second yurt. It took me a moment to get my bearings. The yurt was nothing like the first one. It was nicer than any apartment I had lived in. Here, there were two cots with beautiful linens, some fancy folding chairs I remembered seeing in an airline gadget magazine, a stainless-steel heater and air purifier, and what looked like a portable kitchen with bar and fridge. It also housed an old-fashioned trunk for clothes, which I made a beeline for.

It was filled with beautiful clothes and shoes. I couldn't help but notice the shoes were fancy, as nice as my grandmother's, and pretty close to my size. I quietly slipped off my sneakers and tried on a pair of Louis Vuittons I saw hanging off the side of the trunk. They were excruciatingly painful, but they were gorgeous.

I hadn't been feeling all that sexy lately, but walking around in those shoes made me feel sexy as hell. I had just the right dress for those shoes, I thought, and if I got a good manicure, Holden would swallow his tongue when he saw me.

It was such a relief to think about shoes instead of crazy women chasing me down the street with a knife. I had been having too much of a stressful time lately, a lot like the whole town. How did everything get so turned upside down? Spencer was hiding from women, Holden was hiding from me, a dead dentist with no face fell on me, and Belinda might go to jail before I could match her.

I was in the middle of searching the trunk for more shoes when I heard men's voices approaching. I panicked and threw myself under one of the cots, bruising my knee pretty good. That's when I recognized one of the voices. It was dreamy, like butterfly kisses full of testosterone.

"Thank you for meeting with me, Mr. Steve. I was pleasantly surprised when I saw you were in town. Good luck for me. I've wanted to talk to you. This means a lot to me," he said.

"I'm very busy, as you can imagine. I hope this won't take long, Mr. Holden," the other voice said.

"I'm sure it's very complicated organizing all this. You have a lot of followers," Holden said.

"We are all followers, followers of the Arrival. This is a very exciting time."

I squished my body into the ground and prayed that no one could see me under the cot. It smelled of earth and dirty socks. I wondered if other matchmakers went through this. Grandma never left her house and was probably at that moment sitting on the couch watching *The View* on TV.

As much as I loved Whoopi Goldberg, however, nothing could stop me from listening to Holden's conversation with what appeared to be the leader of the end-of-worlders' cult. Technically, I was spying on Holden, but, I told myself, I was still a long way from stalking him with designer cutlery.

"I understand that. This will only take a minute," Holden told Mr. Steve. "It's my understanding that you may know where Becky went. It's imperative that I contact her."

"If Becky doesn't want to be found, I don't see how I could help you to find her."

"Really? I think it's crystal clear how you could help." Holden's voice was different than I had ever heard it. Cold with a hint of a threat.

"All right, I understand," said the cult leader. "Maybe we can wash each other's backs, as it were. Tell me again what Becky is to you."

And that's when a spider crawled over my hand, and I screamed like a blonde in a Hitchcock film, jumped up, and threw the cot off me and across the yurt, which ripped the nylon bindings that held it together, making the whole structure collapse like a house of cards on top of me.

Surprisingly, the yurt made a lot of noise as it fell apart. When the ruckus finally died down, I stumbled to a crawling position and struggled to make my way out of the yurt, which was now a pile of nylon and sticks. I pushed the material off of me, and just as I made my way outside, I felt a hand grab the back of my sweatshirt and pull me to a standing position.

"What the hell?" Holden asked, looking at me as if I were the last thing he ever expected to see in the cult leader's yurt, and maybe I was.

"I was just visiting," I said for no apparent reason. He was angry, like steam was going to shoot out of his ears and make a train-whistle sound like in cartoons.

"I was looking for Belinda," I added, coming to my senses. "She followed the donkey."

"Shut up," he said between clenched teeth. "Shut up and don't say a word. Nothing. Not a squeak."

My jaw clamped shut in surprise. Holden had always been kind and gentle with me. He had never told me to shut up, that's for sure. I took a step back to leave and find Lucy and Bridget, but I forgot I was wearing the heels and tripped. Holden caught me easily. "Not a sound," he repeated.

We watched as Mr. Steve the cult leader climbed out from beneath the rubble. Quickly, other cult members circled him, concerned for his safety.

"What happened?" Mr. Steve asked. "I thought it was the Arrival for a moment," he said to Holden, and then his eyes cut to me and down to my stolen shoes. He was not pleased.

"Uh . . . ," I started, but heard Holden's molars grind together.

"There must have been a defect in the construction," Holden said. "How about I buy you a cup of coffee and we'll continue our conversation?"

Mr. Steve studied me and wagged his finger in my direction. "You're the witch's granddaughter, the one who found Simon Dulur's body."

"Uh, that's a misconception about my grandmother. She's just highly intuitive," I said.

"The motive for Simon's murder is obvious. I don't know why the police can't figure it out," he continued.

"It is? You don't?" I asked.

"Of course. It was a hate crime."

"You mean, Dr. Dulur was . . . ?" I asked.

"Yes, one of us," he said, completely shocking me. "Simon was a devotee of the Sacred Mountain, waiting for the Arrival. Holy shit!" His head shot up, and his mouth dropped open. Holden, the other cult members, and I followed his gaze.

Above in the sky, the unfortunate Christmas pageant donkey floated by, suspended by a red, white, and blue parasail. The animal looked down and brayed pitifully.

"Uh," Holden said.

The donkey kicked its legs, trying to get free, and then gave up, letting its body go slack.

"This is what happens when we are threatened, I'm afraid," the cult leader explained after a moment with a shrug. "It becomes an exaggerated tennis game, a competition, as it were."

I leaned into Holden. "I guess it's pagans one, townsfolk zero."

Chapter 10

✦ ♥ ✦

Matchmakers need to be glass-half-full kind of people. How else could we squeeze love from a stone? There's a lot of stones out there, dolly. A lot. So, we hold out hope that matches will click. Eventually. But it doesn't always start out that way. Sometimes matches clunk, clunk, clunk along before they get it right. Dates are disasters where everything goes wrong. He spills his drink on her. She has a near-death experience choking on her steak. He breaks wind after ordering. She laughs her martini out through her nose. And that's when they call us, when the date is the hurricane, tornado, earthquake of dates, and they're ready to give up. So, here's what I tell them: Stick with it. It will get better. Or, between us, bubeleh, it could get worse. Much worse.

Lesson 10,
Matchmaking Advice from Your Grandma Zelda

SIRENS CAME from all over. Police cars, an ambulance, and two fire trucks careened around the corner, seemingly following the donkey's path as it floated over the town in order to catch it before the poor creature fell to its death or got caught in a power line.

We could hear the donkey's pathetic cries for help as it floated above us. We could also hear giggling from some of the cult members, who were no doubt responsible for the vengeful act.

I caught a glimpse of Sergeant Brody driving by, his gaze toward the sky and the flying donkey. In fact, all law enforcement was looking up, watching the donkey's trajectory as they drove to its rescue.

It wasn't the safest way to travel.

They swerved through the streets. I gasped as I watched three near misses, and then finally there was an explosive sound as metal met metal and two police cars sideswiped each other.

Mr. Steve the cult leader hovered over my shoulder. "This town is so strange," he said. He put his hands on my shoulders and turned me around. "Strange but lovely," he added, throwing a look down at my stolen shoes and then into my eyes. His breath smelled of stale cheese, making my morning's latte back up on me. He gripped me hard. I tried to wiggle away, but I couldn't break his hold.

In an instant, Holden was there and peeled Mr. Steve's hands off me and moved me to stand behind him. "So, about that talk," he said to the cult leader.

"Inopportune moment," he said. I couldn't see them with Holden in front of me, but there was a small, almost imperceptible shuffle and Mr. Steve had a change of heart. "Fine, then. Tomorrow night. You can come for the firelight vigil. And bring your lady friend. I like her taste in shoes."

Mr. Steve stepped away from us and ordered his minions to rebuild his yurt. The street, once deserted, was now a hive of activity between law enforcement managing their car accident, the cult managing the aftermath of the stampede, and the stragglers who wandered, pointing upward at the donkey, who was floating in a southeasterly direction.

Bridget and Lucy appeared as well. I was happy to see them safe, and I couldn't wait to go home. Before we could say our hellos, however, we were interrupted by

Mayor Robinson running through the street with his costume half torn off his body.

"Dulcinea! Dulcinea!" he shouted to the heavens. "My donkey! Look what they've done to my donkey!" He ran in the donkey's direction, shouting for it. The donkey seemed to recognize him and brayed even louder.

"Best Christmas pageant *ever*," Lucy said cheerfully.

"Did you find Belinda? We came up empty," said Bridget.

With no sign of her, we decided to double back and look for Belinda at Bridget's condo.

But Holden had other ideas. He held on to my arm a little too firmly. "Ladies, Gladie and I are going to walk home together," he told my friends. He used his authoritarian voice, which was out of character for him. I got goose bumps. I wasn't scared, exactly, but he had my attention.

"Oh, my," Lucy said, fanning herself.

"Okay," giggled Bridget.

HOLDEN ESCORTED me by my arm away from Main Street, and in a short while, I found myself back in the alley where Rosalie had had me cornered only minutes before. Holden steered me up against a wall and planted his hand above my head. He leaned into me, his face about an inch from mine.

"What were you doing in the yurt?"

He was good-looking. More than good-looking. He left Brad Pitt in the dust in the looks department. But at that moment, he was all business. I had been a bad girl, he seemed to say with his eyes, and Holden didn't like bad girls.

"I was looking for Belinda," I croaked, my mouth dry all of a sudden.

"Under the cot? You thought Belinda was under the cot?"

"I heard your voice and got scared."

Holden raised an eyebrow. "My voice scares you?" He took a strand of my hair and curled it around his fingers. "I was hoping my voice had another effect on you."

I swallowed.

"What did you hear when you were listening to my scary voice?" he asked.

"You wanted the cult leader's help. You asked about Becky."

"And who is Becky?"

"I don't know," I said. But I suspected her thighs were thinner than mine, and I hoped she wasn't too pretty.

Holden caressed my cheek. "You are lovely," he said like he was trying to convince himself. "And I can't seem to stay away from you."

"Are you trying to stay away from me?"

"It might be wiser," he said.

"Ouch."

"No, there's no ouch." He leaned in, pressing his body against mine, and captured my mouth with his. His face was scratchy with the start of a beard, but his lips were soft and warm, and I sank into him. He was yummy, even better than ice cream. My head swam, and I could swear I levitated. I wondered vaguely if I was going to float away and then they would have to chase me along with the donkey.

Holden kissed me like he meant it, like he never wanted to stop, but after a while, he did stop, and he rested his forehead against mine and caught his breath. I had stopped breathing altogether. I was past the need for oxygen.

"No more hiding under beds, all right?" he said, bringing me back to reality.

"Well . . . ," I started.

"Well what?"

"About this cult. I mean, what do you have to do with them? Are you a member like Dr. Dulur?"

"No, I'm not."

"So, how do you know the leader?" I asked.

"Gladie, I'm not prepared to get into this with you."

"Who are you prepared to get into it with? Becky?"

Holden put his finger under my chin and tilted up my face. "No more hiding under beds. Stay away from the cult. I mean it, stay away. I don't want to see you hurt."

I didn't ask him how getting close to the cult would hurt me. And I didn't tell him about Rosalie. I didn't have a lot to say. Instead, I did a lot of thinking. Holden took my hand and walked me home, and the entire time I thought. I thought about Holden trying to stay away from me. I thought about the creepy cult and Dr. Dulur being one of them. I thought of Dr. Dulur as the sadistic dentist. I thought about a pretty woman named Becky and Holden's desperation to find her. I thought about Holden telling me to shut up.

When we got back to the house, Grandma was waiting for me outside. "There you are," she said to me. "You're late. Say goodbye to Arthur. You're needed inside."

I started to walk up the driveway, but Holden took my hand and pulled me close.

"Are we good, you and I?" he asked me.

"Yes." But I wasn't sure about that.

"Are you sure? I want us to be good." He said it like he was used to getting what he wanted. It was another side of Holden, a side I wasn't used to.

"Gladie needs to come inside now," Grandma said a little forcibly to Holden. "She has work to do."

Holden let go of me, and I walked up the driveway, looking back at him a couple times. "You've had a complicated day," Grandma said when I reached her. "It's time to be inside. Promise me you'll stay inside the rest of the day."

"I promise, Grandma." She handed me a Pop-Tart and walked with me into the house.

With all the excitement, I had missed lunch, but Grandma had thought of that. "I've got fried chicken and mashed potatoes," Grandma told me as we walked inside. "Don't worry about you know who and that lunch situation. I took care of it."

I had almost forgotten about you know who. I wondered where he was in the No-Face Case investigation. I had been racking up suspects all day long. Between Rosalie and Spencer's other loony lady friends, Rosalie and the other parents of children the dentist allegedly abused, people opposed to Dr. Dulur's membership in the cult, and the cult itself, there were more than a few directions to go.

I made a beeline for the kitchen, but I was stopped dead in my tracks by Grandma's visitors in the parlor. Sister Cyril, the nun who ran the women's shelter outside of town, sat there and stared at another woman, who stood in the center of the room.

There wasn't anything odd about the standing woman except for the fact she was topless, and Sister Cyril was inspecting her boobs. "Will you look at those," exclaimed Sister Cyril.

"Yvonne Richardson just got a new pair, and we are admiring them," Grandma informed me. "Grab a plate and join us."

"I think I'll just eat in the kitchen," I said. I wasn't a big fan of other women's breasts.

"No, join us. I want Yvonne to talk to you."

I couldn't imagine why Grandma wanted me to look at someone's fake knockers, but it was the most normal part of my day.

I piled a plate high with fried chicken, mashed potatoes, and gravy. I took Bird's Chinese diet tea out of my purse and brewed a cup. I took a sip. It wasn't bad. It tasted like regular tea with a hint of licorice. I brought my plate and cup into the parlor, joined the women, and got an eyeful of boob.

"Yvonne, this is my granddaughter, Gladie."

"Nice to meet you," Yvonne said, completely unconcerned to be naked in front of a perfect stranger. And a nun. And an old-lady matchmaker.

"Uh . . . nice to meet you, too. Nice to see you, Sister," I said, happy to turn my attention to Sister Cyril. "I didn't see you at the Christmas pageant."

"Christmas in December is plenty for me," she said.

"Uh-oh," Grandma said, sitting down. "That fool mayor just ran after his donkey into the lake, and he got kicked in the head. Kicked in the head by a donkey . . . maybe it will be an improvement."

Nobody asked how Grandma could know that. Instead I wondered if the mayor could still go out with Belinda even if he had a concussion or worse. That is, if Belinda ever showed up again.

Grandma threw me a look and tsked.

"I know," I told her. "But it's just one date until I can find someone suitable for her."

"Cutting corners just makes a lot of weird shapes," Grandma said. "It never helped anyone in the long run. You know better. You've got the gift. You are a born matchmaker."

I sighed. Grandma was convinced I had the gift and was just like her, but I thought the only thing we had in common was our metabolism.

She clapped her hands together. "Okay, Yvonne, now that you have the jugs out, I want you to tell Gladie what you were telling me earlier. The hooters are part of the story," Grandma explained to me.

"Should I start from the beginning?" Yvonne asked,

cupping her large silicone breasts like she was holding on to them for balance.

"That would be fine," Grandma said. "You might as well give her the full rundown."

Yvonne took a seat facing me and crossed her legs. She studied me a moment, perhaps wondering if I could handle a story that started with big, naked hooters sitting in my grandmother's favorite parlor chair. It was hard to look her in the eyes; my focus kept drifting south.

"Last year, I was an obese spinster with a job as a janitor at Lou's auto mechanic place. You know the one?" she asked.

I nodded, but I was transfixed by her boobs, which inflated and deflated with her breath.

"I had had enough. While I was sweeping up at Lou's and eating Mallomars, a show was playing on the TV in the waiting room. It was that one where all the different professionals get somebody on, tell them they are ugly, fat, and don't know how to dress, and then change them. So, you know what I thought?"

"Excuse me?" I asked.

"Focus, Gladie," Grandma said. "They're just breasts."

"So, you know what I thought?" Yvonne repeated. "You know, about that show?"

I knew the show she was talking about. They made women lose ten pounds, shoved them into uncomfortable clothes, added fake hair, and smeared on a lot of makeup. It gave me hives. "No, what did you think?" I asked.

"I thought, 'This is the show for me.' I was about to call the producers and ask if I could get on the next episode when Lou's phone rang, and guess who was on the other line?" Yvonne snapped her fingers. "Gladie? Are you with me?"

The boob thing was getting to me. I didn't understand why she had to be naked the entire time, unless she was trying to get her money's worth, showing the world the whole enchilada instead of the normal amount of ample cleavage other breast-implant recipients liked to display.

I was obsessed with her nudity. My mind tried to make sense of it. Would she leave the house this way, completely topless? Would she drive around with a boob perilously close to the steering wheel? What if she had to make a U-turn? I hoped she wasn't a coffee drinker. I hoped she didn't order soup at dinner. It was dangerous being a nudist.

"I'll tell you who was on the phone," Yvonne continued, tired of waiting for me to answer. "Your grandma. She said if I wished, she would give me a makeover. Like she knew, you know. Like she knew."

"I remember that," Sister Cyril piped in. "It was like watching a disappearing act. You lost all that weight, you changed your appearance from top to bottom. It was almost a miracle."

Grandma blushed. I guess she liked being called a miracle worker. "But the new breasts weren't my idea," she pointed out. "She had perfectly respectable B's." I looked down. I was a solid C cup, but Yvonne was currently topping double-D status. Easily.

"No, I did that on my own," Yvonne said. "It was a bad idea. 'Cause I wanted them cheap, you know?"

I nodded. "Your boobs don't look cheap to me. You know, not that I'm looking or anything."

"These?" she said, cupping them high and pointing her nipples at me like they were going to shoot out daggers, just like in a James Bond movie. "These aren't the cheap ones. These are the new, expensive ones."

"Tell her who was with you at the cheap place getting her own cheap body parts," Grandma prompted.

"Holly Firestone," Yvonne said. "Holly Firestone got a huge deal from the doctor because she bought in bulk and because she did the doctor favors, if you know what I mean."

I wasn't surprised a bit. In fact, it wasn't anything I didn't suspect already about Holly the hygienist. I ate a forkful of mashed potatoes and leaned back.

"Tell her the rest about Holly," Grandma urged Yvonne.

"She and I bonded," Yvonne explained. "That was before, you know, when her face still moved. When I told her I was looking to change careers, she said she had a sweet job at Bliss Dental. You know why, Gladie? Can you guess?"

"Free dental work?" I asked.

"In a manner of speaking. Holly was cooking the books, skimming off the top."

I leaned forward. "Are you sure?"

"She told me."

"She told you at the plastic surgeon's office that she was stealing from Bliss Dental?"

"No, she told me that later when we were drinking Harvey Wallbangers at Bar None. She said she was saving up to buy a Camaro and later she was going to get a nice condo in Houston, where she had family."

"Tell what happened after that," Sister Cyril said excitedly. "Tell her about the Pilates."

"So, I take my cheap boobs to Pilates class, and I had a little incident."

Sister Cyril bounced up and down in her chair. "Gladie, one of Yvonne's cheap mammaries was sucked up into her chest cavity when she was doing a Pilates exercise."

I swallowed and then raised an eyebrow. I had so many questions, I didn't know where to start. There was the obvious how-do-boobs-get-sucked-into-chest-cavities question, edged out only by the is-that-how-a-nun-says-tatas question.

"My hand to God," Sister Cyril said. "I was in the same class when it happened. One minute she was completely symmetrical and the next minute, *whoop!*" she exclaimed, making a loud sucking noise. "Her right side was gone."

"Holy crap," I said.

"I had to go to the hospital," explained Yvonne.

"She married the EMT who drove the ambulance," Grandma said with a twinkle in her eye.

"Yep," Yvonne said, flashing me a huge ring. "Zelda had set up the Pilates class for me. It was painful, but I wouldn't trade Paul for anything. He paid for these new ones, and they are guaranteed not to get sucked up into my body."

"That's nice," I said. "I should probably go upstairs and do some work." I was developing a boob-inspired migraine, and I wanted to tell Spencer that Holly was the one embezzling from Bliss Dental.

"Wait, Gladie," Grandma said. "Yvonne, tell her the rest. Tell her the important part."

"About Dr. Dulur?"

"Yes."

Yvonne leaned back and tried to fold her arms in front of her, but her boobs got in the way, so she dropped them to her sides. "When I was in the hospital after they dug my boob out, I stayed in a room with a crazy woman. She told me she had been chosen by aliens. She was part of this cult, the cult the wackos belong to over here, you know?" I nodded. "Anyway, at some point during the day, Dr. Dulur came in and visited her. They closed the curtains for privacy, but of course I could hear every word."

My head was throbbing. "Yeah, the leader of the cult told me that Dr. Dulur was a member."

"Oh, yeah?" Yvonne said dramatically. "Did he tell you he was battling him for leadership?"

"Gladie," Grandma said. "Dr. Dulur was number two, and he was trying to be number one."

Chapter 11

✦ ♥ ✦

Matching a doctor is child's play. Any hack can do it. Matching a fence builder is another story, bubeleh. If you can get a fence builder married, you are a star. I've matched three of them. Sure, they were good-looking and made a good living, but they were like Killer, the Rottweiler guard dog at Joe's dump. I'm talking territorial. They're so used to fencing off boundaries, their heads can't entertain the idea of welcoming someone into their life. Of sharing. It's all about your space and my space and never our space. As matchmaker, you need to make your matches willing to break through their fenced-in ideas. Love flows. It can't be fenced in.

Lesson 93,
Matchmaking Advice from Your Grandma Zelda

FOR A moment, I forgot about Yvonne's knockers, and I had a flashback to Dr. Dulur's smiling face, telling me joyfully that I had a mouth full of cavities. But his face had changed in my mind from that of the happy, disco-loving dentist to one that fit a sadistic, power-hungry cult member. He was almost the man of a thousand faces, I realized, and suddenly the murderer's grisly act made sense to me. What better statement to make than to remove his face?

With Dr. Dulur turning into the bogeyman, the question wasn't who wanted Simon Dulur dead; the question was who didn't want him dead?

"I have to get going," Yvonne said. "I have yoga at three."

Sister Cyril jumped up from her seat. "I'll go with you, dear. I've always wanted to try yoga." She winked at me. "Just in case there's another emergency," she mouthed in my direction.

Yvonne grabbed her purse and what I was relieved to see was a bra and was just about to hook herself into place when Grandma's front door burst open and the mayor marched in with Bridget, Lucy, and Belinda trailing behind him.

"Good day! Good day!" he announced, stumbling slightly when he noticed Yvonne's rack. She paused and posed for him a moment before putting her bra on. "Plans, ladies, plans. Let's make them!" he cheered, regaining his composure and clapping his hands together.

Mayor Robinson was soaking wet, half his clothes had been ripped off him, and his head was wrapped in a bandage. He became distracted by dust motes in the air and clutched at them.

"He won't go to the hospital," Bridget explained, pushing her way in front of him. "The donkey kicked him in the head. The paramedics said he's lucky to be alive."

"Beezow Bee Bop," the mayor exclaimed, giving up on the dust. "That's a much more fitting name for a mayor, don't you think?"

Grandma leaned into me. "I was wrong. The kick didn't improve his brain. He's got scrambled brains now. No different than the omelet special at Denny's."

"Mr. Mayor, wouldn't you like to sit down and rest a bit?" Lucy asked.

"Fine, just fine," he said. "I've got a big of vitiligo. The room is spinning."

"That's vertigo," explained Belinda. "Vitiligo is what Michael Jackson had."

"No, vitiligo. I know what I'm talking about. I Googled it."

Belinda was slightly dazed but all in one piece. I was relieved. I figured she had had a fifty-fifty chance of getting trampled to death. "I'm so happy you're okay," I told her, patting her back.

Lucy looked through Grandma's booze cabinet and poured herself a drink. "We drove around all hell and gone looking for her. Finally found her at the lake, where the whole town wound up following the flying donkey." She snickered. "Flying donkey. Hey, that's kind of funny."

"My donkey!" the mayor yelled out.

Grandma patted him on his knee. "There, there. Dulcinea is fine, now. She's forgotten about it already."

"Is that true, Zelda?" the mayor asked, his eyes big and round.

"Yes," Grandma said, as sure as only Grandma could be about a donkey's state of mind.

"Good, because she's the only one who understands me," the mayor said.

Lucy punched back her drink and Grandma wordlessly joined her for another.

"Should we go check on the donkey?" Belinda asked. Her hair had come undone, and her tracksuit had green stains on the knees, where I supposed she took a tumble in the stampede. I made an excuse and pulled her out of the room.

"I'm on the case," I told her. "I'm getting really close." I didn't want to come right out and tell her that Holly was stealing money from Bliss Dental for fear that Belinda would try to take revenge and get into trouble with Holly, but I wanted her to know she would be okay. "You won't have to worry about the police, and on the romantic front—" I started, but Grandma came up behind me and tsked loudly.

"Bridget and Lucy want the keys to your car. They're going to fetch it for you later," she said, eyeing me pointedly.

I pretended not to take the hint. I didn't have a clue who to fix Belinda up with, and the mayor would just have to do for the moment until I could find someone better. It wasn't that I was giving up on Belinda, I just needed a stalling tactic. Besides, the mayor shouldn't be alone just now, I figured, and Belinda could watch him to make sure he didn't get kicked in the head again.

I handed Grandma the keys and gave her a little nudge in the direction of the parlor before turning back to Belinda.

"Isn't the mayor handsome?" I asked her. "Did I tell you he was single?"

"Was he the one you picked out for me?" she asked, craning her head to get a better look at Mayor Robinson.

"Yes, and he may be a bit damaged now, but he cleans up nice," I said.

"He drives a Lexus," she said, her mind in fast-forward.

"Okay. Would you consider going on a date with him?" I asked, but she was already in the parlor, planting herself next to the mayor and whispering something in his ear.

"Off we go!" he announced. "After you, my lady." He held his hand out gallantly for Belinda. She giggled, and they left Grandma's house with Yvonne and Sister Cyril behind them.

I took a deep breath. Grandma arched an eyebrow at me, her disapproval of my matchmaking shooting out of her eyeballs. Lucy handed her another drink. There was a lot of alcohol flowing in the middle of the day.

"Is it my imagination or have things turned a little *Twilight Zone*-y lately?" Lucy asked.

Bridget stared at the chair where Yvonne had sat. She shook her head like she was trying to wake up. "Hey, was Yvonne naked?" she asked.

LUCY WENT home to nap, and Bridget went to do the books over at Pete's Market. With the house quiet, I only had to contend with Grandma's disapproval. So I feigned exhaustion (not really a lie) and went upstairs to check on the other problem in my life: Spencer.

My room was oddly quiet when I opened the door. Spencer was standing shirtless, his back to me, dusting my nightstand. The muscles in his back moved and bulged while he dusted. I bit my lower lip, and my breath hitched. The sound made him turn.

"Put a shirt on," I grumbled.

"Hey, Pinkie, what's up?" he said.

His chest was wide and hairless except for his treasure path of love. "Put on your damned shirt!"

"Okay. Okay. You don't have to get pissy." He grabbed a shirt and then paused, studied me a minute, and arched an eyebrow. "Does my manly torso make you uncomfortable, Pinkie?" He flexed his pectoral muscles, and I took a step backward.

"Put the shirt on," I managed.

Spencer slipped a T-shirt over his head. It was another Padres shirt, his favorite baseball team. It was bulky and hid some of his body. I took a deep breath of relief.

"Holy crap," I said, taking a seat on the bed. "You're up."

"What does that mean?"

"Normally, you're lying around with a bag of chips, watching *Family Guy*."

"It starts in five minutes." He opened another bag of chips and popped open a root beer. He passed it to me, but I refused.

"You better watch out," I said. "You're going to get fat."

"Don't worry about my body. I don't get fat."

"I thought I saw the start of a roll just now," I lied. "You might want to lay off the Ruffles."

"There's no roll, Pinkie." I thought I detected a trace of doubt in his voice. "But if there is, how about you help me work it off?"

"Okay, that's it. That's it!" I threw a pillow at him, truly angry now. "Do you know how I spent much of my day, Spencer? Can you guess?"

"Did it involve a bikini wax?" He smirked his annoying smirk, and it was everything I could do not to belt him.

"Rosalie Rodriguez. Does that name ring a bell?"

"It might," he said. He fluffed the pillows and leaned back against the headboard.

"Rosalie ran after me through the streets with a knife."

Spencer sighed. "Yeah, she does like to do that, doesn't she?"

I blinked. "What's with you? You've changed. You're still a philandering jerk, but now you're wimpy, too."

Spencer grabbed me, pulled me to the bed, and rolled on top of me. "Wimpy?" he asked in a whisper. "I don't think so."

His eyes were huge and dark, and focused. "Your breath smells like barbecue chips. Get off me before I gain five pounds smelling you."

He rolled off and tossed a chip in his mouth. I punched him in his arm. "No more fooling around. You have to leave. You can't stay here anymore. You have to deal with Rosalie. She's got a whole set of Rachael Ray knives, and she wants to use them on someone."

"That's what I'm afraid of."

"Do something, Spencer. You got yourself into this mess. Get yourself out of it."

Spencer grunted and turned on the television. It was like living with Archie Bunker.

"And that's not all," I continued. "The town has gone berserk. Spencer, donkeys are flying over our town. Flying. What do you say about that? And the mayor has brain damage, and there is a murderer on the loose with Dr. Dulur's face."

"The mayor has always been brain damaged," Spencer said.

I kicked off my shoes and got into bed, pulling the covers over me. I was exhausted. What a couple of days. My world was in chaos, and I didn't know how to fix it.

"You want to know what I'm thinking?" I asked him.

"Is that a trick question?"

"I think the suspects in the No-Face Case are mounting."

Spencer put the TV on mute. "Pinkie, are you sticking your nose in?"

"Well, someone has to." I looked at him pointedly and punched my pillow. "I would love to have my bed back. If I knew I would have to share with a behemoth, I would have bought a queen."

"I hate to tell you this, but your friend Belinda looks like a good candidate for murderer," he said, chewing on a chip.

"Are you kidding me? She wants to be fixed up. She's looking for love, not murder."

"So maybe she was looking for love, and the doc rejected her." He tossed another chip in his mouth and chewed. I thought about his theory a minute but threw it away. Dr. Dulur looked nothing like George Clooney. She wouldn't have killed him for love.

"And there's the problem with the missing money," he said.

"Oh!" I shouted. "I almost forgot. Yvonne Richardson just told me that when she was having her first boob job, Holly the hygienist told her that she was the one taking the money from Bliss Dental. She was using it for plastic surgery, a Camaro, and a condo in Texas."

"Why is Yvonne telling *you* that?"

"I'm a good listener."

Spencer ran his fingers through his hair, leaving remnants of chips speckled through it. "We'll check out the Holly angle, but Holly has an alibi. She was at Bar None all night, according to a dozen witnesses, and your friend Belinda says she doesn't remember where she was that night. That doesn't sound suspicious to you, Miss Marple?"

It did sound suspicious to me. I had forgotten that fact. What was Belinda hiding about that night? I would have to get it out of her somehow. "I don't think it's suspicious at all," I said.

Spencer counted on his fingers. "Belinda doesn't have an alibi, the money is missing, and Nathan described the perpetrator as *big*. Well, have you seen Belinda?"

Belinda was bigger than most, but I didn't know if she could overtake the dentist. "Belinda is not that big," I said.

Spencer crossed his arms in front of himself and closed his eyes. "Let the professionals handle the case, Pinkie. We're on it." He was insufferable, especially when he was trying to prevent me from working a case.

"And how about Dr. Dulur and the cult?" I asked. "Have your professionals looked at that angle?"

Spencer opened his eyes. "The cult?"

"Dr. Dulur was a member and trying to be the leader. He was in some kind of battle for the leadership."

"I can't imagine Dr. Dulur as the leader of a cult," he said. "He looked like a Bee Gees reject. He was more disco than transcendental."

"Dr. Dulur wasn't all that he seemed," I said. "According to Rosalie, he was sadistic. He broke her son's arm."

Spencer sat up straighter in bed. "According to Rosalie? Did you talk with her?"

"Why? Does that frighten you?"

Spencer's jaw clenched and made a grinding noise. "Don't worry about the No-Face Case or Rosalie. I'm working on it, and I will have it wrapped up sooner or later, so you can stop your *investigating*." He bent his fingers into the air-quotes sign and made a squishy face. He got me so mad.

"Did you just do air quotes?" I demanded.

"I might have. Something wrong with that?"

"No. Nothing. It's just that I didn't figure you for the air-quotes kind of guy."

Spencer cocked his head to the side. "What kind of guy is an air-quotes kind of guy?"

"I don't know. Let's forget it." I turned over and buried my head deeper in my pillow.

Spencer tugged at my shoulder. "No. What kind of guy?"

"I don't know."

"You know. Otherwise, you wouldn't have said anything. Tell me."

I sat up and stared him down. "Panty wad."

"Panty wad?" he asked.

"Yeah, the panty-wad kind of guy."

"Pinkie, you wound me."

"Sorry," I said with air quotes, and lay back down, rolling over.

I DOZED through two *Family Guy* episodes. In the middle of one, Spencer whispered in my ear that he promised to be out of my room as soon as possible. He was almost apologetic and very nearly vulnerable. Who would have thought women would be Spencer's weakness? He had turned from predator to prey, and he couldn't handle it.

I took a shower to clear my head. With so much chaos in town, I had become disoriented. I couldn't make out what was important anymore. Holden, the cult, the mayor's donkey, Dr. Dulur, Rosalie, Spencer. They had all infiltrated my life in one way or another, and I felt forced to deal with them. But I was only one woman, and a tired one at that. It was time to prioritize.

I let the warm water wash over me, and as I shampooed, I realized that matching Belinda with someone who wasn't an idiot should be my first priority, and coming a close second was proving her innocence. The rest would have to fall into place after I had Belinda taken care of. After all, she had come to me for help. She was my first real matchmaking client, and I wasn't going to let her down and have Grandma disapprove of me forever.

I had already planted the seeds of doubt in Spencer's mind about Belinda's innocence. I mean, he hadn't arrested her or anything, so I didn't think he was sure about her being the murderer. Now I needed to get her to reveal her alibi, and we could move on and let the "professionals" find the No-Face Case killer.

And I would let Spencer worry about Rosalie and his pack of Facebook stalkers and let Holden worry about Becky and where I fit into the picture. For now.

With my priorities straight and clean hair, I put on comfortable sweats and a T-shirt and joined Grandma downstairs in the sunroom. She watered plants while I sat on a yellow polka-dotted garden chair and cranked up her old laptop to Google Arthur Holden.

I couldn't find a thing about my mysterious pseudo-boyfriend. There was an Arthur C. Holden in Cleveland, but he was a sixty-five-year-old retired police officer, and he was Asian.

"Sometimes secrets are secrets for a reason," Grandma

said, pruning a plant. "Sometimes a person is a secret. A tall, handsome secret."

I thought about what Spencer said about my grandmother not liking Holden.

"You know something I don't, Grandma?"

"Years' worth, dolly. Years' worth."

The rest of the afternoon was unusually quiet. It was like the town was catching its breath before the next round in the battle against the cult. I hadn't heard from Belinda or the mayor since they left the house, which I thought was a good sign, until I remembered that I hadn't paid my cellphone bill. She couldn't get in touch with me if she wanted, because she refused to call the home line in fear that she would have to speak to my grandmother.

With the coast clear, according to Grandma, Spencer was allowed to come downstairs and eat spaghetti and meatballs for dinner with us in the kitchen. We were a strange little family, but Spencer seemed to take it in stride, and Grandma was all but euphoric at having him at our table.

She picked his brain for an hour about polygamy laws in the state of California, completely ignoring the obvious topics of conversation she could have with the chief of police in a town where a cult had invaded, donkeys flew overhead, boys peed from the trees, and cop cars were used for coitus.

"Rain," she said as I sopped up pasta sauce with my slice of garlic bread. She clutched my arm tightly. "Remember your promise."

The only promise I remembered was not to lose my virginity during the homecoming dance in tenth grade, and I broke that one, big time.

"The promise not to go outside," she reminded me.

"Forever?" I asked. "Don't go out for the rest of my life?" I wanted to be a matchmaker like Grandma, but I wasn't prepared to be exactly like her and not leave the house forever.

"No, just for tonight." She pointed to the ceiling, and Spencer and I looked up. It was the normal ceiling, white with a circa-1930s lamp. "Rain," she said. "Bad things come with rain."

"We're set for clear skies all week," Spencer informed her. I had caught him watching more than his share of the Weather Channel lately, but it was foolish to question Grandma about these things. "Fine. Rain," he said after a moment.

"Don't go out," she urged me.

IT WAS a good meal, and it ended with coffee and cheesecake and a long discussion about the history of the mountain, and how there had never before been any mention of it being sacred or housing aliens. "People are more or less lunatics," Grandma explained. "We're just getting a large influx of more."

Surprisingly, Spencer offered to do the dishes and to change my much-used sheets, and I decided to go upstairs to the attic and do some work on Belinda's love life.

A month ago, I had cleaned out all of Grandma's old "files," which were just some dusty, yellowed index cards and bits of papers. There was precious little to work with, but it felt good to sit at the desk again in front of the big circular window that looked out over the street. I felt professional, like a real matchmaker. I wasn't much for commitment, but the idea of finding love for Belinda gave me a warm feeling all the way down to my toes that wasn't so bad.

With the warm feeling came a twinge of guilt about fixing her up with the mayor. Even before he was kicked in the head by his donkey, he wasn't all there, and it was unfair to saddle Belinda with him. I was determined to find her someone better.

I thought back to my hospital idea. There were plenty of people visiting the ER lately, I reasoned, and I bet I could find a good match who had a broken leg or some other minor injury without much trouble.

Belinda would be so grateful, I thought. She would tell me where she had been the night of the murder, and I could help her there, too. I slapped my hands together in triumph just as a clap of thunder ripped through the night. As I went to close the window, I saw movement at the house across the street. It was falling apart and up for sale, but it hadn't gotten any takers yet, either because the market was sluggish, or because it was a major fixer-upper. Or maybe because a man had died in it the month before.

I jumped when I saw a shadow on the front lawn, and a feeling of icy dread slid down my back.

"I don't believe in ghosts," I said out loud. But I wasn't so sure I was telling the truth. I couldn't get behind aliens, but I was pretty scared of hauntings.

I closed the window and threw the latch just as I saw the movement again, but this time I got a good look and realized it was Shlep, the dog from down the street.

"What are you doing, Shlep? You are going to get all wet," I said, even though he couldn't hear me.

I watched as he crossed the street, intermittently sniffing the ground and the air, following some scent to our house and right into our backyard. I pictured him digging up Grandma's tomatoes, and the thought drove me to run downstairs and out the back.

"Shlep, Shlep," I called quietly. It had gotten late, and I didn't want to wake up Grandma or Spencer.

The lightning cracked through the dark, and I spotted Shlep still on the scent, heading right for Grandma's tomatoes. "No, Shlep!" I called, but he ignored me, intent on whatever it was he smelled.

I tiptoed out onto the back stairs in my bare feet and after a moment's hesitation trotted out into the yard. "Don't you dare, Shlep. Grandma will be so mad."

The ground was cold under my feet, and I knew I only had a moment before it would start to rain. I ran after the dog and had almost caught him when he cried out in pain and ran out of the yard.

"What was that about?" I called after him. "I'm not that scary."

I was answered by a thud, a movement in the yard. I looked around, but without the lightning, it was dark.

"Shlep?" I called out, but I knew it wasn't the dog. Someone—a person, not a canine—was walking around Grandma's backyard at night.

I swallowed with difficulty. "Spencer?" I tried again, but there was no answer.

I froze in fear, sure that I was being watched. As I took a step toward the house, the sky opened up and began to pour down rain. I was instantly soaked through my clothes. I started walking faster, but I heard the noise again, as if it had moved into my path, and I quickly jogged to the right to avoid whatever it was that was there, only to stumble into what I at first thought was a man.

I screamed but stopped just as suddenly when I realized it was only a scarecrow.

"When did Grandma put you up?" I asked the scarecrow. The lightning cracked, illuminating the backyard and giving me a good look at the figure. And its face. A long white scar glowed down its right cheek.

"Oh, hello, Dr. Dulur," I said to it. And then everything went black, and I slipped down into unconsciousness and onto the muddy ground of Grandma's backyard.

Chapter 12

Fifty shades of smut! That's what the folks want these days. If there isn't an orgy or a whip in a book, it's not good literature anymore. If Hemingway were alive today, he would be forced to write To Have and Have Some More *or* For Whom the Bell Slathers You in Whipped Cream and Takes You on a Ride Like a Whore at a Rodeo. *So, you may get some clients who are searching for something unconventional. Something out of the box. A three-way, for example. Don't be shocked, bubeleh. I've been around the block. I know about three-ways. But orgies aren't our department. We are a traditional sort of shop. Three's a crowd, as far as we are concerned. Don't get me wrong: Three is sexy. Three is fun and athletic. But three is complicated.*

Lesson 69,
Matchmaking Advice from Your Grandma Zelda

I WOKE to someone shouting my name. "You're not Dr. Dulur," I said, opening one eye.

For a moment, I had thought it was a ghost, but it was Spencer, kneeling over me, a gun in his hand and a look of concern on his face.

"Are you hurt?" he asked.

I took stock of my body. I was wet, dirty, and cold, but I wasn't hurt. "I think I fainted," I told him. "I thought I saw the craziest thing."

Spencer nodded. "I heard you scream. Can you stand?" He helped me up. The rain was coming down in sheets, making it difficult to see, but the bolts of lightning illuminated the scene as if taking snapshots of the action. I staggered back when I saw the scarecrow.

"I thought it was my imagination," I said, more to myself than to Spencer.

"Holy Christ," he said, noticing it in detail for the first time. Sewn onto the head of the scarecrow was Dr. Dulur's face. "What kind of sick fuck," Spencer began, reminding me of Nathan's words. And then we heard a thud and heavy breathing, and I knew we were not alone. I *had* been watched, and whoever it was was still around.

Spencer raised his voice so I could hear him over the thunder and rain. "Get back in the house," he shouted, aiming his gun at the dark beyond us. "Get in, now!"

"Not without you," I said, surprising myself.

He turned around, obviously surprised himself. His face was inches away from mine, but he yelled to make sure I would hear him. "You are the world's biggest pain in the ass!"

I put my hands on my hips and dug my heels into the mud. "More of a pain in the ass than your Facebook friends?" I asked like an idiot who wasn't standing in a thunderstorm next to a dead man's face with a killer nearby.

Spencer smacked his forehead with his non-gun hand. "Do what I say, woman. Get inside. Now!"

The lightning cracked through the night, shining a light on Dr. Dulur's face, and then suddenly a shadow appeared from the bushes and took off running through the backyard's gate out to the front. Spencer went after him like a shot, and I followed him.

We ran into the dark through the rain in our bare feet. I was only dimly aware of stones and twigs scraping my feet as I ran, slipping in the mud, trying to keep up with Spencer, who was running full out as if he could see the shadowy figure in front of us. I saw nothing, only darkness, rain, and the occasional lightning bolt. But I could hear him. He was breathing hard, and he was wearing heavy shoes that slapped the wet ground as he ran.

"Stop! Police!" Spencer shouted, and tried to take aim with his gun. "He's going into the Ternses' house," he said. "Go back inside!" he shouted at me, as if he was surprised I was still behind him.

"No way," I said. "I'm sticking with you." It wasn't all about stupid bravery or feeling protective of Spencer. I had no intention of going near the face again. At least not alone. Even if we were running in the direction of a homicidal maniac, at least I was with an armed cop.

We were across the street in a matter of seconds, staring at the house's front door, which creaked as it flapped open and closed in the storm. Spencer took a step toward the door, his gun raised. I grabbed his torso and held strong. "No, don't go in," I said. "Spencer, wait for backup. Don't go in."

He squirmed away from my hold. "Go back to your grandmother's," he said. "Gladie, do as I say." And he took a step into the house. I followed him in.

It was instantly quieter, but it was even darker inside the house. I had been there several times before, but it had been filled with furniture and knickknacks, and now it was empty, abandoned. And quiet.

I had stopped breathing, and so had Spencer and the shadowy figure. I knew he was in there somewhere, but we couldn't see or hear him. On the other hand, he could probably see us in the doorway, and Spencer quickly pulled me to the side to rest in the corner a moment, allowing our eyes to adjust to the darkness.

"Spencer," I whispered, but he shushed me. Then we

heard a thud on the floor and running footsteps. "He's in the kitchen," I told Spencer. "That's the sound of the linoleum."

Spencer held my hand while we ran toward the kitchen. And we got him.

Well, almost.

The shadowy figure, dressed all in black from head to toe, skulked in a corner like Boo Radley in *To Kill a Mockingbird*. We could almost make out his form, but just as Spencer shouted *"Freeze!"* I slid on the wet floor and careened into Spencer, sending his pistol flying from his hand in a high arc to land in the kitchen sink and sending us falling on the floor like dominos, with me as the top domino. Boo Radley hopped in place and swung open the kitchen door and fled out of the house.

"Oops," I said.

BY THE time Spencer recovered from getting the wind knocked out of him and fished his gun out of the sink, the man in black was long gone. Spencer didn't say a word to me, nothing at all about me foiling the apprehension of the No-Face Case killer.

"Well, obviously, that wasn't Belinda," I told him as we dripped muddy water on the floor of the Ternses' kitchen. "She can't run nearly that fast."

Spencer didn't say anything for a long time. I could almost hear his blood pressure rising, and if Dr. Dulur's face hadn't been on a scarecrow in Grandma's backyard, and a killer hadn't been on the loose in the neighborhood, I would have run as far from Spencer as I could.

"I should have left you up on that telephone pole the first time I saw you," Spencer said after a while. He grabbed a fistful of my shirt and tugged, pulling me behind him out of the house and across the street.

I stumbled after him as he marched us back to Grandma's yard, my shirt wadded up in his clenched fist. "I wish you would never speak about the pole," I said. It wasn't that great of a memory, not my finest moment.

"Fine, Gladys."

"Don't call me Gladys," I said, swatting at his hand. "You are not allowed to call me Gladys."

"Stay here, I'm going to get a flashlight." He left me next to the scarecrow. I hadn't had the presence of mind to refuse to stand there by myself, and by the time I realized where I was, Spencer was in the house and I was too scared to move. I tried to recall a self-defense class I watched when I worked as a janitor in a karate dojo for four days, in case the killer returned, but I couldn't remember a thing, and besides, it only took Spencer a few seconds to come back.

Spencer shined the light on Dr. Dulur's face. He studied it for quite some time, squinting his eyes as if to see it better or to better believe what he was seeing. "Okay," he said finally. "I've called a couple officers. We're going to keep this very quiet for the time being. No sirens, no one will know we found the face, no one will know I'm here."

"The killer knows you're here."

"That might work to our benefit."

"I don't understand."

Spencer knocked on my forehead. "When are you going to get it through your thick skull that you don't need to understand? I am the chief of police. I am the investigator. You are a matchmaker. You fix people up so that they can be miserable together for the rest of their lives. You do not solve murders. You do not get involved in police business. Got that?"

"It's not my fault dead people follow me," I said. "Besides, the chief of police is hiding in my bedroom. So, technically, you got me involved in police business. You and your happy-pants penis are dragging me into this investigation."

Even in the dark and through the rain, I could see Spencer's face turn red, his eyes large and furious. "Go inside and get cleaned up while I wait for them!" he ordered. "Go or I will shoot you. You got that, Gladys?"

"Are you going to call me Gladys forever?" I asked. I hated my name. I tried to change it to Fantasia when I worked in the box office at a burlesque show for a month, but my grandmother gave me a guilt trip. Gladys had been my great-great-grandmother's name, she explained, and it was good luck.

I stood in the pouring rain, covered head to toe in mud, staring up at poor Dr. Dulur's face sewn onto a homemade scarecrow in my grandmother's backyard, and wondered if the name really was good luck or not. "Well, at least I'm not dead," I said, and spit against the evil eye.

INSIDE, GRANDMA was waiting for me with a towel and a cup of hot chocolate. "Strip down here," she said. "No sense traipsing through the house like that. I told you not to go outside. Why don't people listen to me?"

"I know. I'm sorry, Grandma."

"And that mayor. You were thinking all lopsided with that one. Well, you'll have another chance with Belinda."

"I will?"

"Yes, that fool went on about Barbra Streisand again, and Belinda took off. She's been trying to call you for hours."

"I need to pay my cellphone bill."

"You still have the pen in your purse?" she asked me.

"Yes, I think so."

"Good, dolly. Keep it there."

I TOOK a long, hot shower and got into bed. Spencer had changed the sheets and made the bed with hospital corners. It felt great on my clean body. I snuggled under the covers and tried to wait up for Spencer in order to get an update on the face and the killer, but after fifteen minutes, I was fast asleep.

I woke for a moment when I heard Spencer turn on the shower and then again when he got into bed and wordlessly gathered me to him like a spoon, and then I fell into a deep, dreamless sleep.

I woke to featherlike kisses on my ear. "You better stop that, or I will bean you," I yelled, slapping him away.

"Sorry." Instead of Spencer, I realized quickly, it was Holden's lips on my earlobe. He had brought me breakfast in bed and was lying next to me, kissing me.

I looked around quickly for Spencer, but he was nowhere to be found. The clock read 8:00 A.M., and I hoped Spencer had decided to finally face the music and go home.

"Oh, sorry, I was dreaming," I told Holden. "How did you get in here?"

"The front door was open, and I let myself in." I doubted the front door was open, especially after last night, but I let that slide, since he had brought lattes and bagels.

"You look beautiful in the morning," he said, and kissed me, letting his tongue slide into my mouth. It was a fabulous way to wake up. We kissed for ages, long languid kisses like we had all the time in the world. We had had a lot of practice kissing each other, and we had become really good at it. He was my Brad Pitt, and I was his Angelina Jolie. Without the kids.

It was perfect.

After about fifteen minutes, we rested our lips, enjoying looking in each other's eyes.

"Are those lattes from Tea Time?" I asked.

He nodded, and I went to grab one from the nightstand, letting a napkin drop to the ground. I was leaning over to pick it up when a hand shot out from under the bed and grabbed me. I stifled a shriek when Spencer's head peeked out and made the international shushing gesture, his index finger touching his mouth. My forehead began to sweat, and I thought quickly.

I pulled away from his grasp and snapped back onto the bed. "How about we go downstairs and enjoy this?" I asked Holden, holding up a latte.

"I thought we could spend a moment by ourselves," he said, pulling me closer to him. "Maybe continue where we left off the other night."

"Uh," I said, pulling back. The situation had all the parts of a fantasy I had played out in my mind on several occasions, but in my fantasies, Spencer was not under the bed, and besides, I didn't think either Spencer or Holden was the sharing type. Holden misread my apprehension.

"I understand, Gladie. We have unfinished business about yesterday, about what happened with Mr. Steve."

I had elected to omit that bit of information from Spencer. I didn't want him to know that Holden had dealings with the cult or that he was searching for a woman named Becky.

"Oh, we don't have to get into that. Really, not important at all."

"No, I'm ready to talk about it, at least part of it," Holden said. He looked deeply into my eyes, making me blink furiously as the powerful pungent wave of sexy hit me like a jalapeño.

"Oh," I said. "That's not necessary, really. Let's go downstairs and eat up." I moved to get out of bed, but he pulled me back.

"It will keep," he said. "Won't you allow me to look at you a little? You are so beautiful in the morning light."

I heard Spencer make a noise under us, either a chuckle or some kind of vomiting noise, and I pretended to cough and hack to cover up the sound.

"How beautiful am I?" I asked Holden after I cleared my throat. It was time for Spencer to get a little lesson on how to treat a lady. Spencer was a player of the worst sort, but Holden was all class and dreamy-eyed, yummy, sexy body.

"Oh, that's the start of great poetry," he said. "Byron, Browning, poets like those might be able to take a stab at describing your beauty." He took a deep breath. "I can't take my eyes off you. I can't stop thinking about you."

He looked me in the eyes, unblinking, as if he was seeing me down to my soul and all the building-block truths that made me up. I held my breath while he studied me. Finally, he blinked and arched an eyebrow. "And you have a great ass," he added.

And then he was on top of me, and it was going awfully fast. I was tempted to let it go fast, because I was pretty hard up. I had almost made it all the way with Holden several times, and if I just let things play out, in a few minutes I would be singing in a happy soprano voice.

It was tempting, all right, to let Holden fondle all my lady parts and give me the world's biggest orgasm. But the faint smell of Spencer's aftershave wafted up from under the bed, which effectively threw cold water on doing the big nasty with Holden. No matter how hard up I was, I could not have sex with Holden while Spencer lay under us.

No, even though it would be a great story to tell Lucy and Bridget, I couldn't bring myself to let it happen.

Luckily, Grandma was on top of things. She burst through the door in her royal-blue sateen-finish housecoat and plastic house slippers, her hair in rollers and her face greased up in circa-1950 cold cream. Holden was oblivious, as he was on top of me, his back to her, and he was working to touch every inch of me under my nightgown.

"There you are, Arthur. I'm so happy you came to visit us," Grandma announced loudly and a little out of breath.

It took a minute for Holden to understand what was happening, but as soon as he turned his head and saw Grandma in the doorway, he jumped off me like a Mexican jumping bean, almost flying into a standing position in the middle of the room.

"Just the man I wanted to see," Grandma continued, as if this was the most normal situation in the world. "I have a light bulb that needs fixing. Yes, indeedy."

She winked at me and unceremoniously pushed Holden out of the room. Then she walked back in, wagged her finger in my direction, and tsked again before joining Holden, wherever the light bulb in need was located.

Spencer slid out from under the bed. "You're killing me," he said, staring me down and wiping dust bunnies out of his hair.

"You are so bad for my sex life, Spencer."

"What did he want to talk about? What happened between you two? Is there trouble in paradise?" he asked, dusting himself off and taking his place on the bed. I ignored all his questions, grabbed the lattes and bagels, and ran after Holden before he could come back and discover Spencer in my bed.

• • •

I FOUND Holden standing precariously on a tall ladder on the stairway landing. The rickety ladder must have been as old as the house, and Grandma had dragged it out of the shed to offer a good distraction from the man under my bed. I was about to object to Holden risking his life just to change a light bulb, but he seemed very comfortable straddling the ladder about twelve feet in the air.

"There you go, Zelda," he said, sliding down. "All fixed. You got anything else?"

"No, that's enough. Isn't that right, dolly?" she asked, looking at me.

"Fine for me," I said. "Let's eat."

The kitchen was clean, with no sign of the previous night's activities. Grandma must have cleaned up the muddy tracks Spencer and I had brought in. I made a show of putting on a pot of coffee in order to look out back.

The storm had laid waste to Grandma's tomatoes. I could see where our footsteps had torn up the wet ground and a large hole where the creepy scarecrow had been.

I still didn't know what Spencer and his men had discovered about the scarecrow. Were there clues about who had made it or where it had come from? The rain had probably washed away prints and DNA, I reasoned, but I was sure some answers could be gleaned from the scene. Grandma took a bagel from the bag Holden had brought, and sliced it in half.

"Cream cheese?" she asked Holden.

Absent was any mention of last night's events. Spencer wanted to keep it quiet for some reason, and so now Grandma and I had to keep it secret from Holden, like nothing out of the ordinary had happened. That is, nothing except for the alien cult, the donkey, crazy Rosalie, and Dr. Dulur's murder.

I was keeping secrets from Holden and secrets from Spencer about Holden. In fact, I was keeping a lot from Spencer. He didn't know that Holden was dealing with the cult, that he was searching for a woman. And with all my secrets from Holden and Spencer, I wondered what secrets they were keeping from me.

Grandma smeared cream cheese on a bagel and poured cream in her coffee, rejecting Holden's offer of a latte. I imagined she could help me regarding Becky and Holden's secrets, but so far she had been awfully quiet. Maybe she was keeping secrets, too.

"So, today is Belinda day?" she asked me.

"Yep, I'm going to get her fixed up no matter what."

Last night's activities pretty much proved Belinda's innocence. We hadn't made out the shadowy figure in the dark and the rain, but there was no way Belinda could have outrun Spencer.

"Sometimes clients have a mind of their own," Grandma said. "It's unfortunate, but sometimes we don't have a thing to say about it. Sometimes they run wild, like *Lord of the Flies*. Blech."

I couldn't imagine Belinda running wild like *Lord of the Flies*. I imagined her pretty domesticated, actually. Nevertheless, Grandma's point was well taken. Sometimes clients went off and matched themselves. I would have to get on the stick and get her matched off before she did it herself.

"So, you're busy all day?" Holden asked me.

"Why, you're not?" It was an honest question. He had been occupied most days, unable to be with me so much that I had counted him out altogether.

"No, but that's all right. But how about tonight after my meeting?"

Holden offered me a late dinner at ten that night after

he met with Mr. Steve. With the dinner was the unspoken promise to finally finish what we had started. I accepted and after breakfast walked him to the door.

He was wearing worn jeans and a white T-shirt, which outlined his muscular chest and arms. He must have worked out a lot, but I had never seen him out jogging like so many in town did. He embraced me and gave me a chaste kiss, one eye watching Grandma watch us, standing nearby.

"He hikes, dolly. That's what he does," she announced.

"That's true," he said, surprised. "I like the outdoors." He lowered his voice and whispered into my ear. "Don't come out to the lake. Stay away from the cult, especially Mr. Steve. I like when you're nosy, but now is not the time. Stay away from them. Do you understand?"

No, I didn't understand a damned thing. I didn't like being warned by Holden, no matter how sexy he was. "Yes, I understand," I said.

WITH HOLDEN gone, Spencer ran downstairs and ate some breakfast before Grandma's Forget Me Not class showed up. He was a little ornery after having to hide under my bed while I made out with Holden.

After some badgering, Spencer said he didn't have any updates on the murder or the scarecrow.

"Why did the killer come here? Why did he leave the face here?" I asked.

"I don't know," Spencer said.

"Is he trying to send a message?"

"I don't know."

"Who's he sending a message to? Me? Grandma? Does he know you're here?"

"I don't know."

"Maybe it's Rosalie! Maybe she found out you're here."

Spencer poured himself another cup of coffee. "If Rosalie knew I was here, she would find another way to send me a message, and she wouldn't be quiet about it."

He had a point. Rosalie wasn't much for stealth.

"What were you trying to get out of Holden?" Spencer asked me, squinting as if he was trying to see the truth. "I mean, besides the obvious. What were you trying to learn?"

"None of your business. That's between us."

He scrunched his forehead, making thick lines appear between his eyes. "Us," he repeated.

Grandma stood, went to the refrigerator, and studied its contents.

"Us," I repeated. "Us, us, us. I don't care if you don't believe it. Us."

Spencer stood up and threw his hands up into the air. "You don't even know what he does for a living!"

"He hikes," I said.

"He hikes for a living?"

"I don't think so," I said. "But he likes to hike, and he likes using organic shampoo."

Spencer stared down at me as if he was watching corn grow out of my ears. "You are a nutcase," he said finally. "Pathological."

"Hey, your last girlfriend is running around town carrying a cleaver. Maybe you need to consider your own taste in soul mates."

"Maybe I should," he said, never taking his eyes off me.

"I don't have time for your crap," I told Spencer. "I have a match."

"Listen, Pinkie. You should stay close to the house for a while. Let me keep an eye on you. Keep you safe."

"Funny, Spencer. I'm staying far away from you. You

have work to do. You have to solve this case. I have work to do, too."

I looked for my cell in order to pay my bill and finally be able to use it. I was pretty proud of myself for my focus on matchmaking. It had taken me a long time to commit to something, and it looked like I was finally getting the hang of my new job and career. Maybe I would become a good matchmaker. Maybe I had the gift, like Grandma said I had.

I looked all over for my cellphone but couldn't find it. Grandma didn't know where it was, either. I turned over every cushion in the house and looked under my bed. Nothing. I would have to go over to Belinda's to find out why she'd been trying to get in touch with me the night before.

Just as I was about to leave, the house phone rang. Holly the hygienist was on the line. "Gladie Burger, I need to talk to you," she said.

"What is it?" I asked, not too patiently. The woman rubbed me the wrong way. I really didn't like her.

"I have to talk to you. Don't get all pissy with me."

"I don't have a lot of time today, Holly. I have work."

"This is more important than work. Listen, I don't have a lot of time, either. But I need to talk to you."

"About what?"

"Politics, religion, what do you think? I have to talk to you about the murder. I need to tell you what really happened that night."

Chapter 13

✦ ♥ ✦

One beer good. Three beers bad. Martini with dinner good. Tequila shots before dinner bad. A woman goes into a first date and drinks more than normal, more than she can handle. She's nervous and wants the date to go well. She wants to show her date she's a fun party girl that he will enjoy being around. If I had a drink for every time one of my matches did this, I would be very drunk, dolly! Tell your ladies to cool it with the schnapps. Tell them to take it easy, maybe do deep breathing instead of drowning their anxieties in hooch. Alcohol makes you stupid. And it makes your face red and blotchy, too. Remember your Aunt Ida? One Manischewitz at Passover, and she looked like Danny Partridge. Don't let your matches turn into Danny Partridge. Keep them sober.

Lesson 74,
Matchmaking Advice from Your Grandma Zelda

"IS THIS some kind of joke?" I asked Holly.

"Does it sound like some kind of joke?" she sneered.

"Yeah, it does."

"Gladie, I'm not exactly the yuk-yuk kind of person. This is not a joke."

"Holly, I don't have time for this. I know what happened that night. I was there, remember?"

"I remember, but you were out cold, under the gas.

Maybe you forgot. You were only awake for the last part of the evening."

For the life of me, I couldn't take her seriously. I more than disliked her. I had disdain for her. I couldn't respect her in any way.

"Meet me tonight," she ordered. "I'm going to the cult meeting at the lake at seven."

"I can't go to the lake," I said.

Holden didn't want me to go to the lake. I didn't want to go to the lake. I didn't want to see the cult members or aliens, and most of all I didn't want to see Holly. I no longer had to prove Belinda's innocence. In fact, with a killer coming as close to me as he did last night, my goal was to stay far away from the suspects.

Holly wasn't the big figure that Nathan described the night of the murder, but she was the embezzler and she looked spry, like she could outrun Spencer with no problem. I didn't want any more dead faces in my life, not Dr. Dulur's, not Holly's. I didn't want Rosalie chasing me with her cleaver, and I didn't want anything to do with the wackadoo cultists. The alien worshippers were not all crystal-carrying, incense-burning love children. They hooked up a donkey to a parachute and made it fly over town. Things were heating up in Cannes, and I wanted to stay clear.

Those were my reasons for staying away from Holly and the lake. But that was my brain talking, and I've always had a hard time listening to my brain. Just ask my high school teachers.

Holly's offer to tell me what had happened while I was under the gas had me tempted. I had been out for hours that night, completely helpless while a killer was on the loose. Even if I didn't believe she had information about the murder, I couldn't say no to the chance of finding out what had happened to *me*.

"Fine, I'll meet you at seven at the lake," I said.

"Good. See you there. Be careful, Gladie. Trust no one."

OUTSIDE, IT was a beautiful September day. Not a cloud in the sky, but chilly. I wore a turtleneck, jeans, and comfortable sneakers, but I had to cross my arms to brace against a cold wind. It looked like fall was going to come early to Cannes and our summer days had ended mid-September. I regretted not bringing a jacket and then remembered my winter clothes were still in storage in Grandma's shed with the rest of the things I had accumulated in my years of traveling from one job to another.

Luckily, it was only a short walk to Belinda's place. She lived over the pharmacy in a two-bedroom apartment with a view of Main Street. I could smell it before she opened the door, like a tropical paradise.

"It smells like tutti-frutti ice cream exploded," I commented as she welcomed me in. At the thought of ice cream, my stomach growled with hunger, even though I had just eaten two breakfasts.

My eating had gotten completely out of whack since I had moved in with my grandmother. If I couldn't get my jiggle under control, I would have to move to get away from her junk food habit, perhaps back to Wisconsin, where I had worked for a month on an alfalfa sprouts farm. My butt was really firm back then.

"Thanks!" gushed Belinda. "This is my little slice of paradise. Don't you think a man would love to share this with me?"

Belinda had picked orange for the day: orange stretchy pants, an orange terrycloth sweatshirt with a giant orange blossom bedazzled on her chest, and orange Keds with little white socks folded over at the ankles.

"Any man would love to share this with you," I said.

It *was* a slice of paradise. Flowers bloomed from every corner and surface. It looked like a high-end flower shop with cheap furniture and rust-colored shag carpeting, but I had been in close contact with two men lately, and neither seemed to have any interest in flowers.

"Hey, Belinda, I just came by because I heard you wanted to speak to me, and my cellphone is dead."

"Oh, that explains it," she said. "I called you about fifteen times yesterday when I was with the mayor." She looked up at the ceiling and sighed, lifting and dropping her shoulders with the effort.

"Did he talk about Barbra Streisand?" I asked with sympathy.

"Huh? No, it was weirder than that."

I was racked with guilt. Grandma was right to tsk me. I shouldn't have let Belinda go off with Wayne Robinson. I should have found her a good match instead of the idiot mayor.

"I need a latte," I moaned.

"You should try tea. I lost another pound," Belinda announced. "The Chinese tea is better than Jenny Craig!"

"I tried the diet tea last night. It didn't do a thing. I ate two breakfasts this morning."

"Did you steep it for three minutes?"

"Steep?" I asked.

BELINDA INSISTED that we go to Tea Time, where Ruth had a special teapot that did something magical to the diet tea, helping it to melt the fat right off a body. I had my doubts that it could do anything more than a latte, but I owed it to Belinda to follow her to Tea Time after leaving her with Wayne Robinson for a day.

The tea shop was almost back to normal. Gone were the naked people and the backpacks, but there was still a group of hairy people at one table and clean-cut Dockers-wearers at another, all sitting, sipping tea. As we entered, I heard quiet murmurs of "*The energies of tomorrow . . .*" and "*The Arrival . . .*"

Belinda was oblivious, clutching her box of diet tea to her chest. We sat at a center table and waited for Ruth to show up and take our order. I looked longingly at the espresso machine on the counter.

"That man was a little weird," Belinda confided.

"The mayor? Was he?" I asked.

"He's very attached to his donkey," she explained, like that said it all. "He's obsessed with it. He's angry that the cult hurt the only one who understands him."

"Oy," I said.

"He made me talk to it," she continued. "I had to say . . . things."

"I wonder where Ruth is," I said, looking around. I didn't want to know what things Belinda had to say to the donkey. I felt miserable I had let her down. I should have matched her with someone good, or at least sane.

Ruth finally appeared out of the back room and marched up to our table. She looked old, older than she was, which was saying something. She was disheveled from head to toe. Half her shirt was untucked and wrinkled, her pants soiled. One shoe was untied, and her hair was greasy. She looked utterly exhausted.

"What the hell do you want?" she demanded.

"Could you brew us a special pot?" Belinda asked, holding out the box of diet tea.

"Are you drinking this nonsense, too?" Ruth asked me. I shrugged my shoulders. "Not an ounce of fat anywhere on you," she sneered.

"There's some fat," I said, delighted she didn't think so.

Ruth grabbed the tea. "Not any fat that shouldn't be there."

She shuffled back to the counter to make the magical tea. "I'm so sorry about the mayor, Belinda," I said.

"Do you have anybody else, Gladie?"

"Not just yet, but I promise to do my best for you." It was good to finally be honest with her.

Belinda sat back in her chair. "That's fine. I know you're doing your best. I trust you."

My breath hitched. I was overcome by her belief in me and my abilities, and I was gripped with a desire to run as fast as possible away from her trusting eyes and her need to rely on me to make her happy in life.

At least I could give her some good news. "I don't think you have to worry about the police anymore," I told her. "I think they've ruled you out as a suspect."

"Really? Gee, thanks, Gladie. You work quick," she said, genuinely pleased, but not quite as much as if I had told her I had found her the perfect match. I made a show of looking for something in my purse, as my eyes had misted in the emotion of taking care of another soul.

Ruth plopped a tea tray onto the table and sat next to us. "I'll join you," she said. She had brought a teapot, three cups, and a mysterious bottle without a label. She poured tea for Belinda and me but filled her own cup with a brown liquid from the bottle.

"Private stock," she explained. "I'm not saying the wackos have me beat, but they got me weary."

I downed my diet tea in one gulp and extended my cup for her to fill with her private stock. "Good girl!" she exclaimed, filling it to the brim. It burned like hell going down.

"What is this? Battery acid?" I choked.

"Only partly," she said. "What's your story?" she asked Belinda.

"I don't have a story," Belinda said with an edge of regret to her voice, but then she thought about it a moment and her face brightened. "I talked to a donkey yesterday."

Ruth slammed back some more private stock. "I have lived a long time, but I have never seen a donkey with as much bitchitude as the mayor's Dulcinea."

I finished my drink, and Ruth poured me another cup. "I fixed up Belinda with the mayor," I admitted to Ruth. "They went out yesterday."

"No greater fool ever walked the earth on two legs," Ruth said about the mayor. "Not off to a good start in your grandmother's business, I see." She wagged her finger at me. "Crazy woman says you have her gift. So much for her third eye."

Ruth had begun to slur her speech, and I realized with surprise that I was seeing double and feeling no pain.

"I love you," I said, and hiccupped. Ruth refilled my cup.

Belinda took my defense against Ruth, telling her how hard I was working, and hinted that my grandmother was a witch. My focus was elsewhere. Through my hazy eyesight, I thought I recognized a man sitting nearby. I got up and clutched the table as the world spun around. After a moment, it slowed down enough for me to manage to stumble over to him.

"Hey, you," I said, falling onto the chair next to him. "Penis Pipe Guy, you made it. I had my doubts. Are you still, you know, in one piece?"

The last time I saw him, his penis was wedged in a silver pipe, and Cannes's rescue professionals were about to hack it away with an industrial grinder. I peeked down at the bulge in his pants. Medium-sized, but two bulges. I rubbed my eyes to clear my vision and get his bulge down to one.

"Hey, Underwear Girl!" he said, smiling. "Yeah, it was a hairy pickle, but they freed old Winston. He's a little bruised, but he's breathing easy now. I'm not wearing any underpants," he added with pride.

"Old Winston!" I shouted, and exploded into laughter. My body heaved with uncontrollable giggles. I slapped the table and tried to catch my breath. My hair flopped over my face, and I brushed it to the side with my hand. The penis-pipe guy leaned back as if my head had caught fire and he didn't want to get burned.

"I drank some tea," I explained. "I might be a little eneeb—eneeb—eneebiated." I snapped my fingers. "Eneebiated? That's not right," I said. "Eneebeeted. Eanie Meenie ated? Nope. Hey, is it hot in here?"

"Maybe," he said, tugging at his collar.

"Drunk!" I shouted. "That's the word." I scooted my chair close to him and leaned in. "So, tell me, Peter," I said, tapping his chest with my finger. "What makes Peter, Peter?"

"I don't know. My name's Tim," he said.

"Are you sure?"

Tim scratched his head and seemed to think about it.

"Why did you stick your penis in a pipe?" I asked.

"It wasn't my fault!"

I patted him on the back. "I understand. I understand. Things are crazy!" I waved my hands wildly to show him how crazy things were. "Did you see the donkey flying in the sky?"

"A donkey?"

"And that's not the craziest. I saw a face," I told him. "I saw it after I didn't see it. It wasn't where it was supposed to be. Neither time."

Belinda tapped me on the shoulder. "Gladie, are you coming back? Ruth kind of fell asleep."

I turned around. Ruth had slumped backward on her chair, and she was snoring loudly through her open mouth.

"Wow, that tea packs a wallop," I said. "Must have been the steeping."

"I think it was Ruth's private stock. Your face is all red," Belinda noted.

"Huh, that's funny. I feel all red. You're not red. You're orange. Peter, doesn't Belinda look pretty in her giant orange flower?" I palmed the flower on Belinda's sweater, accidentally cupping her breast. "Firm flower," I said.

Belinda jumped back like she had been electrocuted, and more or less fell onto the chair next to me. If my thinking was foggy, Belinda's was crystal clear. Her eyes locked onto Tim's ringless hand and she recovered quickly, her focus sharp and her mind one-track, like it was riding on rails.

"I'm Belinda Womble. Never been married." She put her hand out and waited for Tim to take it. There was an awkward moment where he seemed to debate the wisdom of shaking her hand, but he came out on the side of optimism and grabbed her in an energetic hand-shake, baring his teeth in a wide smile.

"Hi there, Belinda. I'm Tim."

Grandma was right. Sometimes clients decide to match themselves. I couldn't blame Belinda for taking matters into her own hands, since I was doing a miserable job as her matchmaker. Still, something—a feeling, an instinct—told me that Tim was not the man for her.

"Tim stuck his penis in a pipe," I said. "It swelled up, and they had to cut him out with a big machine." I scissored the air with my fingers to illustrate my story.

"It wasn't my fault!" Tim yelled.

Belinda caressed his arm. "I'm sure it wasn't. I work in the medical field. Maybe I can help."

Ugh. Belinda was giving him big cow eyes, and he seemed to like the attention. I slapped the side of my head. It must have been the word "swelled" that got her.

"I'm the light-bulb-eating champion for the lower Southwest," Tim boasted to Belinda.

"Excuse me?" I asked.

Belinda batted her eyelashes. "Fascinating. How many did you eat?"

"Only one. It's a speed contest. I did it in less than thirty-three seconds."

I belched flame. Chinese diet tea and Ruth's private stock were a lethal combination. "Did the aliens make you do that?" I asked.

"I eat all kinds of things," Tim explained. "I could eat at least a dozen of those silver teaspoons they got here. But light bulbs are tricky."

"I bet," Belinda gushed. I had to hand it to her. I would have run screaming, but she was sticking it out, holding out hope that Tim would wind up being half decent. But enough was enough.

"He was out in the street for all the world to see with his *shmekel* in a pipe!" I explained to her, thinking that would be a deal breaker for any relationship.

"It wasn't my fault! It was the cult." Tim stood up and pointed to the sky as if the cult had flown in and had done the dirty deed to him.

I stood up, too. I stuck my finger in his face, and then it hit me. My insides rolled and pitched like it was the *Titanic* all over again.

"Holy crap!" I yelled, and ran for the bathroom.

"Oh, good!" Belinda called after me. "The tea hit! I told you we needed to steep it!"

I don't know how long I was in the bathroom, but when I came out, Belinda and Tim were gone and so were the rest of Ruth's clientele. Outside, the sun was setting. I was a little light-headed, but my jeans were noticeably looser.

I sat at Ruth's table, and she opened another bottle of her private stock.

"Oh, no," I said. "I've had enough. I'll stick to tea. I'm still a little tipsy."

"Your grandmother called. You're going to need to get good and drunk."

"Why?"

"Trust me," Ruth said, and poured me a drink. Ruth's eyes were bloodshot, and her hair was standing up on the right side of her head. She clanked her glass against mine. "Down the hatch," she toasted. "Don't spit in the wind. Don't sit on frozen toilet seats. Don't crap where you eat."

She looked at me expectantly.

"Uh," I said, "don't eat light bulbs and don't stick your penis in a pipe."

We downed our shots, and Ruth refilled my glass. Then the door blew open, and in walked Trouble.

Trouble Weiss ran the chocolate shop just outside the historic district, and that's the only reason anyone spoke to her. Her chocolate was to die for. But Trouble herself made you want to kill yourself.

"Gladie Burger, I have been looking all over town for you. If I didn't know better, I would say you were hiding from me."

When she spoke, it was like fingernails on a chalkboard, her voice was so unnaturally high and squeaky. It resonated painfully in the brain.

I caught Ruth staring at me, a sly smile on her lips. "If I knew I should be hiding, I would have," I mumbled in Ruth's direction.

Trouble was annoying in every way except for one. She made the best chocolate on the planet. I heard her hot chocolate gave the widow Frances MacDonald an orgasm at her shop's counter in the middle of the afternoon on a Tuesday. I stayed clear of her shop. For one, I couldn't afford it, and two, if I was going to break my diet, I was more than happy with a Hershey bar.

"Come along, Calamity," she screeched, pulling her daughter in tow. Calamity Weiss was a twenty-something girl who worked in her mother's shop and, as far as I could tell, had never uttered a single word. Her hair was fire-engine red, straight, greasy, and falling in her face. She wore blue-and-white polka-dotted pajama pants and a T-shirt with NOTHING'S SWEETER THAN TROUBLE emblazoned on it.

She looked miserable. I half expected her to shout "*Help!*" at any moment.

"Time is ticking away," Trouble continued. She had a habit of sniffing when she spoke, as if everyone smelled distasteful to her. "We have to get the bridesmaids' dresses made pronto. They don't make themselves, you know." She pulled a tape measure out of her purse and charged me like a rhino.

I yelped and tried to make a run for it, but Trouble was strong and caught me by my collar and yanked me up, almost knocking the table over.

"Easy, Trouble," Ruth scolded. "You're like a bull in a china shop. Always was. Just like the rest of your family. I wouldn't even let your mother, Tragedy, in here. Crazy woman nearly ran me over one day, riding a backhoe through town."

Trouble squeaked, sounding like an organ grinder's monkey. "Old woman, I have a wedding to organize, and I don't have time to speak to crones with uncombed hair."

It was an odd thing to say, considering the state of her daughter's hair. Ruth ran a self-conscious hand over her head and poured herself another drink. Trouble pulled at me, getting my measurements. My brain was in a thick, alcoholic cloud, and it took me awhile to understand what was going on.

"Am I Calamity's bridesmaid?" I asked.

"Maid of honor," Trouble said, sniffing. "Not my first

choice, of course. But your grandmother won't leave her house for anything, even though I explained to her that this wedding would be the finest Cannes had ever seen. Do you know how hard it is to put on a first-class wedding when every crazy in the country is wandering our little lanes and walkways, shouting about aliens? You would think your grandmother would put aside her phobia and come to the event of the decade. The matchmaker should be the matron of honor. It's just the done thing."

I had never heard of the matchmaker being a matron of honor, but Trouble had her own way of looking at the world. Calamity was looking at the ground, and I thought I heard her moan. I wondered who Grandma had set her up with.

"Your waist is a lot bigger than I imagined," Trouble said, shaking her head in disapproval as she measured me. "The least you could have done was get in shape for the wedding. Haven't you given a thought to how you would look in your dress? In Calamity's wedding photos?"

Actually, I hadn't given it any thought.

"Gladie is in shape, you freak," Ruth said. She was slurring her words pretty good now, and I could barely make out what she was saying. I realized that I was half in the bag, too, because I wasn't the least bit tempted to punch out Trouble.

SLOSHED UP to my eyeballs, without Belinda, my cellphone, or good sense, I asked Trouble to drive me to the lake for my seven o'clock appointment with Holly. I wedged myself into her Smart car between Calamity and the passenger door. I sucked in my stomach and made myself small, but the door handle stuck into my side, making an indelible impression. I caught Trouble staring at me, as if my struggling to squeeze into her Oompa-Loompa car was proof that I was an obese ogre and would be an eyesore in my maid-of-honor dress.

The traffic grew heavy as we got nearer to the lake. Whatever was going on was drawing a huge crowd. I wondered how many actually expected to see aliens and how many were just hoping to see if another donkey would fly.

"This is as far as I can get you," Trouble announced, sniffing. We were caught in traffic about a half of a mile away from the lake. There was a steady stream of humanity walking toward it. It wasn't unreasonable for me to join them.

I managed to open the passenger door and tumbled out onto the asphalt.

Calamity's face peered down at me from inside the car as she silently closed the door behind me. Not a word.

I was lying there for a moment to get my bearings when I recognized familiar orange legs walk by.

"Isn't that your friend? The drunk one?" I heard Tim ask. "She's lying in the street."

"What on earth?" Belinda said when she got a good look at me. They helped me up, and I clutched Tim's shoulder while the world stopped spinning. I was not much for holding my liquor. I promised myself never to drink Ruth's private stock again. I could feel my brain cells dying from fumes.

Tim and Belinda weren't alone. Nathan Smith, the Bliss Dental dental assistant, was with them. He was dressed in khaki Dockers and a striped shirt. He still wore a bandage on his head, but he looked reasonably healthy. He smiled at me, and again, I thought he looked awfully familiar.

"You remember Nathan, right, Gladie?" Belinda asked.

"Sure. Sure," I said. "I guess the whole gang is here."

"I hear it's going to be a really entertaining night," Nathan said. "I thought I could use the distraction. And besides, there's a barbecue after."

We walked with the crowd, which was a mixture of cultists and Cannes townspeople. It was like whatever crazy events we'd been having were all coming to a head tonight, and everyone wanted to witness it.

Hundreds of folding chairs were lined up facing a stage by the lake. Half the seats were already taken, and some people were sitting on their own chairs or blankets, making a picnic of it nearby.

Representatives of the varying factions of the cult handed out fliers with different alien themes on them. I scanned the chairs for Holly but came up empty. It was almost impossible to find anyone in the thick crowd.

But I seemed to stand out like a sore thumb, because before I could say goodbye to Belinda, Tim, and Nathan, Mr. Steve and Holden found me.

Mr. Steve seemed delighted to see me, but Holden was expressionless. Even in my intoxicated state, I could feel the disappointment coming from him in waves.

"Lovely. Lovely," Mr. Steve said. He hugged me tightly to him, pressing my body up against his. I pulled away and staggered back. "I'm so glad you decided to join our little gathering," he said. "But no shoes? Pity."

I opened my mouth and hiccupped loudly.

"Mr. Holden didn't tell me you were coming. Naughty Holden."

The entire group squirmed. Mr. Steve had that effect on people. I couldn't understand how he wound up being the spiritual leader of so many followers.

"I'm not here for long," I explained more to Holden than to Mr. Steve. "I'm here to talk to someone, and then I'm off. I'm a little tipsy," I said to Holden in a stage whisper. "Which way did she go?" I looked around with my hands wrapped around my eyes like binoculars. "Holy crap!"

Coming my way was Rosalie, still dressed to the nines. I couldn't make out any cutlery in her hands, but I didn't want to stick around to find out. How she found me in the crowd was beyond me. I quickly said goodbye and trotted away, hiding in the crowd.

I ran blindly, not daring to look to see if Rosalie was following. That's how I ran into the chairs, taking a tumble and bringing a couple chairs down on top of me.

"What the hell?" Holly spat at me, helping me up from the chairs. I had narrowly missed her and had almost literally fallen into her lap.

"Oh, Holly, thank goodness I found you," I said. "I'm so glad you don't like to cook."

"What are you playing at?" she said, her eyes scanning the area I had come from. "Why did you bring the killer here?"

Chapter 14

+ ♥ +

Snatched from the jaws of victory! That's just how it is sometimes, dolly. You get so close with a match. It all lines up perfectly. She's the one for him. He's the one for her. They were made for each other. Then something happens . . . the stars fall out of alignment. The earth revolves backwards. It's a huge fakakta mess. You want to scream at them to make it work, but it's too late. They've moved on, and no matter what you say, they cannot see the other as their soul mate. You can't make butter from an egg. You know what I mean? When this happens, it's not your fault, bubeleh. Just apply pressure, stanch the wound, and find them new matches. Quick.

Lesson 61,
Matchmaking Advice from Your Grandma Zelda

THE GROUP I had walked in with had been swallowed up by the huge crowd of people, which now filled almost every seat and every patch of ground in eyesight of the stage, as the sun finally set, giving the illusion of it sinking into the lake. Belinda, Tim, and the rest had disappeared into the masses, and I couldn't make out who Holly was looking at.

"What are you talking about, Holly?" I asked. I disliked her, intensely, and it occurred to me that she was playing with me.

"Shh!" she said. "It's starting."

She pulled me down onto the chair next to her and shushed me again. Big lights came on, illuminating the stage, and a gong was rolled onto it by two gigantic, muscle-bound men in loincloths.

"This ain't bad," I mumbled. "I could use some popcorn or something, though."

Holly shushed me again. "Be quiet," she hissed. "This is important. Watch everything."

Her dead-serious attitude sobered me a little. "I thought you were going to tell me about the night Dr. Dulur was murdered," I whispered to her.

But Holly's attention was fixed on the stage. The two he-men gonged the gong loudly. At once, the crowd became quiet, and then just as suddenly burst into chants of "They come, they come" in unison. My skin erupted in goose bumps. As if by magic, a brisk wind started, blowing the trees, which made eerie shadows through the night.

"I'm not sure I like this," I said.

As if through a psychic connection, the crowd changed their chant to "Arrive, arrive," their voices building to a crescendo until Mr. Steve appeared onstage. He wore Bermuda shorts, a pink Izod shirt, and nothing on his feet. He seemed very happy, like it was the most natural thing in the world to appear next to two half-naked bodybuilders onstage in front of a crowd of about one thousand strangers.

"The Arrival!" his voice boomed over a loudspeaker. He must have had a microphone somewhere on his body, but I couldn't see it. The crowd grew quiet and leaned forward in rapt attention to hear whatever Mr. Steve was about to say.

"Yes, they come, my friends," he continued. "They come, and we are unworthy, but we wait for them, and we will do their bidding. No matter what impediments block our path, our path remains a righteous one. More righteous than the so-called righteous townspeople of the Sacred Mountain."

Half of the audience applauded while the other half murmured in what I imagined to be alarm. Mr. Steve paused and removed his shirt, revealing a large red triangle tattooed on his chest. He pointed to it and shimmied his hips.

"Oh, my," I said, and began to giggle. It was one of those giggles that builds on itself, until the giggler is doubled over in hysterics, unable to breathe, with snot bubbling out of her nose. The alcohol didn't help matters.

I clutched my ribs and guffawed, drawing angry stares from the people around me. I tried to get my giggles under control. After all, these were the same people who sent a donkey off to fly over the town. Who knew what they would do to a disrespectful spectator who laughed in the face of their leader's naked torso?

"I'm really sorry," I said in Holly's direction, but she wasn't paying attention to me. She was busy scanning the area for something or someone, I didn't know, but she was intent, and her face moved even less than usual.

I followed her gaze, and my giggles stopped. Holly was studying a tent a little off to the left of the stage. People were walking in and out of it. It was obviously a holding area for tonight's performers. And standing outside of the tent was Arthur Holden, my maybe-boyfriend, the occasional mysterious man in my life.

I sobered up.

"They come! They come!" shouted Mr. Steve, and he was joined by a chorus of cultists, who began to sing their rendition of "The Way We Were" with lyrics adapted to the Arrival. "Aliens, like the probers of our minds," they sang.

I was feeling concerned and jealous, and very impatient with Holly. "What are you up to?" I asked.

Holly clutched my arm. "Listen, I need your help. I know you have connections with the police."

"Oh, that. I'm sorry, I can't do anything to help you. They already know that you have been embezzling from Bliss Dental."

"Focus, Gladie," she said. "I'm talking about the murder."

"Are you confessing something, Holly?"

Holly turned to me. Tears filled her eyes. "Dr. Dulur, he wasn't a good man," she said. "Do you believe me?"

"Yes."

"He hurt people. Children. He had a rage inside him that was something terrifying to behold when he let it out. Do you know why I'm here?"

"Trolling?"

"I'm investigating. I'm doing your job."

"Hey, I'm a matchmaker," I said.

"Yeah, right," Holly sneered, getting my hackles up. "I've been checking out this cult. Did you know Simon was a member?"

"Yeah, I did."

Holly was surprised. I thought I even saw her eyebrow twitch.

"Did you know he was almost the leader of these nutjobs?"

"Yes."

Holly laughed. "Now you're playing with me. Okay, how about this? Did you know that the cult insisted he hurt those children as a test to become leader?"

"That's criminal," I said, shocked. "How did you find this out?"

"I have been hanging out here for days," she said. "I've heard things."

Things had a way of turning out to not be reliable. *Things* usually meant rumors or miscommunication like in a protracted game of telephone.

"Why are you hanging out here? Why are you asking about Dr. Dulur?" I asked. It wasn't like Holly to care about anybody except herself. I couldn't understand why she would be looking into the murder.

"Don't you see? Simon Dulur was a bad person."

"Okay, and why do you need to prove that?"

"Because he deserved to die. It wasn't such a bad thing to have killed him."

Ding! Ding! Ding! Warning bells went off in my head. What did Oprah say about warning bells? Were they good or bad? I had a hunch they were bad.

The warning bells evolved into outright ringing in my ears. I rubbed them, but the ringing wouldn't stop. I scanned the area, looking for Holden. He was still at the tent, and I felt glad that he was within shouting distance.

The stage was filled with cult performers doing a synchronized dance, their hands to the heavens, or in this case, to whatever planet the aliens came from.

"Are you trying to confess something, Holly?" I asked her.

"What do you mean?"

"Are you saying you killed Simon Dulur, but it was okay because he wasn't a nice guy?"

"I didn't kill him," she said, her voice loud. "But maybe it's better he's dead. Maybe it was like a good deed. The murder, I mean. I need a drink."

So did I. The alcohol had evaporated from my system.

"You are creeping me out," I told her. I was about to get up and leave. Hitchhike or whatever it took to get home. It was a long day of nothing. A waste of a Friday. I might even stand up Holden, kick out Spencer, and spend the rest of the evening eating Oreos and watching Spencer's television in bed, I thought, just to finish up the day on my terms.

Then I remembered why I had come to see Holly.

"Tell me about the night it happened," I ordered.

"You said you were going to tell me the truth about what happened that night."

Holly took a deep breath.

"Will you help me with the police?" she asked.

"Tell me about the night."

Holly seemed to weigh the prudence of confessing to whatever it was she was going to confess. Perhaps she couldn't live with her guilt any longer, or perhaps she couldn't live with the secret, or just as likely, maybe she wanted to get it off her chest in hopes that I would understand and absolve her of her crime.

"I'm in deep, Gladie," she said. "I'm drowning in it. I made a wrong turn, and now I'm royally screwed. I'm even scared to go home. I don't see a way out."

"What happened that night, Holly? Spit it out."

"I have always paid my way. Nobody has ever given me a dime. I earned every cent that went through my fingers."

I didn't think it was the best time to remind her that she stole a hundred grand from her employer. Holly was staring out into the night, telling her story to make her seem like the best person she could be, revving up to finally admit to a terrible deed.

"I did go to Bar None that night, Gladie," she said, bringing her attention back to me. "That part wasn't a lie. I went right after you came into the office. Do you believe me?"

I nodded. There was a whole bar full of witnesses that put Holly at the bar that night.

"Good," she said. " 'Cause I want you to believe me. That way you'll help me with the police."

I sighed. If she was the murderer, the only thing I would help her with was the phone call to 911.

Holly rubbed her hands on her lap. "So, I left Bliss Dental and went to the bar that night. I went to the bar, but I came back."

The choir ended their performance, and the audience erupted in applause. Then a terrible sound ripped through the night. At first I thought it was thunder and we were in for another storm. But it wasn't a storm.

Holly slumped to the ground, hitting my legs as she fell. Her eyes were round with horror and blood spilled from a hole in her neck. She made a gurgling sound and then no sound at all.

"She's been shot!" I yelled, which was what started the stampede.

Chapter 15

+ ♥ +

You've heard it before: sometimes too much of a good thing isn't all that good. It's true with tequila, face fillers, and Adam Sandler movies. You know another thing that isn't too good when you got too much? Yep, that's right. Potential matches. Sometimes you get a match who is perfect for at least ten people you know about. All of a sudden, you are surrounded by needy people who want to take a shot at your match. Joe walks in, and you know immediately he would be perfect for Joan, Sybil, Lola, and Maddie. Too much! You have to narrow it down. At times like these, breathe deep and slow so you don't hyperventilate and pass out. Then grab some brain food like a box of Mallomars or a breakfast burrito and think deep and slow. Not all of those women are perfect for Joe, bubeleh. Not all of them are the one. Only one of them will get a shot at Joe. Only one is the one.

Lesson 32,
Matchmaking Advice from Your Grandma Zelda

"SHE'S BEEN shot!" I shouted again. I watched as Holly's blood pooled on the ground by her neck. Her eyes stared up at me, unblinking, without expression. "Please!"

I felt consciousness drain out of me, but I was jarred awake by the push and pull of panicked spectators, trampling people and chairs as they fled for their lives.

I tugged at one person as he ran by. "Help!" But he took off without looking back, tearing his shirt in the process. I was standing with the piece of his shirt in my hand, unsure what to do next, when a man came out of nowhere, dealing me a body blow, throwing me to the ground and crushing me under his weight.

"Stay down," he hissed in my ear. "There could be another shot."

I recognized the smell of meat and organic soap before I recognized his face. His forehead was lined with concern, and his eyes studied me for any sign of injury.

"I'm fine," I croaked. "It's Holly. I think she's dead."

"One shot," he said out loud. "I think you're safe."

"Safe?" I screeched the word, hysteria finally breaking to the surface. Where had it been? Usually hysteria was much closer to my surface.

"Stay down," Holden ordered.

He rolled off me and checked Holly's pulse as the stampede dwindled to a few people running past. "She's alive, but she's choking to death," he said. "She needs a tracheotomy."

He checked his pockets and came up with a fancy Swiss Army knife. "Damn," he said.

"What?"

"I need a tool, a tube, something to do it with." He searched the area, but it was pandemonium, like a tornado had touched down.

"I have a pen!" I announced. "It's a cheap ballpoint pen. Grandma made me bring it."

Holden nodded and put his hand out. I fished through my purse and gave it to him. He unscrewed the pen and tossed the ink cartridge onto the ground. He knelt over Holly. I turned my head as he made the incision in her neck without flinching and inserted the pen to allow her to breathe.

It was like he was a natural at it, or it wasn't his first tracheotomy. Another Holden secret, I guessed.

Only a couple chairs were left standing, and the ground was littered with water bottles, shoes, and bits of trash. Most of the gathering had run away, but some shell-shocked cultists and spectators remained, some wandering the perimeter, some standing in place, wondering, I imagine, what the hell had happened.

The stage was illuminated from only one side. The lights on the other side had been toppled over, and they now pointed upward, lighting the dark sky. The tent that had held Holly's attention was no more.

To my surprise, I spotted Mr. Steve in a deep conversation with Belinda and Tim, and as I turned back to Holden, I caught Rosalie in the corner of my eye. She was more subdued, and I hoped someone had knocked some sense into her.

Nathan Smith appeared at my side, more traumatized than ever. "Is she—?" he asked, his hands up at his mouth. He had gone through a lot in the past week, and I feared he would slip into shock.

"She's breathing," Holden told him. "But we need the paramedics in here, quick."

As if on command, the sound of sirens ripped through the air, drawing nearer.

Holly was unconscious, covered in Holden's jacket, with her wound stanched and a pen stuck in her neck. Nathan was transfixed, as if he was incapable of turning away from the sight, a look of pure horror on his face. Yep, Nathan was going to need counseling. I wondered if he could get a two-for-one deal and take me with him.

Thankfully, emergency services arrived within a couple minutes. The paramedics, a fire truck, and police cars drove up onto the grassy area. I had been seeing a lot of them lately, and they waved when they saw me.

Holden guided them to Holly, and they began to work on her.

I stood there, unsure what I was supposed to do. Should I leave? Should I stay and make some kind of statement? I didn't have to wait long for my answer. A familiar car skidded onto the grass and squealed to a stop near us. Spencer hopped out and marched right at me. He looked mad, and I flinched and hid behind Holden.

"It wasn't my fault!" I yelled as Spencer got nearer.

He tried to get to me, circling around Holden, but I danced away to avoid him. Finally Spencer caught me in his arms and held me by my shoulders.

"They told me you got shot." His voice was rough with anger or some other emotion, I couldn't tell what. I braced myself, expecting him to slug me or shake me or arrest me. Instead he wrapped his arms around me and pressed his lips against mine.

My exhausted, traumatized body reacted to him. I was at once energized, a warmth filling me as if he was blowing life into me. My mouth opened and welcomed his tongue, and I pressed myself deeper against him.

Little fireflies of arousal buzzed in my head, and I was swept away from everything to a place where there wasn't murder or violence or dentists without faces, a place of warmth, acceptance, want, and desire. Holden was a good kisser, but Spencer *transported* me.

At the thought of Holden, I pulled back. Spencer's eyes were wide open, and he looked almost as surprised by the kiss as I was. We dropped out of our embrace and stood in awkward silence for a moment before Spencer regained his composure and went to work assessing the scene. I stood rooted to the spot, waiting for my fireflies to stop buzzing and my breathing to return.

Holly had been treated and was on her way to the hospital in the back of an ambulance. The rest of the police and first responders, as well as Holden, Belinda,

Tim, Nathan, and the remainder of the stragglers, were entirely focused on me. Tim had a big, shit-eating grin on his face. At least Nathan looked better. He had been pale and shocky before, and now he was flushed.

I didn't dare make eye contact with Holden. Not only had I betrayed him, but I betrayed him in front of half the town. I shifted my gaze to Belinda, who looked suitably impressed, undoubtedly figuring that I was the latest person to succumb to the "magic penis."

I groaned.

Spencer moved on to interview witnesses, bypassing me entirely. I guessed he was saving me for last. He talked for a little while to a large woman in a maxi dress and cardigan, jotting down notes. She didn't seem to know anything, which was a common story among the so-called witnesses.

Belinda was Spencer's fifth interview. "I don't know. I was watching the performance when I heard the shot, and then it was chaos," she explained. I caught her eyes shifting downward, probably searching for evidence of Spencer's magic body part.

Tim belched. "Must have been something I ate," he said. Belinda handed him a bottle of Tums, and he took four.

"You two together?" Spencer asked. Belinda thought about it a moment, and Tim belched again.

"I'm not feeling very well," Tim explained.

"Those are my guns. Mine!" One of the mostly naked bodybuilders who had so recently gonged the gong that got the evening started ran barefoot after Officers James and Brody across the grassy area toward us. James and Brody held armloads of weapons. The naked bodybuilder's weapons, according to him.

Before Conan could reach the police, Sergeant Fred Lytton, my first client, tried to tackle and handcuff him. But the bodybuilder was big. Fred jumped on his back, but instead of taking him down like a linebacker, it looked more like a failed game of leapfrog. Fred held on for dear life, clutching the bodybuilder's back, his legs wrapped around his waist. It was as if the behemoth had decided to wear a tall, gangly Irishman as a back-pack.

James and Brody, finally noticing that Fred needed help, dropped their collection of guns and ran to the sergeant's aid. "No! No!" shouted Fred. "I've got him. I think he's slowing down."

Fred grunted, trying to take down the bodybuilder, his spindly legs squeezing around the man's eight-pack. The muscle man swatted at Fred like he was a pesky fly and tried to pry his limbs off him. I had to give it to Fred, he had staying power. James and Brody cheered him on.

"You can do it, Fred! You've got him where you want him!" they called to him at a safe distance, the guns on the ground at their feet.

Spencer's eyes grew to twice their normal size as he watched his police force at work. I couldn't imagine what he was thinking, but I would bet homicide or suicide was in there somewhere.

"That's the way, Fred!" yelled Officer James. He hooted and hollered, drawing a crowd of law enforce-ment, firefighters, and cult stragglers.

Spencer ran his fingers through his hair.

He walked toward the bodybuilder and Fred, still locked together in struggle. "Stop," he said, monotone. "Jump down." He never raised his voice, but his tone brooked no discussion.

The bodybuilder stopped struggling, and Fred jumped down and cable-tied his wrists. "I don't want any trou-ble," the bodybuilder said. "I was just telling you that those guns are mine."

"Actually, they are mine."

Mr. Steve sauntered over. He was barefoot, like the bodybuilder, except his toenails were painted bright red. A thought flickered through my mind about the owner of the beautiful shoes in Mr. Steve's yurt.

"All registered, of course," he told Spencer. "Completely legal. We live in a scary world. Can't be too careful."

Spencer looked at the large pile of weapons on the ground. "You're a very careful man, Mr.—"

Mr. Steve introduced himself, and Spencer took him aside under some trees to interview him. Meanwhile, Fred put the bodybuilder in the back of a police car, and the guns were bagged and driven off to the police station.

"Do we just stand here?" asked the woman in the maxi dress.

"Maybe we should sit down," I suggested. Nathan was dead on his feet, and Tim was green around the gills. The night had taken a toll on all of us. I was surprisingly well, considering a woman got shot right next to me. The alcohol and Spencer's kiss seemed to have dulled my trauma. Either that, or I was getting used to my bit part in my new *Reservoir Dogs* life.

We arranged the chairs and sat in a circle like we were at a Girl Scouts meeting. It was almost congenial. I caught Holden's eyes, but he slid his attention away to Mr. Steve and Spencer. I didn't know which one he was focusing on, but I figured it would be a long time before I ate duck again.

Spencer spoke to Mr. Steve for about ten minutes before he released him. Holden watched him go. I tracked his line of sight, studying Mr. Steve's back as he walked to where the tent had stood, his posture relaxed as if he didn't have a care in the world.

Holden's posture was different. Rigid, his jaw clenched, his bloody hands splayed, outstretched on his lap so as to not infect the rest of him. Saving Holly's life had been hard work, and despite the chilly evening, his shirt stuck to him, wet and transparent with sweat.

He wasn't as big as the bodybuilder or even Spencer, but he was all muscle. Long and lean. Heroic. It was hard to imagine hiking could make a Holden body. I wondered if my kiss with Spencer had lost me my shot at having Holden's body on top of me ever again.

"I hate you, Spencer Bolton," I muttered. Nathan's head whipped around toward me, and I blushed.

"Do you think Holly will be okay?" he asked me. Nathan was fragile and about to break apart into little pieces, I thought.

I wished Spencer would hurry up the process and let us all go home. He was walking our way while reading through his notes. He seemed relatively calm, but that was destined to change.

Rosalie Rodriguez was running full out, closing in fast on Spencer's back. She was a woman on a mission, that much was clear. She was impeccably dressed, running a nine-minute-mile in four-inch pumps. She had murder on her mind, or something worse, her face set firm with determination. Spencer had finally come out of hiding, and she was not going to miss her chance. Luckily, she left her knife set at home, but she was armed with acrylic nails that could take down a man with little effort.

Holden stood up and pointed at Rosalie. "Spencer, your back!" he yelled.

Spencer froze and turned. He was quick. He ran to the lady in the maxi dress, pulled her up from her seat, and laid on a huge kiss. Not as passionate as the one he gave me, but bigger, juicier. More theatrical.

"Boy, he gets around," Nathan said.

"Magic penis," Belinda breathed.

Rosalie stopped in her tracks. The air had gone out of

her like a balloon. Actually witnessing Spencer's lips on another woman, especially a woman with far less fashion sense than Rosalie, put everything into perspective for her. Spencer was not a man to be controlled. Impossible to tame. Rosalie didn't stand a chance. Even though she was possibly a homicidal maniac, I felt sorry for her.

But Spencer's strategy was successful, and he knew it. He broke off the kiss with the maxi-dress lady and lowered her to her chair. She stared straight ahead, unblinking. I knew that look. She would never be the same again.

"All right. So, back to you, Belinda and Tim," Spencer said, slapping his hands together.

Tim responded by hacking. He retched, his body racked with dry heaves. It was contagious. Ruth's private stock started the journey up my esophagus. Nathan was also having trouble.

"What the hell?" Spencer grumbled.

"It was something he ate," Belinda explained.

"Tacos?" Spencer asked. Cannes boasted the best tacos in the world, but they came at a gastroenterological price.

"A gun," Tim managed.

"What?" Spencer asked.

"He said, a gun," Belinda said.

Spencer scratched his head. "Help me out here. What?"

"Tim eats things," I explained.

"I think it was a thirty-eight," Tim croaked.

"Nobody can eat a gun," Spencer said, stating what should have been the obvious.

"It was my first one," Tim explained, clutching his abdomen like he had just eaten a firearm.

"Why the hell would you eat a gun?" Spencer demanded.

"I'd never eaten one before."

"He found it on the ground when we were running away," Belinda said.

Things moved quickly after that. The ambulance came back for Tim, and Spencer insisted Belinda go with him. The moment he released the rest of the witnesses, I cornered Holden.

"You were amazing," I told him. "How you saved Holly."

"I'll have to cancel our date, Gladie. I never got my talk in." He wouldn't look me in the eye. Instead, he scanned the area for Mr. Steve.

"What do you want from him?" I asked. "Who is Becky and what do you want from her?"

Here was my thinking: On one hand, sure, I had swapped spit with the sexy, womanizing chief of police right in front of Holden, and I was probably no longer involved with him, let alone possessed of any moral upper hand or the right to demand anything from him. But on the other hand, I had swapped spit with the sexy, womanizing chief of police right in front of Holden, and since we probably were no longer involved, it was now or never to get the down-low on the haps. Finally time to get the skinny and take a turn on the catwalk.

It was also probably time to get new slang.

"It's important that I speak to him," he said. "It's important that I find her. Do you really need to know more than that?" He had dreamy eyes. I wanted to dive in and swim in his eyes. If I looked into his eyes during an earthquake or some equally vibratory natural disaster, I was sure to have an earth-shattering orgasm.

"I believe in full disclosure." Unless it's in my best interest to lie. "How are you involved with the cult? What is your relationship with Mr. Steve?"

Holden ran his hand over his face and sighed.

"I'm just trying to get my life back." He caressed my

cheek, sending shock waves of desire through me. "Pretty girl. Perfect girl."

"I'm not perfect," I said, flipping my hair and batting my eyelashes.

Holden smiled, but it quickly faded. "If only I was a different man," he said.

"Uh-oh. That didn't sound good. Is that a version of 'It's not you, it's me'?"

"I'm trying to get my life back," he repeated. There was a desperate edge to his voice that I had never heard before. He kissed me lightly, brushing my lips with a feather touch, and left me there, no wiser, to go and talk to the leader of the aliens-are-coming cult.

"Can I talk to you?" Rosalie Rodriguez, the lunatic stalker with high-end cooking tools, had snuck behind me while I watched Holden leave me.

"I'm not in the mood for your crap, Rosalie."

"I guess I deserve that. I was a little . . . crazy." Rosalie's attitude had drastically changed. Gone were the crazy eyes, and she seemed to have rediscovered her sanity.

"No, not crazy at all," I said, just in case there was some residual cuckoo left in her and she was a maniacal killer.

"I want to make it up to you. I know you're investigating the dentist murder, and I want to help, not that the jerk Dulur didn't deserve it."

"I don't investigate, Rosalie. That's a misconception about me. I'm a matchmaker."

"Whatever. I'll take you to talk to some parents of Dulur's victims. I'll pick you up tomorrow morning at eight."

"Uh—"

"Watch out for him," she said, nodding toward Spencer, who was watching our conversation with interest. "He pretends he's sensitive, that he loves you, but he's all lies." With that parting shot, Rosalie left.

I walked back to Spencer.

"What's the matter, Pinkie?"

"My buzz from Ruth Fletcher's homemade hooch is completely gone."

"Ruth Fletcher sells homemade hooch? She must have expanded her menu. Did you have a nice talk with Rosalie?"

"You have terrible taste in women," I said. "She's an idiot."

"She is?"

"Yeah, like you could ever pretend to be sensitive."

"Sometimes it's like you're speaking Greek, Pinkie. Come on, let's go."

He grabbed my elbow and tugged me toward his car.

"Where are we going?" I asked.

"The hospital. On the ride over, you can tell me what really happened tonight."

"What a night," I said, getting into his car. "Everything happened except for the Arrival. At least it's over."

"Pinkie, when you're around, it's never over."

Chapter 16

+ ♥ +

Everybody deserves love. Everybody. Well, maybe not Hitler and maybe not Stalin. Well, actually, I can think of a lot of people who don't deserve love. But everybody else . . . they deserve love, dolly. You and me, we're born matchmakers. We want everybody to find love (you know, except for the ones who don't deserve it). So, you'll do whatever it takes to find love for your client. You won't rest until they are living their happily-ever-after with their soul mate. Unless. Unless you have a change of heart. Unless you begin to doubt your client. There might come a time when you think your client doesn't deserve it, that he or she is not the person you thought they were. In this case, take a breath and a step backwards. Be wise. You don't want Hitler for a client.

Lesson 55,
Matchmaking Advice from Your Grandma Zelda

"I COULD go for pancakes," Spencer said, driving toward the hospital. "Too bad we don't have a Denny's in this town. Can't get pancakes this late."

"Grandma has some frozen waffles in her freezer."

"I could eat some frozen waffles. Hopefully, the hospital will go quick."

We got out onto the road, leaving the lake and the chaos of the night behind us.

"All right, Pinkie, spill," Spencer said. "What did you see? What did you hear?"

It flooded out of me. "Holly called me and told me to meet her at the lake. She told me Dr. Dulur was a bad guy, that he deserved to die, that he was sadistic because he was trying to prove himself to the cult, and she said the night he was murdered, she left, but then she came back. I think she saw the murder or at least knew who the murderer was. She was shot before she could tell me."

It was good to get it out, to say it out loud. I had been so close to uncovering the truth about Dr. Dulur's murder, and then it was snatched away from me. If I didn't solve the mystery soon, I might be next.

"Oh!" I added, remembering. "She also said the killer was in the crowd. But I guess that's obvious, since she was shot."

Spencer cleared his throat.

"So, what do you think?" I asked. "Who do you think did it? Any leads?"

"What do you mean, you went to meet Holly? I told you to stay out of this. You are not a police officer. You are not a private detective. You're not even a real matchmaker."

Spencer gripped the wheel for all it was worth, and I could tell his face was red, even in the dark car.

"That was a low blow about the matchmaker thing. I am so not sharing my waffles now," I said.

"You are pathological. You can't mind your own business. What's wrong with you that you attract wacko killers?"

"You're attracted to me. What does that say about you?"

"It says I need my head examined." We were approaching the hospital. I wondered who we were going to visit first. "Can you mind your own business for once? Can you stay away from trouble?"

I thought about that for a moment. "No," I said, finally. "But I can put on mascara in a moving car, and I can sing the states song straight through to Louisiana."

"You're a hot mess," Spencer said.

We parked close to the hospital entrance. Spencer turned off the car. "The fact that the dentist was a creep doesn't make any difference," he said.

"Maybe someone wanted revenge. Maybe someone was mad at him."

"Why, Pinkie, you *are* an investigative genius. You figured out that someone was mad at the murder victim. What gave it away? The face thing?"

Spencer really knew how to chap my hide. "Whatever," I said.

"Here's one thing you didn't think of, Miss Marple: that bullet that hit Holly could have been meant for you. Maybe someone is sick and tired of you sticking your nose in where it doesn't belong."

My blood ran cold at the thought of being the killer's real target. "The only one sick and tired of me sticking my nose in is you. Do you have an alibi?"

Spencer narrowed his eyes, and I thought I heard his molars grind together.

"Besides," I added, wagging my finger in his face, "I haven't stuck my nose in this time. People keep asking me to look into Dr. Dulur's murder, to listen to their stories, to help them. I'm just trying to mind my own business."

"Pinkie, you are so full of shit."

TIM WAS first on Spencer's list. He was resting comfortably in a bed in a hospital room with Belinda by his side.

"It was just like *Star Trek*," Tim explained. "They used the coolest tool to get the gun out."

"It looked like the creature in *Alien*," Belinda told me, shuddering.

"You don't need to describe it," I said, getting woozy.

"Where did you find the gun?" Spencer asked. He took notes in a small notebook.

"On the ground near the stage," Tim explained. "It was a beaut. I eat all kinds of things, but I never ate a gun before. It might have been too ambitious."

"Any idea whose gun it was? Did you see anyone drop it?"

"Nope. There was a lot happening."

Spencer put away his notebook. Not much of an interview, I thought. I wondered why he had me tag along, except that it was on the way home.

"Belinda, you want us to give you a ride home?" I asked her.

"I'll get her a ride," Spencer said. He pulled out handcuffs. "Belinda Womble, you are under arrest for the murder of Simon Dulur and the attempted murder of Holly Firestone. You have the right to remain silent—"

"What the hell?" I said. "What do you think you are doing?"

"Whatever you say can and will be used against you in a court of law," Spencer continued, ignoring me.

"Gladie, you said the police were going to leave me alone," Belinda whined.

I was outraged. "I thought we discussed this. Belinda couldn't have done it," I said to Spencer.

"Is that right?" Spencer asked me, after reading Belinda her rights. "Belinda has no alibi for the night of the murder."

We turned to her, but she pursed her lips. For whatever reason, she would not say what she was doing that night.

"And now Belinda was at the scene of this crime, of Holly's attempted murder," Spencer pointed out. "And her boyfriend tried to destroy the weapon used in the crime."

"I didn't destroy it," Tim said, panicked. "I only ate it!"

Belinda sniffed and dabbed at her eyes with her sleeve. "He's not my boyfriend. I only just met him."

"He's the wackjob who stuck his penis in the pipe!" I yelled at Spencer. I couldn't believe he was arresting poor Belinda. How dumb could a person be?

"The cult made me do it!" Tim explained. "They lured me!"

"The cult! The cult!" I said, remembering. "They made Dr. Dulur do some kind of hazing ritual to prove himself. That's why he hurt those children. Don't you see, Spencer? They have a history of violence, and we know that Dr. Dulur was vying for power with Mr. Steve. Mr. Steve must have done it."

"Mr. Steve was on the stage when Holly was shot," Spencer said.

"He could have had one of his henchmen do it," I said reasonably.

"Where was Belinda the night of the murder?" Spencer asked me. He tossed the handcuffs in the air and caught them. Suddenly I knew what he was doing, why he brought me with him to the hospital. The police couldn't get Belinda to talk, but Spencer thought I could. He figured I had some influence on her and could get her to say where she had been that night. I wasn't so sure. So far, she was pretty independent, even going so far as to make her own matches.

"And there's the issue of the flowers," Spencer said.

"What's wrong with flowers?" I asked.

"Belinda's flowers are all poisonous," he explained.

I blinked. "What do you mean, poisonous?"

"I mean, every one of the beautiful flowers Belinda grows at Bliss Dental could kill a man," he said.

"Every flower?"

"Every flower," Spencer said.

Belinda was doing a good impression of a deer in head-lights. She took two steps back, cornering herself in the hospital room.

I was creeped out and disappointed in myself. I had pegged Belinda as a nice, unassuming person, not a gardener of death. "So?" I said. "Big deal."

"The toxicology report is due any minute, but it looks like one of her flowers may be the culprit."

"He had no face!" I yelled. Why did everyone forget about the face?

"The face was done postmortem. Where was Belinda the night of the murder?"

"Hold on," I said. I took Belinda by the arm and ushered her out of the room.

"It can't be that bad," I told her. "You have to tell me where you were. Your life is on the line."

Tears streamed down Belinda's face, leaving a trail of black mascara.

"I can't tell," she sobbed. "I can't."

"Why not? Are you ashamed? Is it porn?"

"No," she said, catching her breath through her cries. "I can't tell you."

"Spencer is about to arrest you, Belinda. Tell me before it's too late."

"I love flowers," she said.

"I know you do."

"It started out with some calla lilies, and then a couple elephant ears. Before I knew it, I had the largest private collection of poisonous flowers in the Southwest." She broke down in long, wrenching sobs.

"I understand," I said, patting her back. "I collected Cabbage Patch dolls for a summer when I was fifteen." Try sleeping with twenty Cabbage Patch dolls staring back at you. Not easy.

Belinda wiped her nose on her sleeve. "You don't know what it's like to be me," she said. "You have a boyfriend."

"I think the word 'boyfriend' may be a stretch." A huge stretch. An NBA stretch. I had blown it with Holden, and the bloom was off that particular love affair. I wondered if there was a way I could make it right with him.

"I've never had a boyfriend," she told me. "I've never been loved."

"I'm sure that's not true."

"It's true, Gladie. Do you know what it's like not to be loved? The only thing rubbing my thigh is my other thigh!"

She broke down in more tears. I didn't know how to console her. Grandma would tell her to shut up and give her a cookie and the name of her true love. But I didn't have a cookie, and I didn't know who to fix Belinda up with. Maybe because I didn't really know Belinda.

Obviously, Grandma was wrong about me. I wasn't like her. I didn't have her instincts, and I was a failure as a matchmaker.

"I have to pee," I said.

"Me too," Belinda said. We giggled, probably happy to talk about something as normal as peeing.

"They have communal toilets in jail," I pointed out. That sobered her up quick. She stopped crying and took a deep breath.

"The morning of Dr. Dulur's murder, I got an email."

"From who?"

"I don't know. He called himself 'the Evil Queen,' you know, like the one with the poison apple."

"How do you know it was a man?"

"I could tell," she said. "He said nice things about how I looked, the way a man would."

"So, what did he want?"

"He wanted to meet me," she said. Her breath hitched, as she swallowed a new wave of sobs. "He had a certain flower to give me, one that's not strictly legal, Gladie. One I could get in trouble for."

I knew nothing about flowers or plants or gardening in general. I had worked at a tree farm in Minnesota for one day. Then a giant spider jumped on me from the branch of a Marshall ash tree, and that was the end of my burgeoning horticultural career.

"Why did he offer you an illegal flower?" I asked.

"I don't want to go to jail, Gladie."

"Belinda, Spencer wants to arrest you in the No-Face Case. Dubious flowers come a distant second. You know what I mean?"

Belinda swallowed, making a gulping sound. "I sort of advertised for it. You know, on an Internet forum. I'm kind of a celebrity in the poisonous-flowers online world." She beamed with pride. "It was a crucial flower for my collection."

"So you agreed to meet a stranger."

Belinda's face dropped. "I guess I'm sort of dumb. Anyway, he never showed up. I went way out of town to an empty parking lot and waited two hours for him. I was so mad, being made a fool of like that. But I was relieved after, because I was supposed to do the books at work that night. If I hadn't been waiting for that jerk in the parking lot, I might have been another victim."

My skin crawled like the Marshall ash tree spider was on me again. "Wait a minute. You were supposed to be at Bliss Dental that night?"

"Yes, to do the books."

"Do you still have the emails from the mystery man?"

IT WAS a flimsy alibi, but it was a start. Spencer had a couple cops escort Belinda home and told her to come in to the police station the next afternoon to give her statement.

The gun was taken into custody, as well, to test against the bullet extracted from Holly's neck. It turned out it was a .38 caliber and a good candidate for being the gun that did the deed.

Spencer and I stopped in to see Holly on our way out, but she was unconscious and had a tube down her throat, helping her breathe and preventing her from getting pneumonia. Miraculously, she was going to live.

Her face was peaceful as she lay in bed. Smooth, but not the usual waxy look she had when she was awake.

"I wonder what she wanted to tell me," I said.

"If she wakes up, she'll tell us," Spencer said.

"You weren't going to arrest Belinda, were you?"

Spencer smirked his annoying smirk.

"You wanted me to get her alibi out of her. You used me," I said.

"You make it sound cheap."

"We have a strange relationship."

"Oh, Pinkie, don't use the 'R' word. You know it gives me hives."

"There is no hope for you," I said.

"Still, it is a weird coincidence about Belinda's gardening habit and the use of the scarecrow," Spencer said. "I wouldn't say she's entirely in the clear."

On the way to the elevator, we found Nathan Smith wandering the halls. He looked shell-shocked, pale, and exhausted.

"I was trying to find Holly," he said when he saw us.

"She's still unconscious," I said. "You want a ride home?"

"My car's out front."

We walked out together. It was a peaceful night. Quiet. Chilly. I folded my arms in front of me to brace against the cold.

"What a week," Nathan commented. "Who would

ever guess working in a dentist's office would be hazardous?"

"Are you okay to go home alone?" Spencer asked.

"Yeah, sure," Nathan said. "I got a double lock on my door."

It never occurred to me that Nathan would be afraid for his safety, but it made sense. He had been one of the killer's victims. He was lucky to be alive after suffering a blow to the head. It was reasonable that he feared the killer would try to finish what he started.

"Hey, Nathan," I called after him as he made his way to his car. "If you ever want to talk or just want company, come on over to my grandmother's house and see me. The door's always open."

I DOZED on and off on the way home. Spencer parked in the driveway. He was no longer in hiding and didn't care if people knew he was at my house.

I unlocked the front door and Spencer followed me in. His duffel bag was packed and waiting for him in the foyer.

"Oh, good, you're leaving," I said, eyeing the bag.

"Huh," he said, running his hand through his hair. "Your grandma must have packed my stuff."

"I've got the bed all to myself!"

"Don't sound so gleeful, Pinkie, about kicking me out of your bed."

We walked into the kitchen, and I took out a box of frozen waffles. "I'm not shedding any tears, Spencer. I'm sure you'll find another bed within the hour."

"No, not me. I'm taking a break. Women are a lot crazier than they used to be."

"Duh. That's because you make them that way. It's the Spencer effect. You turn women into psycho lunatics."

Spencer popped open two root beers and handed me one.

"At least Rosalie has been subdued," he said.

"You sound happy about being hated."

I poured maple syrup over a waffle and took a bite.

"You know what?" he said, cutting into his waffle. "I've discovered being hated is better than being loved. Safer."

"Well, then you are the safest man in America, Spencer."

"Amen to that."

"Nathan's injury couldn't have been self-inflicted, could it?" I asked.

Spencer put his fork down and swallowed. "Where did that come from?"

"I want to be safe, too. And Nathan looks spry, like he could outrun you."

"According to the doctors, it's not a self-inflicted wound," Spencer said. "Also, he was very lucky it wasn't a fatal blow. At the very least, it knocked him out, and there was no weapon left at the scene. So the poor bastard was another victim. He ran; the killer knocked him out and left him for dead and then went back to the dentist to finish him off and butcher him."

I pushed my plate back. "Can I have your TV?"

IT WAS the middle of the night before I finally got into bed. I had taken a long, hot shower, deep-conditioned my hair, and slathered my feet in Vaseline and covered them in clean, thick athletic socks that Spencer had forgotten under my bed. I changed my sheets, put on a pretty linen nightgown, snuggled under my covers, and turned on the TV to the old-movies station. I was asleep in five minutes.

I woke up a little before dawn to Rhett Butler giving

Scarlett the business. What a man. Why did hats go out of style? Clark Gable wore them well.

I felt someone watching me, and I jumped when I noticed a figure sitting on the chair next to my bed.

"I'm sorry I startled you," he said softly. Holden's long body sat rigid and his expression was serious.

"What are you doing here?"

"I'm saying goodbye."

Chapter 17

✦ ♥ ✦

We're in the happily-ever-after business, but sometimes The End comes before the happy ending. Romance can burn hot and burn itself out. Romance can also explode and fizzle to nothing, like fireworks. When this happens to one of my matches . . . well, it breaks my heart. Dolly, it's important to accept the goodbyes and move on, no matter how much it breaks your heart. But emmis, my hand to God: Sometimes the embers continue to burn below the surface, and the romance will reignite. Sometimes, goodbye doesn't mean goodbye.

Lesson 86,
Matchmaking Advice from Your Grandma Zelda

I TURNED off the television and sat up in bed.

"Goodbye?" I stopped breathing. My jaw clamped shut, and my tooth pain returned with a vengeance. "I'm sorry about Spencer. I didn't want him to kiss me. It was his idea, not mine."

Holden moved to the bed, sitting by my side. He put his hand on my leg and caressed me through the covers.

"No, pretty lady. I don't care about Spencer. I don't think of him as a threat. Truthfully, if I did, I would have beaten the hell out of him long ago."

"Is it me? I'm sorry about my hair."

"I love your hair."

"I started drinking Chinese tea."

Holden laughed. "Your body is perfect. The first time I saw you, I wanted you."

"You first saw me at night in the dark."

"I saw your silhouette. Your breasts. Your hips. And I wanted you."

I wanted him, too, like a diabetic wants a chocolate chip cookie. I took his hand and rubbed his palm with my thumb. "And now you're saying goodbye."

"I've traveled around the world at least a dozen times," he said.

"I went to Epcot Center once," I said.

"I've paddled down the Amazon, followed in John Hanning Speke's footsteps to the source of the Nile, sailed from Tahiti to Hawaii with only the stars to guide me, and climbed the heights to Tibet. I'm an explorer, Gladie. That's how I've made a living since I was sixteen years old."

"Are you sure?" I asked.

"Am I what?"

It occurred to me that Holden might have been drinking his organic shampoo. "I've had a lot of jobs in my life," I told him. "I never knew you could make a living exploring."

"I wrote about it, took photos," he explained.

"The women in town have been trying to figure you out. They guessed the craziest things. Bird thought you shot Osama bin Laden, but Bridget thinks you were a butt model. Nobody guessed explorer," I said.

I must have looked doubtful. "You Googled me," he guessed.

I had found nothing on him. No books. No photos.

"So, one day I was in New York City, giving a lecture to the National Geographic Society," he continued, "and I witnessed something. I testified in a trial about the incident. Do you get where I'm going with this?"

"Holy crap, you're in witness protection. That's why

there's nothing on you, like you dropped from the sky." It all clicked together. The secrets, paying for his house in cash, and the weird fact of a gorgeous intellectual moving to our small town.

Holden nodded.

"Who's Becky?" I asked.

"A woman who can get me my life back. With her help, I can get to the man who wants me dead. Get to him before he gets to me."

"You sure you don't want to be a butt model?" I asked. "Less dangerous, and I bet you would be good at it."

Holden smiled. "There's a spot I want to share with you in the desert along the Red Sea. The moon is so big there, you can almost reach up and touch it."

I exhaled, and to my horror, a tear rolled down my cheek. "You talk good," I said.

And then we stopped talking. We sat on my bed in silence, staring into each other's eyes, trying to read each other's thoughts, as the light from the sunrise filtered through the curtains. He was a beautiful man. Kind and strong.

"When are you leaving?" I asked, finally.

"Soon. Now. Mr. Steve gave me a lead, and I don't know how long it's good for."

"Are you allowed to leave?"

"No."

The next, obvious question was whether he would take me with him. I was surprised to realize that I didn't want to go.

"It would have been easier if you were hiding from your Facebook friends," I said.

"Excuse me?"

"When are you coming back?"

Holden didn't answer. He looked out the window and exhaled.

"Does Spencer know?" I asked.

"I don't think so."

I wondered about that. Could Spencer keep a secret like this?

"We have a lot of unfinished business, you and I," Holden said.

"Are we going to finish it now?" I wanted him, but I knew it would make it more painful after.

"I'm not a jerk, Gladie. We have time. We'll get down to business when I come back." He looked out the window again.

He kissed me lightly and stood up.

"Wait," I said. "What's your real name?"

Holden smiled, surprised. "Between you and me, it's William. William Burton. Friends call me Burton."

And then he was gone, and I was left alone with a toothache and a miserable sense of loss.

I HEARD the door click closed behind Holden. Sleep was impossible. I walked downstairs to make a pot of coffee.

Grandma was waiting for me at the bottom of the stairs.

"I tried to steer you clear of him," she said.

"He's a good guy," I said. "But he's going away for a while."

"A pot's on, and I'm defrosting the Sara Lee."

Half a cherry cheesecake later, I was feeling better, despite the throbbing in my tooth. "It's been a bad month for love," Grandma said, her mouth full of cake. "People all turned around and moving backwards. Just like this town. We've got a surplus of crazy happening here. Can't wait for it to end. If I hear one more word about that *fakakta* donkey . . ."

"When is it going to end?" I asked.

"I can't get a reading, but I think it will end in a blaze of glory."

"That doesn't sound good."

I WENT back to bed and turned on the TV. *Gone with the Wind* was playing again. I fell into a deep sleep as Atlanta burned.

I woke to a voice in my room. For a moment I thought Holden had returned, but this voice was higher and crazier.

"It's 8:05. Do you think I have all day?"

Rosalie stood over me, her eyelash extensions batting at an alarming rate.

"It's 8:05," she repeated. She pursed her lips, forcing her lipstick to ooze into the tiny lines around her mouth.

I screamed. I screamed really loudly. Rosalie took a step back. That's when I noticed she wasn't armed and I remembered I had made a date with her.

"Are you ready to go?" she asked.

"I'm in bed. Today's not a good day. How about tomorrow?"

"No, I'm going to a wedding tomorrow. It's now or never. They're waiting for you."

I threw back the covers. "Fine!"

There's nothing like getting dumped to change my mood. I ran into the bathroom and slammed my legs into a pair of jeans and threw on a T-shirt. When I went back into my room, Rosalie's eyes grew big.

"Yeah, that's right," I said. "No bra. You want to make something of it?" The truth is I forgot to put on a bra, and when I remembered, I didn't want Rosalie to know I was that stupid.

"No, that's fine." Rosalie was blinking a hundred miles an hour. My boobs are too big for me to go braless, especially in a threadbare Porky's Pig Farm T-shirt. I was probably quite a sight, but it was too late to go back now. Besides, I was in a foul mood, and I just didn't care.

Downstairs, Grandma's house was filling up with the Saturday morning Cooking for Love class. I found Grandma supervising the setup.

"Grandma, Rosalie is taking me—"

"Holy hell, it's the sixties all over again," Grandma exclaimed. Her eyes were glued to my chest. I resisted the urge to cover myself with my arms.

"I'll be back soon."

"Don't be gone long," Grandma said. "Trouble is coming over at ten with some seamstress she found. The wedding is tomorrow, you know."

I moaned and stomped a foot on Grandma's kitchen linoleum.

"You can't get out of it," she said.

I wanted to get out of it. I wanted to get out of all of it. After all, I had been dumped by the sexiest man alive, a man who wanted to take me to the Red Sea. I didn't want to be a maid of honor or be dragged around town by whiny, complaining Rosalie Rodriguez. I wanted to throw my own fit. I wanted to wallow. I wanted my own set of Rachael Ray knives.

"Fine," I said. "I'll be back by ten."

Rosalie and I got to the front door just as Lucy and Bridget opened it. Lucy was soaking wet, her silk dress glued to her body, and her once perfectly done hair stuck to one side of her head, dripping down her face.

"You will never believe what happened to us!" Lucy shouted.

With the week I had been having, it could have been anything.

"Uh," I said.

"Darlin', who are you supposed to be today? Jenna Jameson?"

"Right on, sister," Bridget declared with glee, and

proceeded to take off her bra. It didn't have the same effect. Bridget was an A cup at best and was wearing a blousy top. Still, she never lost a chance to fly her feminist flag, so to speak.

I wanted to tell my best friends that Holden was leaving. They would have wrapped me up in love and understanding. But I didn't want to say anything in front of Rosalie. Not only wasn't it her business, but I didn't want to remind her of being dumped and be responsible for giving her a relapse of crazy.

"We were just going out to interview mothers of kids who were abused by Dr. Dulur," I said. "Supposedly," I added.

" 'We'?" Lucy asked. She arched one eyebrow so high it almost reached her hairline. "That's quite all right. Give me two minutes to right myself, and we'll go with you."

Rosalie wasn't happy about the delay, but Lucy was true to her word about only being two minutes. She changed into an emergency dress she kept in her purse, one that you can scrunch up and unroll without a wrinkle, and emerged from the bathroom a moment later completely made up.

We left the house and had just gotten to the driveway when Nathan Smith arrived in his Geo and parked at the curb. All of a sudden, I was the world's most popular woman. Nathan ran up the driveway and waved at me. He tried to look me in the eyes, but his gaze kept slipping to my chest.

"You said I could come anytime," he said, slightly breathless.

"Sure, why don't you tag along," I said.

The five of us squeezed into Rosalie's BMW. Bridget called shotgun, and that's how I wound up wedged between Nathan and Lucy in the backseat.

"So, how did this little party come together?" Lucy asked me. "I mean, Rosalie and you."

"We talked last night after the hygienist got shot," Rosalie explained as she drove.

"After the what got what?" Lucy asked. "Bridget, I think we missed something."

Rosalie gave the rundown on Holly's shooting. She had more information than I thought she would, like the fact that Holly was stable in a coma in the ICU.

"Gladie, you were almost killed again," Bridget noted. It was getting to be my theme, almost getting shot or killed.

"You should get a vanity license plate," Lucy said. "'Magnet for Murder and Mayhem.'"

"I think that's too many letters for a license plate," I said.

"Who are you? You look familiar," Lucy said to Nathan.

"I assisted Dr. Dulur with your root canal."

Lucy pointed at him. "Oh, yes. That's it. Everything's a bit fuzzy from that day. Loved the gas."

"I'd love some gas right about now," I mumbled.

"What's that?" Nathan asked.

"I was just saying I'd like some gas. My tooth is throbbing."

"Oh, I have good news for you," Nathan said. "The replacement dentist arrived last night. He's taking patients starting this afternoon. I can get you in as an emergency."

My throat constricted and my stomach dropped. Little beads of sweat erupted on my forehead. "I'm sure I'll be fine," I said.

"Let me take a look." Nathan turned in his seat, grabbed hold of my chin with two fingers, and tugged my mouth open. He murmured all kinds of dire sounds. "Doesn't look good," he said. "You better come in. You're working on an abscess."

Rosalie whistled. "Ouch. You don't want to go there,

Gladie. My cousin had an abscess, and they had to re-move part of his jaw before the infection traveled to his brain."

"I've got a slot open at eight tonight," Nathan said.

I felt the blood drain out of my head, and I saw stars. It wasn't even the thought of getting my tooth filled that sparked terror in me. It was going back to the scene of the crime and being helpless on the dental chair, under the gas.

Nathan surprised me with his sensitivity. "We don't have to put you under the gas this time," he said, read-ing my mind. "We'll numb the area. You won't feel a thing. I promise."

Infections traveling to my brain didn't sound too good. I agreed to the appointment before I could think about it any longer.

"Hey, where are we going?" Nathan asked.

"We're going to visit Tiffany Theroux to talk about what a sadistic bastard that boss of yours was," Rosalie explained.

"What?" Nathan asked, startled.

But Rosalie didn't answer. She was focused on her rear-view mirror as she swerved onto Orchard Road, the road that led out of the historic district east toward the apple orchards. "What the hell?" she grumbled. "The world is full of nutjobbers."

We let that go without comment, but I could tell it was killing Lucy to remain silent. Considering only yes-terday Rosalie was running through town clutching a cleaver, she was a pretty black pot to diss any other nutjobber.

Rosalie sped along the road, swerving in and out of the lane. I got nervous. Maybe her crazy quotient hadn't diminished at all, and maybe she was planning on fin-ishing me off here in the back of her BMW. I turned around to see what Rosalie was looking at.

Trouble Weiss was behind the wheel of her Smart car, chasing after us. I could barely make out the small *toot-toot* of her car horn as she frantically tried to get our attention and, I figured, make us pull over.

"What is in there with her?" asked Bridget. "It's hurting my eyes."

It looked like Trouble was being swallowed alive by a cloud of neon pink so bright the color could provoke seizures.

"That's tulle," Lucy said with confidence.

"Are you sure?" asked Bridget.

"Honey, I know tulle. And I would imagine there's about nine yards of it in that clown car."

I had a bad feeling about the tulle.

"Maybe you should pull over," I said.

"I drove three years for an oil executive in Cartagena, and I never got carjacked," Rosalie said, driving like a madwoman, all the while keeping her eyes on the rear-view mirror. "I'm not going to let a ballerina in a Smart car take me down now."

Spencer really had bad taste in women. I couldn't for the life of me figure out what attracted him to Rosalie.

"She must be a hot tamale in bed," Lucy whispered in my ear.

I sighed. My sex life had taken a big hit today. Who knew when I could be a hot tamale again? Maybe my hot tamale days were over. Maybe with all my inactivity, I was a lukewarm enchilada.

"Maybe we could stop for lunch," I said.

"I ain't stopping for nobody!" Rosalie announced. She made a hairpin turn and headed back toward town.

"Does this car have air bags?" Bridget asked.

"Whose idea, exactly, was it to have Rosalie drive?" Lucy asked.

"I think it was Rosalie's idea," I said. "I think you lost her," I told Rosalie. Sure enough, Trouble's Smart

car just couldn't keep up with a Colombian-trained professional driver in a turbocharged BMW. We finally
made it to Tiffany Theroux's condo complex.

We tumbled out of the car and followed Rosalie as
she marched up to Tiffany's front door.

"So, what are we doing here?" Nathan asked me. He
was a little green around the gills, and I sensed he was
regretting his decision to seek me out for company and
comfort.

"I don't know," I said. "But I'll buy you lunch after."
What was I saying? The only money I had was ear-
marked to pay off my cellphone bill. "Or we could eat
at my grandmother's house," I amended. "The Cooking
for Love class usually has great leftovers."

"Is Rosalie driving us home?" he asked.

TIFFANY WELCOMED us in. "Oh, my, look at
you all. What fun!"

She was the polar opposite of Rosalie. Where Rosalie
was put together in sharp lines and designer clothing
and exhibited an eternal-victim complex, Tiffany was
homemade chic and radiated happiness. She was bedazzled, knitted, and macraméd. I recognized her at once
as one of those people who in the face of tragedy says,
"I am so blessed."

"Please sit. I hope you're hungry."

Tiffany put out quite a spread. There was quiche,
salad, assorted breads and cheeses, and a chocolate
cake.

"I almost didn't get back in time to meet you," Tiffany said, smiling. "I was helping the committee against
the alien lovers."

"Tiffany, tell Gladie what the dentist did to your
Sam," Rosalie said.

Sam, it turned out, was Tiffany's son. Five years ago,

when Sam was thirteen, Dr. Dulur bruised his arm when he wouldn't sit still in the chair. It wasn't much to go on, not much in the way of proving Dr. Dulur was a sadistic dentist. And besides, I couldn't believe Tiffany Theroux would avenge her son's abuse with murder. She might needlepoint an angry letter, but I bet that's as far as she would go.

Nathan jumped up from the couch. He held a plate of chocolate cake with one hand and with the other he pointed at the front window. "Look at that, she found us," he said.

Storming up the walk was Trouble Weiss. Calamity was a few steps behind her, more or less drowning in a sea of neon pink tulle.

"Shit," I said. "Here comes Trouble."

Chapter 18

+ ♥ +

*A*ccessories don't get the respect they deserve. A woman will sweat about what outfit to wear on her first date. Sweat about it, max out her credit cards, get her friends to vote on it, even cry. Cry? That's nothing. . . . A woman will have a complete nervous breakdown over a dress. I had one client run naked down Main Street screaming, "Anne Klein, suck my wiener!" when her new dress wouldn't fit five minutes before her first date. Luckily, she had a great body, and she wound up marrying that match. But your matches don't need this kind of tsoris. The dress doesn't matter all that much. A simple black dress from Target is good enough. Because it's the accessories that make the outfit, dolly. Anne Klein without a nice necklace is Anne Nothing Special. But an Hermès scarf can make jeans fabulous. Focus on the accessories. It's like my grandmother told me years ago: Wear the right shoes, bubeleh. It can mean the difference between love and bunions, which is a big difference, let me tell you.

Lesson 26,
Matchmaking Advice from Your Grandma Zelda

TROUBLE KNOCKED on the window and wagged her finger at me. "I see you in there, Gladys Burger!" she yelled through the glass. "How dare you make me chase after you the day before my daughter's wedding!"

She had a point. I'm sure she had more important things to do the day before Calamity tied the knot.

Tiffany let Trouble in, and Trouble ordered me to strip down right there so I could be fitted. I protested.

"Trouble," I pleaded, gesturing toward Nathan.

"Don't tell me you're shy," Trouble said. "Your boobs are hanging out for everyone to see. You have precious few secrets this morning."

But I didn't have to worry about my honor: Calamity held up the fabric, which effectively blocked Nathan from seeing anything crucial. She pulled it up over my head, and I tugged my arms through.

The dress was much too tight on top and ridiculously big on the bottom. There was poof and ruffles and swirling cascades of tulle.

"I don't think I'm wearing it right," I said.

I pulled at it and twisted it to try and make it fall correctly. The room had grown quiet. Bridget and Lucy had their mouths open.

"What?" I asked. "Does it look okay?"

"It's a dream!" Trouble gushed. "Absolutely gorgeous!"

"Bridget?" I asked. "What do you think?" She didn't answer. Her eyes were enormous, even bigger than her giant hoot-owl glasses.

"Where's a mirror?" I asked.

Bridget and Lucy jumped up. "No!" they shouted.

"Don't look in a mirror," Bridget commanded. "It looks fine."

A door opened and closed somewhere in the condo, and heavy feet marched down the hallway toward us.

"Criminy!" A tall, dark-haired man stood in the living room, seemingly transfixed. He was about forty years old and was wearing dirty jeans and a T-shirt that said A FLOWER IS FOREVER. He looked a lot like Tiffany but with a George Clooney edge to him. My skin prickled, and I began to hyperventilate a tiny bit.

"Isn't she breathtaking?" Trouble said to the man. "Just like Scarlett O'Hara."

"She takes my breath away, all right," he said. "Like napalm."

"You don't have a mirror, Tiffany?" I asked.

"Whatever you do, Tiffany," Bridget said, "don't let her go near a mirror."

"It just needs to be taken in here and there," Trouble said. She pulled a sewing kit out of her purse and started pinning the bodice.

"I don't think it can be taken in up there," I said. My breath was being cut off by the boning in the bodice, making me pant like a Pekingese. My boobs were inching their way out, trying to escape the confines of the dress. It was only a matter of time before we had full nipple exposure.

"This is my brother, George," Tiffany said.

"Oh, that's just too perfect," I said. "You married, George?"

"Recently divorced," he said.

"Gladie is a matchmaker," Lucy explained before he could get the wrong idea and run screaming from the scary, overly forward, neon lady.

"Anybody would be better than his ex-wife," Tiffany said.

"She wasn't very supportive of my vocation," George explained.

"George is a flower grower," Tiffany said. "Exotic, rare flowers."

Jackpot. *Ding! Ding! Ding!* I felt a rush of happiness. The kind of satisfaction that comes only when the pieces fit together perfectly. Maybe there was some hope for me as a matchmaker. Maybe Grandma was right about me.

Suddenly, nothing else mattered. The dress, the murder, a crazy killer on the loose, Holden. All took a backseat to the knowledge that I would match Belinda Womble.

Trouble pinned and sewed me into the dress. The tulle swirled and billowed, eliminating my view of my body's lower half. Ribbons weaved their way around the polyester fabric of my sleeves and dangled down past my fingertips. I didn't think Heidi Klum would approve.

Calamity passed the pins to her mother. At first I thought she had stuck herself when a tear rolled down her cheek, but then she did the unexpected. "Love is the exquisite bloom that gives beauty to life," she said.

It was the first time I had heard her speak. Her voice was soft, rich, and melodic, nothing like her mother's.

"I love Dan so much," she continued. "He's my flower, and I'm his. I'm his neon pink flower, and you're my neon pink fairy godmother, Gladie. The tulle was my idea. I think it makes you look dreamy, just like a Disney movie."

"More like *Gone with the Wind* on crack," Rosalie said. But we ignored her. The air was thick with a pleasant romantic air, and no one wanted to spoil it.

That's when I started to cry.

Bridget knocked Trouble aside, taking me into a bear hug, flinching slightly, probably because of a pin or two. "What misogynistic jerk is making you cry?" she asked.

"He's not misogynistic," I said.

"So, Holden is making you cry?" Lucy asked.

"He's—he's—he's leaving town," I said. I gulped air between my sobs, and a nipple popped out of my dress.

"I'm going to call a cab," Nathan announced, and went out to make the call.

"I'll make you some tea," Tiffany said with a smile. "You'll be right as rain."

I couldn't give specifics about Holden's departure. No, I didn't know where he was going; I thought he was going away on business; no, I didn't know when he would be back or if he would be back; no, he didn't say he might not be back.

It was a pretty pathetic reason to cry. I couldn't tell them that Holden was going to risk his life to get his old life back, his life where he wasn't Holden and he wasn't living next to me or in the same town. So I looked like I was one notch above Rosalie. Whining about the loss of a man but without the knives.

"It will be fine," Tiffany said, handing me a cup of tea. "He'll be back soon enough, and you know what they say: distance makes the heart grow fonder. He will be over the moon to see you again."

I gulped down the tea. She was right. It did make me feel better.

Nathan's cab arrived, and he said goodbye. "Don't forget, Gladie. Eight o'clock tonight. It won't hurt a bit."

"Hey, Nathan," Rosalie said as he walked out the front door. "That dentist of yours was no good. He hurt my boy, and he hurt others."

Outside it had grown dark, even though it was a little before noon. "The weather's changing," Trouble noted. "Not a big deal. Rain is good luck on a wedding day, Calamity. Onward. We have to finish the chocolate sculpture."

They gathered the sewing supplies and leftover material. After reminding me to be at their house at ten sharp the next morning, they scooted off in their Smart car.

"You're popular lately," Bridget said.

"We have to get going, darlin'," Lucy said. "We have to get my Mercedes out of the lake."

"Okay, but this time, you're leaving it to the professionals. You almost killed yourself with that crane from the do-it-yourself store," Bridget said.

"You don't have to tell me twice. It dumped me so far in the lake, I almost made it out to sea. And I don't have another outfit in my pocketbook. You coming, Gladie?"

I was exhausted, both physically and emotionally. I wanted to go to bed and hopefully sleep through my dental appointment. But I wanted to strike while the iron was hot. I was within spitting distance of matching Belinda. I was sure of it.

"George, would you give me a lift?" I asked him. "There's a lovely woman I think you should meet. At the very least, you should see her flower collection." *Her poisonous flower collection. And she'll be available just as soon as the police are through interrogating her about a grisly murder.*

"I guess that won't hurt," he said.

We thanked Tiffany for the brunch and her hospitality and then every cellphone ringtone in the room went off. My phone was still dead.

"Change of plan," Lucy told Rosalie. "Emergency town meeting. They're coming up with a plan against the end-of-worlders."

"Where are my clothes?" I asked. And then it hit me. Hit me like a bargain vacation to Mexico in the middle of the summer. My stomach rolled and pitched and made a sound similar to the one Dulcinea made as she flew over town in fear for her life. I had a nasty suspicion. "Tiffany, what kind of tea did you give me?"

"Chinese diet tea. Very good for the body. All-natural. I got it from Bird Gonzalez, my hairdresser. Do you know her?"

I lifted up armloads of tulle and ran for the bathroom. Chinese diet tea seemed to work for everyone in Cannes except for me. In my stomach, it acted like a thermo-nuclear device, leaving destruction in its wake.

I left the bathroom after about thirty minutes. My dress was slightly looser, and I stuck my boob back into the bodice.

The condo was empty except for George, who I found in the kitchen, washing the dishes. He was careful not to look me in the eye. Lesser people would have been embarrassed, but considering I was wearing a neon pink monstrosity, everything was relative.

"Did you find my clothes, by any chance?" I asked George.

"Tiff thought the chocolate lady took them by accident."

I sighed. "Fine, we'll make a quick trip to meet Belinda, and then I'll change at home."

"You're going out like that?"

"Why? Does it bother you?"

It did. And if I was honest with myself, it bothered me, too. The tulle was itchy, and I could hardly breathe through the bodice, even after the Chinese diet tea. It was also ugly, probably the ugliest dress I had ever seen.

George offered me some of his sister's clothes, but it turned out Trouble had sewn me into the dress, and even with George's help, I couldn't get out of it without ripping the seams.

"My grandmother will get someone to help," I said.

So it was back to Plan A. George helped me into his truck, piling the tulle onto my lap. There was so much material, I couldn't see past it out of the windows. But I could tell the weather was changing. It had grown dark, and a wind was picking up.

"I'd sure like to go to that meeting. It's supposed to be a humdinger. Things are sure heating up," George said.

"Well, it will be on for a while, I'm sure. Maybe you'll bring Belinda with you." The thought pleased me. It would be a great relief to have Belinda fixed up. A good match and healthy teeth would go a long way to getting my life on track.

"Does Belinda work at the police station?" George asked as we parked in front.

"Something like that."

I literally swept into the station, my crinkly dress skirting the floor with a loud crackling sound. I drew a lot of attention, like a sideshow freak or a bad car accident on the side of the road.

My first client, desk sergeant Fred Lytton, greeted me when I entered with George. "Hey there, Underwear Girl," he said. "Gee, you sure do look pretty."

"Thanks, Fred. This is a maid-of-honor dress for Calamity Weiss's wedding tomorrow," I said. It was important to me to distance myself from the dress as much as possible.

"It's good you're getting a lot of wear out of it," Fred noted. "It would be a shame to wear it just for one day."

"Is Belinda Womble here? Is she, er, done with her interview?"

"I think so. Let me get the chief."

I tried to stop him, but he had long legs and was much faster than I was, especially in my dress. I held my breath and tried to become invisible. Then a miracle happened. Instead of Spencer Bolton appearing, Belinda Womble, in her finest purple-flowered ensemble, walked right toward us, most likely on her way to the exit. She didn't recognize me at first. The moment she did registered on her face. Disbelief. Disgust.

"What in the h—" she started, and then noticed George and his shirt—in that order—and her mouth dropped open but nothing came out. George seemed equally impressed.

He pointed at her chest. "Autumn crocus. The beauty of the deadly flower."

Belinda giggled and patted her hair into place. I expected a Matchmaker of the Year award. A medal. A parade in my honor.

"I hear there's some lavender blooming chaparral just outside of town. It should be quite a sight. Care to join me?"

He put his arm out, and Belinda slid her arm in the crook of his elbow. She giggled again but never said a word. There was nothing to say. She had found her George Clooney.

I watched them go. He held the door open for her and escorted her outside to his truck, where he opened the passenger door and helped her up. It wasn't until after he drove out of the parking lot and they were out of my line of sight that I realized I was alone at the police station, in a giant pink polyester-and-tulle *Gone with the Wind* reject, which I had been sewn into, without a ride home. And to make matters worse, Fred had found the chief of police.

"Pinkie, Pinkie, Pinkie. Or should I say, *Pinkie! Pinkie! Pinkie!* 'Cause that's a hell of a lot of pink, Gladys Burger."

"Don't call me Gladys, Spencer."

Spencer wore a form-fitting suit and shiny shoes. He was clean shaven and not a hair on his head was out of place. Obviously, he was no longer worried about his Facebook friends, because he was the old Spencer again. Cocky, arrogant, with his annoying smirk permanently planted on his (more than likely) moisturized face.

"New look for you?" he asked.

"I'm the maid of honor at Calamity Weiss's wedding tomorrow."

"And you wanted to get a head start on it? Show off your pretty dress in town? To me?"

"Trouble took my clothes, and I can't get the dress off."

"So you came to me," Spencer said, smirking his annoying little smirk. "Because you know that if anybody can get a dress off you, it's me."

"You are five years old."

"Me? How about you? 'Can't get the dress off.' Sounds like a line to me."

I grabbed a fistful of Spencer's perfectly ironed shirt and pulled him close. "She sewed me into the damned thing," I hissed between my teeth. "I can't get it off." I let go of his shirt, and he straightened himself out.

"All right, come into my office and I'll get some scissors."

"No! I need it for tomorrow. Get me home. Grandma will know what to do."

"Fine," he said. "I need to pick up my TV, anyway. I had no *Family Guy* with my breakfast this morning. Made my Frosted Flakes soggy."

"I can't keep the television?" The question came out whinier than I had planned. I really enjoyed watching old movies in bed. I would miss it.

"You wanna work out a trade?" He smiled and arched an eyebrow.

"I have to hand it to you, Spencer. At least you're consistent."

AS WE walked to Spencer's car, I updated him on Dr. Dulur's sadistic behavior.

Spencer stopped dead in the parking lot. "You went with who to where?" he asked. "Have I gone deaf? Has your dress affected my hearing as well as making me half blind?"

"I didn't have a choice," I said. "Rosalie asked me to go."

"Listen, Disco Scarlett," he said, sticking his finger under my nose. "Stay away from the crazies. Stay away from the killers. Stay away from my cases. You got me?"

"Uh—"

"You got me?" he asked, raising his voice.

I stuck three fingers in the air. "No crazies. No killers. No police cases. Girl Scout's honor." Not that I had ever been a Girl Scout, but I loved their cookies.

"Meanwhile, what have you learned about the cult and

Mr. Steve?" I asked. "Maybe he thought of Dr. Dulur as a threat and offed him. He gives me the creeps."

"Maybe you don't understand English," Spencer said. "You just said you wouldn't get involved in my cases."

"He pretends to be reasonable, but he's not," I said. "I mean, he's the leader of a cult, Spencer. Sure, he has great taste in shoes, but I don't think we can trust him."

" 'We'?"

"And it doesn't matter if he has an alibi, because he has henchmen. Did you see those bodybuilder gong guys last night?"

"I think your dress is giving me seizures. My eye keeps twitching."

"Sometimes I don't think you take me seriously," I said.

"Sometimes?"

"I would hit you, but I can't move my arms in this dress."

IT HAD started raining by the time we made it to Spencer's car. Big drops hit the windshield. "Wet autumn," I said. "I wonder what this means for the apple season."

Spencer turned the ignition. His car came to life and so did his police radio. "Freaks in sector three!" The town was still complete mayhem with the townsfolk battling the cultists.

"You know, this town is getting weirder," Spencer said. "I didn't think it was possible, but it's like a lunatic factory on this mountain."

Meryl the librarian, dressed in overalls and carrying a saw, waved at us, and Spencer rolled down his window. "I thought that was you, but I wasn't sure," she said to me. "What are you made up as? Some kind of play on Scarlett O'Hara? Are you going to a costume party or something?"

"I'm Calamity's maid of honor."

Meryl shook her head. "Oh, that Trouble. Putting on a wedding in the middle of all this mess. What is she thinking?"

I was feeling weak since my Chinese diet tea ordeal, and I had missed lunch. I wished Spencer would hurry up and get me home so I could get out of the dress and grab something to eat before I had to go out to Bliss Dental.

"That material doesn't look like it breathes too well," Meryl said.

"I'm sweating gallons under here," I told her. "And I think I've got the start of a rash."

"Looks like your boobs are going to explode out of there any minute," she said. "They are like springs strung tight. I keep staring at them, waiting for them to pop out like a jack-in-the-box."

Spencer shot a quick look at my cleavage and then turned to Meryl. "Ma'am, where are you going with that saw?" he asked her.

Meryl tucked it behind her back. "What saw?"

"See? Librarians are running around with saws," he said to me.

"Meryl, where are you going with the saw?" I asked diplomatically.

"To show those pagans once and for all the real reason why this mountain is sacred. That cult is dangerous. Did you hear what they did to Holly Firestone?"

"That might not be strictly their fault," I said.

"And Dulcinea," Meryl continued. "She's chewed off half her hair after what they did to her. The mayor is fighting mad about his donkey."

I nodded. "You shouldn't get between a man and his donkey," I said.

Chapter 19

✦ ♥ ✦

Why don't people find love? How does it get so bad that they have to come to us to help them discover their soul mate? So many reasons, dolly. So many reasons. Here's one reason: kvetching. If I had a dollar for every kvetch who walked into my house looking for love . . . Anyway, you know the type. They complain about everything. They whine. They say, "Why me?" A lot. Nothing is good enough for them. Nothing is the way it should be. It's never their fault, always someone else's. A kvetch is a kvetch until the day he dies. You can't change him. Let him kvetch until he gets tired. Then, if you want, if you need to, you can kvetch about him all you want.

Lesson 9,
Matchmaking Advice from Your Grandma Zelda

IT TOOK awhile, but Spencer convinced Meryl to hand over the saw. Then he started the car up again and peeled out of the parking lot while he whistled a tune. I think it was a Nicki Minaj song.

"You're in a good mood," I noted.

"You're not?"

"I have to see the dentist, there's a killer on the loose, and I'm hungry."

"I can solve the third problem," he said. "I'll take you to Herbie's Hoagies. I hear he's got a new meatball sub that's out of this world. Out of this world!" he repeated, and broke out in hysterics.

"You're back to your old self," I said. "You're not scared of your Facebook friends anymore?"

"They seemed to have quieted down after Rosalie stopped her rampage. Besides, I wasn't really scared of them."

"Are you kidding? I think you peed in your pants at one point."

Spencer put his arm around the back of my seat and leaned in close. "I love when you talk about my pants."

HERBIE'S HOAGIES and Pies had transformed itself into battle headquarters for the townsfolk. A sign on the front door read: WE RESERVE THE RIGHT TO REFUSE SERVICE TO ALL ALIEN LOVERS.

We grabbed a seat close to the counter, and Herbie himself took our order. "Holy cow, that's a bright color," he told me.

I had stuffed most of the skirt down under the table, but enough had poofed out to make me look like I was being strangled by a large pink inner tube.

"It's a maid-of-honor dress," I mumbled. I crammed a little more skirt down under the table.

"It's burning holes through my cataracts," Herbie said.

"It will be less painful if you're in the back, making our sandwiches," I said.

"Are you sure it doesn't go through walls? Like Superman's laser vision?"

Spencer patted my hand. "I think you look great," he said. His eyes flicked down to my cleavage. "Like you're some kind of deranged disco Scarlett O'Hara."

"Thanks, Spencer."

"Like Scarlett O'Hara on ecstasy."

"Thanks a lot."

"Also, in a pinch I could use you to control traffic at night," he added. "Or guide in aircraft."

"Are you done?"

Spencer tapped his forehead and looked up at the ceiling. "Um . . . ," he said. "No, I've got one more."

I put my hand over his mouth. "Save it. Unless you want to sing soprano in the Vienna Boys' Choir, I would be quiet if I were you."

Herbie's meatball hoagie was delicious, even though my tooth shot pain into my head with every bite. I could feel my body swell up after eating a half of a sandwich, my breasts pushing upward against the bodice. I needed to get out of the dress as soon as possible before I popped out altogether. I caught Spencer ogling my chest, his eyes moving with the rise and fall of my breathing.

"Your dress is growing on me," he said, his mouth full of sandwich. "I'm not at all embarrassed to be seen with you anymore."

"Hard to believe women were chasing you," I said. "I could understand if they were fleeing *from* you."

Spencer downed his root beer and wiped his mouth. "So, what's new with you? I mean, besides the dress and the tooth and loverboy."

"Loverboy?" I didn't put it past Spencer to know every detail of my relationship with Holden, Holden's true identity, and the fact that he was leaving town. But there was a chance Spencer was in the dark about all of it, and I had made a promise to Holden not to say anything.

"Yeah, I don't want to hear about the neighbor," he amended. "How's the matchmaking going?"

I had almost forgotten that I had matched Belinda with George. My week wasn't a total bust after all.

The bell on the door rang as two women walked into the hoagie shop. The blonde and the brunette, both attractive and middle-aged and perfectly made up despite the rain, froze when they saw our table. "Look who it is. Spencer Bolton," said the brunette, approaching.

"Oh, Lord," I said to Spencer. "Tell me she's not holding a cleaver."

"Hi, Joanne," Spencer said to her. "You're looking good." He tapped his foot on the floor, and his knee knocked the table. Nervous.

"What the hell?" she said, noticing me.

"It's a maid-of-honor dress," I said. I had had enough. If I had had scissors, or at least a sharp knife, I would have cut myself out of the dress right then and there.

"Joanne unfriended you," the blonde announced. "So did half the women in this town."

"You're a Facebook pariah," Joanne said. "A leper."

It was meant to be a dramatic pronouncement, but I caught Spencer trying to hold back a smirk, the corners of his mouth curved up in a tiny smile.

"Come on, Joanne," the blonde said. "Let's grab a seat before it fills up."

The door dinged again and a large group entered.

"Wow, Herbie's meatball hoagie sure is popular," I said.

"I think something else is happening here," said Spencer.

He was right. The townspeople had united to strategize. So far they had failed miserably at getting rid of the cult, and it looked like the alien lovers had settled into Cannes for the long term. Not only was it upsetting to the day-to-day life in town, but the apple season was coming, and the cult invaders could possibly disrupt Cannes's number one moneymaker.

Spencer threw some cash on the table, stood, and put out his hand to help me up. "Let's get out of here before I hear something I shouldn't. I'm tired and want to call it a night."

"What time is it?"

It was seven forty-five. I had fifteen minutes to get to Bliss Dental. Not enough time to get home and have the dress removed.

"Maybe I should skip the dentist," I said. "Maybe my tooth will be better in the morning." With the moment upon me, I was gripped with fear. Not only did I not want to have dental work, I didn't want to go to Bliss Dental, especially at night.

"You can't chicken out now," Spencer said. "It's bad enough I am seen with you while you're wearing that dress. What would people say if you were toothless, too?"

"Well, I wouldn't want to sully your reputation, Spencer. Lord knows you're nothing without your reputation."

He held the door open for me, and I stepped outside. The rain had calmed down to a light misting, but it had turned cold. I shivered, and Spencer put his arm around my shoulders. He was warm and strong, and I could feel my hormones pop despite myself.

"I want to make sure you get there and stay there," he said. "That's why I'm going with you."

It was a thinly veiled act of kindness and sensitivity. I would feel a lot safer and more confident having Spencer with me.

"Don't say thank you," he said seriously. "It will give me a chance to study the scene of the crime, and besides, I might owe you for your hospitality."

He had a point. He did owe me, but nevertheless, I was grateful for his presence. It was nice to have someone look after me, especially after Holden's rejection.

Spencer was parked right outside. A steady stream of people walked by us on their way into Herbie's Hoagies and Pies. I was surprised to see Bridget and Lucy among them. They went right past us without recognizing me.

"Hey, it's me, Gladie!" I yelled after them.

They turned around and stared at me for a good minute.

"It glows at night. Amazing," Bridget said.

"I thought Calamity's wedding was tomorrow," Lucy said.

"It is."

"Can this wait?" Spencer asked.

"The cop!" Lucy shouted. "I thought you were hacked to death by your girlfriends."

"Buried under the pears," Bridget added. "How did you make it out?"

"I don't stay dead for long," he said. "We got to go. Gladie has a dentist appointment."

"The dentist was murdered, darlin'," Lucy said. "He was shot or hacked to death or something himself. Or did he cheat death, too?"

"Cause of death undetermined," Spencer said. "And I'm aware he was murdered."

"The replacement dentist, Lucy. Remember?" Bridget asked. "I'm glad Nathan set that up for you, Gladie."

Bridget offered to go with me, but I could tell she was chomping at the bit to see the excitement of the meeting to plan the town's last stand against the cult.

Spencer opened the passenger door of his car for me, and I got inside. It was only a ten-minute drive to Bliss Dental.

"NO LIGHTS outside, but I see a couple on inside," Spencer said, parking the car.

It was spooky, and I was having flashbacks to the night of the murder. Spencer read my mind. He took my hand and gave it a squeeze. "I won't leave you for a second," he said.

"Thanks."

"No problem. I'm hoping I can see up your skirt when you're lying on the chair."

Inside Bliss Dental, it was business as usual. Bright fluorescent lights blotted out any malevolent feeling, and I was calmer, almost relaxed. We were the only patients in the waiting room. Spencer sauntered over to the window separating the waiting room and Belinda's office and dinged the bell several times.

"You got a patient here!" he yelled toward the back.

My heart skipped a beat, and the meatball hoagie turned in my stomach. "We don't have to rush things," I said. "If he's busy, we can come back later."

I turned toward the exit, but Spencer caught my arm. "Not so fast, Disco Scarlett."

Nathan opened the door to the waiting room. He smiled when he saw me. "Here I am," he sang. "Sorry to keep you waiting. I was taking a dinner break. It's been crazy today. Back-to-back patients all afternoon and evening."

Nathan introduced himself to Spencer and shook his hand. "I'll bring her back," Nathan told him. "There's a couple magazines to read while you wait."

"I promised I would stay with her," Spencer said, much to my relief. "I won't get in your way."

Nathan smiled. "No problem. The replacement dentist is pretty laid back."

He took us down the hallway. Belinda's office was sad and empty. All traces of her deadly flower collection were gone.

I peeked in Dr. Dulur's office. The eighties-style pictures were off the wall and had been replaced with black-and-white posters of Paris, London, and other big cities. On his desk were a couple boxes and a computer.

"I'll have you wait in Exam Room One," Nathan said. "He went out to eat and will be back in a jiffy. It shouldn't be too long."

I was relieved to see the carpeting had been replaced, and there was a new chair in Examination Room 2. It was like nothing nefarious had ever happened at Bliss Dental. My blood pressure was almost normal.

"Hey, Nathan, do you mind if I use the computer while I wait for the dentist?" I asked.

"Sure. That shouldn't be a problem."

"I'll go with you," Spencer said.

"No, I'll be right back."

"You're not planning on making a run for it, are you?"

"No. In this dress, the wind would pick me up, and I would wind up in Chihuahua, Mexico, by morning. Hey, that's not such a bad idea."

"Fine. I have calls to make anyway," Spencer said.

Nathan set me up at Dr. Dulur's computer and went back to the exam room to keep Spencer company and to prepare for my filling. I closed the door to give myself extra privacy.

I quickly got to work. I Googled "William Burton," Holden's real name. I drummed my fingers on the desk while I waited for the computer to load. There were thousands of hits on his name.

Holden wasn't lying. He had been an explorer and a successful writer. I clicked on his picture, taken in the Congo on assignment for *National Geographic*. In the photo, he was dirty, unshaven, strong, handsome, and happy. A man like that could never be content in Southern California, I thought.

There were a slew of books by him, the big coffee-table kind, still for sale on Amazon. *GQ* interviewed him in an article on the "Last Real Men in America," and they had a photo of him, shirtless, on top of a mountain somewhere, his face tanned, his hair bleached by the sun. Happy.

And then there were the articles about the case. A

year ago, Holden was in the wrong place at the wrong time, and he witnessed a murder. A hit on a nightclub owner by the head of a crime syndicate. Big Joe Moretti himself had put two bullets in Danny Fiorelli's brain and one in his privates, in the alley behind Danny's nightclub while Holden happened to walk by.

Any sane man would have run in the other direction. But I guessed the last real man in America felt a duty to Danny's family and to justice, and Holden called the cops and testified against Big Joe at trial, knowing that he risked his life by doing so.

Big Joe threatened Holden during the trial. "You're dead, Mountain Boy!" he yelled in the courthouse. "Dead! You hear me?"

Holden was heard to reply, "You're a punk, Joe. I'm not scared of punks."

That was the last anyone ever heard of William Burton. He vanished off the face of the earth. So did Big Joe. He escaped with the help of some dirty cops before his trial was over. There had been reported sightings of him in the Cayman Islands since, but they weren't taken seriously.

Nothing on the Internet about Becky.

I could have Googled Holden for hours. Finally I had the answers to the questions I had been asking for the past month. Finally I knew who my boyfriend was and what he did for a living. Only now he wasn't my boyfriend anymore. Now he didn't live next door, at least not for the time being. I didn't want to stop snooping into his life.

My dress was digging into me something awful, and I adjusted the bodice to give myself some room to breathe. That's when I saw the framed photos in one of the boxes on the desk.

Dr. Dulur on vacation on a beach somewhere. Dr. Dulur at a dinner party, when he was much younger, smiling, his receding hairline already pronounced. Dr. Dulur at Bliss Dental when it first opened.

I was hit with a lightning bolt of realization so strong that I jumped up from my seat. I covered my mouth with my hands to stifle a scream that was threatening to escape.

I knew who the killer was. Knew it as sure as I knew anything in the world. And I probably knew the motive, too.

"Spencer!" I croaked. "Spencer! Hurry! Help!" It all came out in a strangled whisper. I tried to clear my throat, but I couldn't get sound out. I stood frozen in my spot, my chest heaving, pushing against Calamity Weiss's maid-of-honor dress.

Nathan opened the door and peeked his head into the office. "You ready?"

"Did the dentist come back?"

"He called. He's on his way. Let's get you set up."

"Well," I said, "maybe today isn't such a great day for dental work."

"No time like the present," Nathan said, his face all smiles and delight.

Then I found my voice. "Spencer!" I screamed. "Spencer!" I screamed so loud, I could hear the walls reverberate.

I stood back, expecting Spencer to burst through the office door. But there was nothing. Not a sound in answer to my screams.

Nathan raised his right eyebrow. "Is there something wrong?" he asked me.

"Spencer?" I called again. Still nothing.

I took a few more steps back until I reached the window. Quickly I tried to open it to make my escape.

"The window doesn't open," Nathan said. "The office is climate controlled. Why don't you come with me, Gladie, and I'll prep you for your filling?"

I let go of the window and turned around. "Where's Spencer?"

"He's resting. Are you okay? You look like you've seen a ghost." He took a step toward me.

"Don't come any closer," I said. "I'm not feeling well. I think I'll go now. Stand back."

"I'm sorry you don't feel well, but I'm going to have to prep you now."

I dashed to the left and knocked the box of photos onto the floor.

"Don't touch that!" Nathan yelled. "Those aren't yours."

He moved toward the pictures, and I made a run for it out the door. I made it two steps into the hallway, but I got tangled up in the tulle and the dress took me down.

Nathan stood over me, a framed photo in one hand and a needle in the other. "Why are you making this hard?"

He looked at the photo, and his smile vanished. He tossed the photo aside and ordered me to get up. It wasn't easy to maneuver in the dress, and he lost patience with me. He yanked at my arm, and I yelped in pain.

"I prepared Exam Room One for you," he said, like I had hurt his feelings. He pushed me toward the room. On the floor with his back to the wall was Spencer. He was unconscious; a small trickle of blood flowed from his temple down his cheek. A gas mask was tied to his face, and he was trussed up like a Christmas goose.

"Spencer?" Tears bubbled up, and my throat was thick with emotion. "You didn't, did you?" I asked Nathan.

"Not yet," Nathan said, and pushed me down onto the chair. I studied Spencer and was relieved to see his chest rise and fall with his steady breath.

"You know something? My tooth pain is completely gone. Completely. I don't think I need a filling anymore," I said.

"You never needed a filling," Nathan said, matter-of-fact. "Dr. Dulur liked to drum up business any way he could."

I was truly outraged. "That's terrible!" The pain in my tooth vanished like it had never existed.

"Yes! He was a bad man. A bad, bad man!"

It was a common refrain. There was no shortage of people who wanted to tell me just how bad Dr. Simon Dulur was.

"So, he deserved to die," I said.

Nathan nodded.

"Even if he was your father," I added.

He stumbled backward. "What do you mean?"

I sat up in the chair. "I thought you looked familiar, but I couldn't figure out from where. Until I saw the photos. Duh. You look just like him, like Dr. Dulur. You're his son. You told me you were an orphan. Did you know before you came here and took the job that he was your father, or did you find out after you started working here?"

A perfect tear rolled down Nathan's cheek. "I found out before. He didn't know."

"I figured he didn't know. He wasn't the most paternal figure in the world. I mean, he was known for hurting children."

"I didn't know that until after," Nathan said.

"Until after you killed him," I supplied. "When did you tell him you were his son? Was it while I was under the gas?"

Nathan nodded. "I thought he would be happy. He had said I was a good assistant. I thought he liked me."

"So, he wasn't pleased to be approached by a long-lost son?"

"He called me a leech. And worse. He said he would call the police and tell them I was extorting money from him."

Nathan was crying in earnest now. He wiped his nose with the sleeve of his shirt. *That's not very hygienic if he's going to work on my teeth,* I thought, like a crazy woman.

"So, you killed him? How? You hit him over the head?" I asked. I tried to think of a way to wake Spencer up so he could save me. What was the good of knowing the chief of police if he let himself get knocked out by a psychopathic killer?

Nathan sniffed. "No, I stabbed him in the eye with a big shot of novocaine. Went right through. It wasn't hard at all."

The memory seemed to please him. He stopped crying altogether and wiped his eyes with the hem of his shirt. He sobered up and seemed to notice me for the first time in a long time.

"Uh, Nathan, is there a replacement dentist?" I asked.

"I think he's coming next Thursday."

"Oh." It was my time to wipe my nose, but I didn't want to wipe it on Calamity's dress. I guess I still held out hope of making it to her wedding. "Are you going to kill me?"

"Yes."

I gulped. I thought of being stabbed in the eye, of having my face cut off. None of it was any good. *I should have had dessert at dinner,* I thought. *Why didn't I get one of Herbie's pies?*

"Is that when Holly arrived? After you stabbed him in the eye?" I asked.

"No," Nathan said, taking a seat. "She came in when I was cutting off his face. He kept staring at me. And it was my face. He didn't deserve to have my face."

"He was a crappy dad."

"Yeah."

"So, you got Holly to stash the face for you and what

else . . . give you an alibi? Give you an injury that couldn't possibly be self-inflicted?"

"Hey, you're smart," Nathan said. "You figured it all out. I heard your grandmother was a witch. Are you a witch, too?"

I wished I was a witch. I would have turned him into a frog, or woken up Spencer, or given myself perfectly flat abs.

Spencer's cellphone went off. I willed Spencer to wake up, but the gas was doing its job. He didn't stir. Just as soon as the phone stopped, it rang again.

"Should we get that?" I asked Nathan. "It could be an emergency."

"I don't care."

"What I can't understand is why Holly went through with it," I said. "The fact that Dr. Dulur wasn't a nice guy isn't enough of a reason. Unless . . . ," I said.

I stood up and wagged my finger in the air, like I was excited by my idea. "You knew about the embezzling, and you threatened her with it. You forced her hand."

"And then she changed her mind," he said. "Said she didn't care if she went to jail, that I was crazy and needed to be stopped. Crazy! Can you believe that?"

I could believe that very easily. Nathan Smith was nuttier than a fruitcake. "No, of course I don't believe you're crazy," I said. I bunched up my skirt in my hands, raising up the dress from the floor ever so slightly.

"She tried to hide out with the cult, but I found her."

"And you shot her," I said.

"I almost shot you, too. When I saw you two together, I thought, 'This is too good. I can get two busybodies at once,' but I couldn't get a clear shot at you after I took Holly down."

I swallowed. "I could go for some water," I said.

"You'll be dead soon. You won't be thirsty then."

Nathan was nothing if not pragmatic. He was getting

very good at killing people. "If you think I'm a busy-body, why did you come to my house that night with the face?"

"To scare you. To get you to stop sticking your nose in. Besides, it started to smell. The cop was a surprise." A tear rolled down Nathan's cheek. "He didn't love me."

Spencer's cellphone went off again. "Would you like a tissue?" I asked Nathan. I bent down to get a Kleenex and then I was off, running down the hallway for all I was worth. Suddenly the lights went out. I dropped to the ground and crawled into Dr. Dulur's office.

"Where are you going, Gladie?" Nathan called. His voice drew nearer. "Why are you making this hard? I have to kill you. I knew you had it figured out. You've got your grandmother's gift. That's why I brought you the face. I figured you could do something with it, maybe change him. You know what I mean?"

I heard him shuffle into the office. I heard a click and then the beam of a flashlight illuminated the room. I crouched in a corner.

"I can kill you in here if you prefer," he said. "I have a knife. I'm going to slit your throat. It will probably cut like butter. I got a lot of practice from Simon's face."

What a lousy way to die, I thought, crouching in the corner of the office, the tulle of Calamity's dress billowing up around me. And what about Spencer? Would Nathan kill him, too? That would be my fault, because he came to Bliss Dental to be with me and I got him killed. I started to cry.

I didn't want Spencer to die, and I didn't want to die. Not even from old age. I wanted to live forever. Like *Fame.*

Nathan approached me, shining the light in my face. I could make out the long knife in one of his hands. *That will be the knife that kills me,* I thought.

"I know the truth," I said. "The murder was premeditated. You planned it out way before you confronted him. *If* you confronted him."

Nathan grew agitated. "That's not true."

"You sent Belinda on a wild-goose chase to get that flower. You knew Holly would be at the bar, and you took something from her—her phone or her keys or something—so she would have to come back. And me, well, I was a surprise, but the gas fixed that, and it was good to have a witness to prove your innocence."

"I spent my life in the system. You can't imagine what I lived through," he said.

"I'm sorry."

"And then I found out my father was living in the lap of luxury the whole time."

"And he was a bastard to boot," I said.

"A sadistic bastard!"

"So you planned it all."

Nathan nodded. "It took months to plan it."

"And you took his face," I said.

"That was just for fun."

I shivered. Nathan was bonkers, a crazy, twisted loon who could give Jeffrey Dahmer a run for his money in the nutso department.

"And you always planned to kill Holly eventually."

Nathan gestured with the knife. "I'm going to kill her at the hospital as soon as I'm done with you and the cop. You got in my way last night."

"The night you came over with the scarecrow, did you plan to kill me that night?"

"Nah, I liked playing with you. You're fun." Nathan scratched his nose with the back of his hand. "But I'm done playing with you," he said. "I've got to finish this up."

I tried to think quickly for a way out, but Nathan and

his big knife were in the way. I whimpered, sure in the knowledge that I was about to die.

And then there was a loud explosion as the front door of Bliss Dental was thrown open and ear-splitting screams pierced the quiet of the building.

"We're here! We're here! We'll save you!"

"Darlin', I will not get through killin' that psychopathic looney tunes killer!"

Bridget and Lucy ran through the waiting room with flashlights blazing and stopped short when they saw Nathan with the knife.

"Stand back!" shouted Bridget. "I'm trained in the art of Krav Maga!"

"Somebody get the lights!" I yelled.

"I'm on it!" Lucy called out, and ran for the breaker box.

"If you move, I will kill her," Nathan told Bridget.

"No, you won't. I have lightning-fast reflexes," she said. "Krav Maga is all about kill or be killed, and you're going down, little man."

Her face was set in stone. I hadn't seen her so serious and focused since the Planned Parenthood rally during the summer.

The lights came on, and Lucy ran back into the room. She held a gun in one hand.

"Look what I found!" she announced.

"That's Dr. Dulur's weapon," Nathan said. "It's not loaded."

"Oh," Lucy said, disappointed. She threw it down on the floor, and it went off, shooting Nathan in the leg. He dropped to the floor, writhing in agony. Bridget sat on him and told him to shut up while she called the police on her phone.

"Is that the art of Krav Maga?" I asked her. "Where did you learn that?"

"Yes, two lessons at the rec center," Bridget said. "It came in handy, right?"

I hugged Lucy. "Good shooting, Annie Oakley," I told her. "Oh my God, Spencer!"

I ran into the other room and took the gas mask off Spencer. I was pleased to see that his bleeding had stopped. "Wake up, Spencer!" I called. He stirred, and his eyes opened.

"Oh, thank goodness you're okay," I said. I gave him some water and told him all about Nathan being the killer and how he had used Holly to give him an alibi. Spencer stared at me without saying anything.

"Are you okay? Can you speak? Do you have a concussion?" I asked him.

"What?" he said finally. "I didn't hear a word you said. Your boob popped out of your dress ten minutes ago."

Chapter 20

✦ ♥ ✦

*Men and women are different. Bodies: different.
Minds: different. It makes matchmaking a big headache, I
can tell you. Even how they fall in love: different. A man
will see a woman and within three seconds, he knows if he
wants her, loves her, and whether she should be the mother
of his children. But a woman needs a double-blind study,
a note from her preacher or the president of the United
States. She needs to plan, research, test, and deduce. A
woman, quite simply, can't make up her mind. Sometimes
I want to shake them and say, "Nu? Enough already.
Make a decision. Do you like him or not? It's no longer
chapter one, bubeleh. Finish it up. Make it the end already."*

Lesson 82,
Matchmaking Advice from Your Grandma Zelda

MIRACULOUSLY, SPENCER didn't even need a
stitch. "It's a good thing you have such a hard head," I
told him.

After a checkup at the hospital, and hours at the station
filling out reports, he was allowed to drive himself home.

Bridget, Lucy, and I gave the police our statements.
Bridget and Lucy explained that they had seen Belinda
at Herbie's, and she told them the replacement dentist
hadn't arrived yet. Lucy and Bridget put two and two
together and came to my rescue.

Besides the boob incident, my dress came out unscathed. It must have been made of some supersecret material developed by NASA or the CIA, I guessed. Bridget and Lucy drove me to my grandma's house, and since it was nearly sunrise, we decided to keep me in the dress until the wedding was finished mid-morning. Meanwhile, we made a big breakfast and told Grandma all about our adventures.

Bridget regaled her about her Krav Maga skills, and Lucy described her shooting ability as if they were the Green Hornet and Kato at the O.K. Corral. I enjoyed the company at Grandma's table. I was happy and content, despite all the upheaval in my life.

IT WAS good to feel safe again. Nathan Smith was spending the first of many nights at a psych ward in San Diego. After the hospital in Cannes treated him for his leg wound, he went off in such detail about cutting off his father's face, they decided he needed to be hooked up to a Thorazine drip in a rubber room somewhere.

"Here's to a mouth without cavities," I said, lifting up my coffee mug. "That's the one piece of good news from last night."

"To oral hygiene," Lucy said, and clinked her mug against mine.

I drove out to Trouble Weiss's house for Calamity's wedding. Cannes looked like it had been hit by a nuclear explosion. Papers littered the streets, and there was a post-apocalyptic feel to the place. I stopped at Tea Time to fortify myself with one of Ruth's lattes. I was bone tired from staying up all night, more exhausted still in the aftermath of all that adrenaline from the night before.

Tea Time was back to normal. No more naked people, or color-coded people. No whispers of "the Arrival" as I entered. Ruth stood behind the counter, wiping it down, her familiar scowl on her face.

"The usual?" she asked me.

"No argument for me today, Ruth? No lecture on the depravity of drinking coffee?"

"I figure you got enough problems, considering your wardrobe and all," she said, pointing at my dress. I had been wearing it for so long, I had almost forgotten I had it on. It would be a relief to get it off, though. I couldn't wait to get my hands on a pair of scissors and cut it off in one swipe.

"I appreciate it. I'm maid of honor in Calamity's wedding."

"Lucky you. I'd rather have my eyes eaten by wild dogs than go anywhere near Trouble Weiss. No more vile woman has ever existed." Ruth handed me my latte. "But she makes good chocolate, I'll give her that."

"Hey, no cult this morning, I see."

"Gone," Ruth said. "They filed out of town in the early morning, around sunrise. Just packed up their yurts and went on their way."

"Did the aliens come? Is it the end of the world?" I wouldn't have been surprised if either or both had happened. It had been a very strange week.

"I don't give a damn either way," Ruth said. "Just glad I've got my shop back. I'd even prefer coffee drinkers to those freaks."

Outside, the street sweepers had been called in. They motored down Main Street sucking up the papers and washing away the dirt and debris from five days of battle between cultists and townspeople.

I sipped my latte and enjoyed the fresh air. Autumn was coming fast. Apple season was around the corner, the time Cannes did best. Just the thought of it made me feel cozy. Soon the days would be filled with apple-themed events and the nights filled with hot apple cider and bonfires. Life was pretty good. Sure, Holden had left town, but I had good friends, and my second real match under my belt.

Maybe there was another hideous maid-of-honor dress in my future, maybe for Belinda's wedding.

I got back in my car as the stores began to reopen. Shell-shocked store owners opened their doors with a last look around, as if they expected alien lovers to drop down from the sky. But the cult had definitely left, and it was just a matter of time before the town shook off the last vestiges of the alien invasion and got back to their small-town way of life.

I started up my engine with a roar, just as Meryl the librarian stopped by me on the sidewalk and stuck her head in through my open window.

"Did you hear?" she asked me over the sound of my engine. "We won! We won! They scrammed this morning!"

"How did you do it?" I envisioned a D-Day attack, plotted and planned at Herbie's Hoagies and Pies the night before. "Did you pull out the big guns last night?"

"No, we had the night off. They just ran off. They finally got the picture. The mayor says he told them, 'This mountain isn't big enough for the both of us.' You understand?"

"I understand."

"Now the mayor is a shoo-in for reelection in November. You hear the latest about Holly Firestone?"

"Is she doing better?"

"Yep, breathing on her own. Came out of the coma with a cockamamie story about Nathan Smith and the dentist's face."

I didn't have the heart or the energy to tell Meryl that Holly was telling the truth. Besides, it would all come out in a day or two. She could read it in the paper.

"That's not the craziest thing," Meryl added. "They

found out at the hospital that Holly is six months pregnant. Six months! She had no clue. She almost stopped breathing when they told her."

"Who's the father?"

"No idea, but there's good money on the bartender at Bar None. Although I've heard whispers that the old dentist was the father."

Gosh, I hoped not. If it was the bartender, Holly could get free drinks.

I said goodbye to Meryl and made it to Trouble's house by ten o'clock. The wedding wasn't half bad. Calamity wore a huge wedding gown with a hooped skirt and parasol. Trouble had made a wedding canopy out of pure milk chocolate.

Calamity's husband turned out to be Josh White, a gorgeous stockbroker who had made so much money on Wall Street, he retired at twenty-five and moved to Cannes, into one of the McMansions just outside of town.

He never stopped talking, which seemed all right to Calamity, who never stopped listening to him with a smile on her face. Never saying a word.

After eating a big slice of Trouble's chocolate cake with chocolate mousse filling and chocolate fudge icing, I headed home. I planned to cut myself out of the dress, take a hot shower, and sleep until the next day.

My plans were derailed, however, when I drove into my driveway and saw Holden's truck parked next door. I ran into the house, up the stairs to the attic, and spied on him through the window. He threw a duffel bag in the back of his truck. He sensed my gaze, looked up at me, and waved.

Sometimes it's better to throw caution to the wind, to stop analyzing life and just live it. Either because of exhaustion or common sense, I got to that point that morning.

I ran downstairs and out the door.

. . .

I RANG the doorbell, and he opened the door. He was relaxed, wearing jeans and a sweater. He ran a hand through his hair when he saw me, and arched an eyebrow. Surprised.

"The cult's gone," I announced. "The mayor got rid of them."

"Is that so?" He arched his eyebrow again.

"Why? Do you know something I don't?" I asked.

"Maybe I got rid of the cult, not the mayor. Maybe it was my gift to the town. So it wouldn't have any more fires or flying donkeys. Anyway, Mr. Steve is wanted on five felony counts of grand larceny. His real name is Fred Lewiston. When he found out I was onto him, he left in a hurry."

"Crazy week, huh?" I said.

"I think you make people go crazy, Pinkie. Lots of people, not just me."

"You make a lot of people go crazy, too, Spencer."

"So, to what do I owe this honor?" he asked.

I took a deep breath, but no words came out. Our eyes locked, and my body grew warm.

"I just came over to see what you think," I said.

"Oh, yeah? This is a first."

"So, what do you think?"

Spencer studied me a moment and then leaned in close to me. "My dear disco Scarlett," he said, caressing my cheek. "I think you should be kissed and often and by a man who knows how."

"Fiddle-dee-dee," I said. "Sounds good. You got any scissors?"

I walked into his house, and he closed the door behind us.

Acknowledgments

The author gratefully acknowledges the following people for their assistance: Junessa Viloria, my wonderful, patient editor, who knows all the juicy details; all the editors at Ballantine; godsend associate publisher Gina Wachtel; Random House art director Pablo Picasso . . . I mean, Lynn Andreozzi; production editor Beth Pearson; Alex Glass, the agent of my dreams, and everyone at Trident Media; my beta reader Maria Sanminiatelli, who read the whole thing at the beach; my boys . . . again; Ruth Aguilar, for trying to straighten my hair; and my father, who wasn't Citizen Pain. A special acknowledgment to Stephanie Newton, who walked with me through the cancer book. Finally, thank you to the poor unfortunate donkey, who really did fly.

Read on for an exciting preview
of the next book
in Elise Sax's Matchmaker series

Available from Ballantine Books

Chapter 1

✦ ♥ ✦

Everyone talks about the calm before the storm, but no-body warns you about the calm after the storm, bubeleh. I know . . . I know . . . storms are scary. All that wind blows you to hell and gone and can turn you upside down. Drown you. But in love, dolly—and in matchmaking—drowning can be a good thing. Things should be stirred up. Things should be moving. Chaos is love's friend. You know what I mean? So if your matches are drowning, if they are having their kishkes blown to smithereens, that might be a good thing. Be happy for storms in your matches' lives. Be happy for the couples who are holding on for dear life. But if the wind changes and it becomes dead calm, dolly, be afraid. Be very afraid.

Lesson 57,
Matchmaking Advice from Your Grandma Zelda

I SCREAMED and threw a bucket into the corner of the shed. I heard Grandma's designer heels *click-clack* on the stone walk toward me.

"Don't worry, there's nothing poisonous in there," she called in my direction. "Not since the end of rattle-snake season."

I didn't know there was a rattlesnake season in Cannes, California. I had moved to the small mountain village only five months ago to live with my grand-mother and work in her matchmaking business. If I had known there was a rattlesnake season, I might have stayed in Denver to work on the cap line at the plastic bottle factory for more than the six weeks I was there.

I raised the can of bug spray above my head as a warning to all the creepy crawlies in Grandma's shed. There were a lot of them.

"Are you sure rattlesnake season is over?" I asked as she opened the door wider and peeked her head inside. She was decked out in what I suspected was a Badgley Mischka wedding dress, two sizes too small, her flesh threatening to burst out of the seams.

"Normally it's over by the beginning of October," she said, adjusting her lace bodice. Grandma was a lot of woman, but she had style and was never caught out of her house without full makeup and at least a fake designer ensemble. Not that she ever got past her property lines. She was a homebody—what people uncharitably described as a shut-in. It didn't matter, though—the town came to Grandma, as she was the indispensable matchmaker and all-around yenta. And she knew things that couldn't be known.

"*Normally* it's over?" I asked, peering into the corners of the shed.

"The last one slithered out of here at least a week ago," she said, certain of herself.

I screamed and sprayed the wall. "There's spiders the size of Rhode Island in here."

"If you don't like spiders, don't open your red suitcase, dolly," she told me, shaking her head. "There's some nasty ones in there."

My sweaters were also in the red suitcase. And my good coat. The weather in Cannes had turned cold with the arrival of apple season, and I had been wearing the same Cleveland Browns sweatshirt every day for the past week and a half. It was time to unpack my winter clothes, but I didn't know if I was brave enough to fight off nasty spiders for a wool coat.

"You could borrow something of mine," Grandma told me, seemingly reading my mind. "I have a lovely velour jacket with feather detailing that's very warm, and it's just attracting moths in my closet."

"Hold your breath, Grandma," I said. "I'm going in." I took a gulp of fresh air and started spraying. I made it to the red suitcase, doused it with the last of the poison, grabbed the bag by the handle, and shot out of the shed like a bullet.

Grandma looked down at the dripping suitcase. "Yep, there are some nasty ones in there," she said.

I TOSSED the suitcase in the trunk of my Oldsmobile Cutlass Supreme and closed it successfully after three tries. The rust had overtaken my old silver car, making it look two-tone, with large red rusty patches. I had never minded the rust, but now it had infected the lock on the trunk, making it nearly impossible to close.

"I'll have Dave open the suitcase," I told Grandma. Dave was the owner and operator of Dave's Dry Cleaners and Tackle Shop. He was both fastidious and a lover of bugs. My suitcase was right up his alley, and I would have my winter clothes back clean and pressed within twenty-four hours.

But Grandma wasn't paying attention to me. She stood in the driveway, ramrod-straight, her head raised up and her eyes closed. A cool breeze blew against her bouffant hairdo, making it stir ever so slightly.

"Something wrong?" I asked her.

"The wind has shifted," she said.

"Don't I know it. What a relief." September had been chaos. The whole town had gone crazy. But now we were a week into October, and it was calm and relaxed.

Cannes had settled into its Apple Days events, and apple cider and apple pie were being sold at just about every store in the historic district. Everyone was in a good mood, including me.

In fact, I was in the best mood I had been in since my three days as a cashier at a medical marijuana dispensary in Monterey. My bank account was finally in the black, and I was starting to think I might have the hang of the matchmaking business. My last match was working like gangbusters. Even though it had been years since I'd settled down in one place for more than a couple of months, Cannes was starting to grow on me. It was starting to feel like home.

"An ill wind," Grandma muttered.

I turned my face to the breeze. I could smell the fires coming from the neighbors' fireplaces, nothing else. Nothing out of the ordinary.

"Isn't it time for the Dating Do's and Don'ts class?" I asked.

"Nobody's coming."

"What?" Grandma's house was usually Grand Central, with no end to singles coming to her in their journey to find love.

"Not today. Nobody."

"Did you cancel it?" I asked. "Are you feeling all right?"

Grandma ignored me and walked up the driveway to the front door. I could hear the rustle of her pantyhose as she walked, her thighs rubbing against each other. It was unusual behavior for my grandmother, and I was following her into the house when I heard a car horn.

The sound got louder until finally the most beautiful Mercedes I had ever seen barreled around the corner and up onto the curb at the bottom of the driveway. Without turning off the motor, my friend Lucy Smythe hopped out.

"Help! Now! Come!" she shouted in my direction. Despite her panic, she was impeccably dressed, not a hair out of place, her face made up to perfection.

"Wow, is that a new car?" I asked her.

"Don't just stand there, darlin'. Get in the car."

"What's the matter?"

Lucy stomped up the driveway and tugged at my arm. "No time to talk. Come along."

"I'm on my way to Dave's. I have spider clothes that need to be cleaned."

Lucy seemed to notice me for the first time. My hair was tied in a frizzy ponytail on the top of my head. I was wearing my threadbare Cleveland Browns sweatshirt, torn jeans, and slip-on sneakers.

"What's that smell?" she asked me.

"Bug spray," I said. "I might have gotten some on me."

"You smell like citrus death." She waved her hands in the air. "No time to change."

She pushed and pulled me until I was sitting in the calfskin leather passenger seat of her salmon-colored Mercedes. "My butt is warm," I noted.

"There's also a massage setting." She pushed a button on what looked like the control panel of a fighter jet, and my butt started to vibrate.

"Oh, that's nice," I said.

"Bridget says Mercedes has made a leap toward women's sexual independence," Lucy said. Bridget was our friend, my grandmother's bookkeeper, and a militant feminist.

Lucy raced down the street, driving erratically and nearly clipping a garbage can as she turned the corner. I snapped my seat belt into place.

"Is someone dying? Has someone been murdered?" I asked Lucy. It wasn't a stretch. Since I arrived in Cannes, I had come across a few dead bodies. I was getting a reputation.

"No, why? Have you heard something?"

"No. Should I have heard something?"

Lucy was sweating, and she hadn't blinked since she started driving. It was out of character for her, to say the least. She wasn't the erratic kind of woman. She was a very successful marketer, whatever that was. She was a southern belle who had traveled the world and was calm in every situation.

In fact, I had only seen her flustered on one occasion.

"Lucy, does this have something to do with Uncle Harry?" I asked. Uncle Harry wasn't really Lucy's uncle. He was a magnetic older man with a fortune from a questionable source. He lived in a giant house east of town with man-eating Rottweilers, a gate, and a security man named Killer. Okay, I didn't know the security guard's name, but he looked like a Killer.

At the mention of Uncle Harry, Lucy's eyes glazed over and her hands slipped off the steering wheel. She let out a squeak, as if she were a Kewpie doll and someone had given her a hard squeeze.

"Coffee!" I shouted in warning, but it was too late. Despite Lucy coming to her senses and slamming her foot down against the brake pedal, the front door to the Tea Time tea shop sped toward us, or at least it seemed that way. Actually, it was Lucy's car that sped toward Tea Time's front door, but in the end it was the same thing. The salmon-colored Mercedes with the warming vibrator tushy seats pulverized the massive wood doors of Tea Time and took large chunks of the walls with it.

Tea Time used to be a saloon back when Cannes was a Gold Rush town in the 1800s, but now it was all lace tablecloths, yellow painted daisies, porcelain teapots on every table, classical music piped in at a respectable level, and a rack of crocheted tea cozies for sale at ludicrous prices. It was owned by eighty-five-year-old Ruth Fletcher, a crotchety old lady who despised coffee drinkers. Despite Tea Time's name and Ruth's demeanor, it had the best coffee in town.

I stumbled out of the car, past the deflated air bags and the debris. Miraculously, no one was hurt. The shop had been experiencing a lull in the day, and there were only two people in the shop. Ruth and her danger-prone grandniece, Julie, stood behind the intact bar, their mouths hanging open, the sunlight filtering past the dust through the gaping hole in the wall and onto their shocked faces.

Lucy opened her car door and hobbled out. One of her slingback heels was broken, making her limp. Besides that and her toppled hairdo, she was unscathed.

I saw red. "My coffee!" I yelled at Lucy. "You killed my coffee!" I couldn't live without my coffee, and Ruth made the best lattes on the planet. I needed Ruth's lattes.

"I didn't do it!" Julie squealed, waking Ruth out of her stupor. Ruth threw down her bar towel and stomped over to us.

"This building has been in existence since 1872," she spat at me, her words coming out in clipped consonants as she gestured to Tea Time's destroyed front wall. "Had! Had been in existence!"

"Strictly speaking, I wasn't driving," I said.

"You're just like your grandmother," she said. "Wackos think they know everything. I bet she didn't guess this little event, did she?"

She had a point. Besides saying the wind had changed, it would have been useful to know not to get into the car with Lucy.

I pointed at Lucy. "She did it," I said.

Lucy swiped her hair out of her eyes. She climbed over the debris and hobbled toward us, rifling in her purse as she limped closer. She pulled out her wallet.

"I've got five hundred dollars here. Do you think that will cover it?" she asked Ruth.

I thought I saw steam come out of Ruth's ears. "This is a historic building in the historic district of a historic town," she said. "It will take at least a month to fix the damage, during which I will be out of business. There is no wall here!" she shouted, pointing at the hole that used to be Tea Time's front door.

"You have five hundred dollars in your purse?" I asked. For the first time in months, I was up-to-date on my bills, but I only had $7.50 on me. Marketing sure paid well. Whatever that was.

"I'm in a hurry," Lucy said. "I don't have time to stand here and chat, Ruth."

"Well, then maybe you shouldn't have taken a detour into my shop!" Ruth said, stating the obvious.

"Here's my insurance card. I've got to get to Uncle Harry. He's waiting. Come on, Gladie, let's go."

"Are you serious?" I stammered. "I'm not getting in a car with you!"

"Gladys Burger, did I not save your life not one month ago?"

And there it was, the trump card. Lucy and Bridget had come to my rescue a few weeks back, and I owed her one, to put it mildly.

"Okay," I said. "But not without coffee. I need coffee."

"Don't look at me!" said Ruth. "I'm not about to make you coffee."

I stared Lucy in the eye. "Not without coffee."

It turned out we couldn't start the car with the deployed air bags, and Lucy insisted we leave it there for the Mercedes dealership to come and tow away. We had to walk back to Grandma's to pick up my car. I remembered my red suitcase was in the trunk, but my desire for coffee far outweighed my desire for spider-free clothes, and I didn't think Lucy would take the time to stop at the dry cleaners.

Lucy said Cup O'Cake had fabulous coffee, and it was on the way to Uncle Harry's, just on the edge of the historic district.

"Can you make this jalopy go any faster, darlin'?" she asked me as I chugged down Main Street.

"Are you kidding me, Mario Andretti?"

"Sorry, I'm in a hurry."

"Yeah, I still don't know why. Can you tell me what's going on?"

Lucy dusted off a piece of my car's upholstery that had dropped from the ceiling onto her lap. "Uncle Harry called me and said to get over there right away and to bring you. He was very agitated, Gladie. I've never heard him like that. Flustered."

"Flustered" must have been the adjective of the day. First Grandma, then Lucy, and now Uncle Harry. Three people who were never flustered had suddenly turned flustered. So much for my relaxing apple days.

But from the looks of the historic district, the flustered stopped there. Despite the car accident, the ill wind, and whatever trouble Uncle Harry had, the town was calm, quiet, and doing what it did best. An influx of gentle tourists were eating apple pie, sitting at the outside tables at Saladz, a favorite hangout for Bridget, Lucy, and me.

Cannes was a small village in the mountains east of San Diego. It had had a couple years of prosperity during the Gold Rush over a hundred years before, but the gold ran out quickly, and the town settled into a relaxed state after that. Besides growing apples and pears, it welcomed tourists with its beauty, charm, and antique shops. It was usually very quiet and everyone got along. Not much flustering here.

"Take a right," Lucy instructed.

I turned onto Gold Digger Avenue. Cup O'Cake was on the corner in an old, small Victorian house. It took up the bottom story, and there were apartments on the floor above. The building was painted a bright cobalt blue with blood-red trim. A sign out front read CUP O'CAKE in green letters with the letter "O" replaced by a big cupcake. That cupcake looked damned good.

"I'm supposed to be on a diet," I said aloud, more to myself than to Lucy.

"Again? Darlin', you are on more diets than any skinny bitch I know."

"You think I'm skinny?" I asked, sucking in my stomach. I had put on a few pounds since moving to Cannes, regularly eating junk food with my grandma. I was actually looking for a new diet, something that worked. So far, I hadn't had any luck losing a pound.

"How many calories do you think are in a cupcake?" I asked Lucy.

"Fourteen thousand," she said, opening the door. A bell announced our entrance. Inside was serenity, bliss, and nirvana, all wrapped in an odiferous cloud of chocolate, vanilla, sugar, and yeast. And there was another smell, something really familiar.

"Coffee," I breathed in relief.

Cup O'Cake was laid out more like a large living room than a bakery. Big overstuffed chairs took up most of the floor space, all in bright colors, as if they were cupcakes themselves, left to sit around. Little coffee tables dotted the floor as well, covered in pretty tablecloths and books. There were books everywhere. The walls were lined with shelves bursting with them. The mantel over the fireplace was stacked high with books, too.

Hardbacks, paperbacks, reference, literature, and pulp. Books, everywhere.

A tiny thirtysomething woman with gorgeous long jet-black hair, wearing a brown sweater dress that practically swallowed her whole, picked up a book near me that I had been eyeing.

"That's a good one," she said. "Funny romantic mystery. You can borrow it if you wish."

"I'm not much of a reader," I said. Not since a failed one-week stint as a speed-reading teacher in Austin. I hadn't gotten past the training, and my migraine lasted three days.

Her face dropped in obvious disappointment. "Oh," she said.

"But sure, it looks great," I said, taking the book from her. I'm really bad about disappointing people. I'd rather move towns than disappoint someone. Perhaps I needed therapy.

Or a cupcake.

"Let me know how you like it," she said, her frown turning into a smile. "We can talk about it tomorrow, if you wish."

Drat, now I actually had to read the thing. It was about two inches thick. I wondered if I could find CliffsNotes online.

"I'm Felicia," she told me. "Felicia Patel. I help Mavis run Cup O'Cake. You look like you could use a cup of coffee."

I almost hugged her. I was so used to Ruth yelling at me every time I ordered a coffee. Since she only liked tea drinkers, I had to submit to abuse every time I wanted a latte. All I had to do for coffee at Cup O'Cake was read a book.

"We're in a hurry," Lucy said, adjusting her hair. "Make it to go."

"Sure, sure," Felicia said, still smiling. "It will take just a second."

Instead of a counter, there was a series of tables with assorted pastries and a large table with espresso machines.

"Give her the apple spiced latte, Felicia," an old lady around my grandmother's age told her. She smelled like White Shoulders and chocolate, and she had an air of fatigue about her.

"How are you, Lucy?" she asked. "Haven't seen you in a while."

Lucy looked at her out of the corner of her eye while she reapplied her lipstick in a hand mirror.

"Hi, Mavis. Running late. You know Gladie Burger?"

"Zelda Burger's granddaughter?" Mavis asked.

Everybody knew my grandmother, but I was pretty new in town, and I didn't know everybody. In fact, I didn't even know about Cup O'Cake.

"The matchmaker," Lucy said.

Mavis nodded. "Sure. Sure. You live in this town awhile, you hear about Zelda."

Felicia handed me a red-and-blue to-go cup and a red-and-blue polka-dotted box. "A little surprise for you," she said with a wink toward the box. "See you tomorrow?"

"Sure," I said, smiling. Sweat rolled down my back. I was having flashbacks to high school. . . . I had dropped out. Suddenly, the book felt like it weighed twenty pounds.

I handed her a five-dollar bill. Mavis waved it away. "On the house," she said. "First-time customers get special treatment."

Lucy pushed me out of the store. "We're really late now," she said, trying to open the locked car door. I unlocked it for her and took a sip of the latte.

"Holy crap, this is the best thing ever," I said. "It's not coffee. It's coffee candy."

"Drive!"

Halfway there, I convinced Lucy to open the box for me. She was afraid I would slow down to eat whatever fabulous thing they had given me, but I assured her I could eat while doing just about any activity.

It *was* fabulous. Some kind of apple cupcake with a crumble icing concoction that almost made me crash the car when I took a bite. Even better, there were three cupcakes.

"How come I never heard of this place?" I asked.

"It's pretty new," Lucy said. "A couple years. Mavis Jones is a doll. Felicia's a little odd, though—with all those books, I mean. But Mavis doesn't seem to mind. They're there all the time. You can buy cupcakes late into the night. They live upstairs in two of the apartments, and they'll open up for anyone with a craving."

It was dangerous information. What would I do with the knowledge that I could have coffee candy and cupcakes any time I wanted? "I won't fit through the door," I said. "Let's throw the rest out the window. My waistband is digging into my belly."

"Too late, Gladie. You ate all of them."

Uncle Harry lived farther up in the mountains, in a relatively new gated community of McMansions. His house was one of the biggest, with its own gate and security guard. It wasn't anything like Cannes. There was nothing quaint or old about it, but it was gorgeous.

We were stopped at the security shack in front of the house. The guard didn't seem too happy to see us. "We're expected," Lucy said, leaning toward my open window.

"You one of them?" the security guard asked, gesturing to our right. A group of about five elderly people stood on the sidewalk. They were talking among themselves and looking at their watches.

"We're expected!" Lucy said again. She was clearly agitated and, I thought, not above taking on the guard.

"We should be on your list," I pointed out.

We were. He waved us in, and that's when we saw the

two police cars and another car that I was more than familiar with.

"What the hell?" Lucy asked. "Should I call my attorney?"

Uncle Harry was standing on his front porch, surrounded by police. A very tall old lady stood over him, wagging her finger in his face. Uncle Harry seemed unconcerned as he took long drags of his cigar and blew them out at her.

I recognized all of the police officers. Unfortunately, I had had more than my share of dealing with law enforcement since moving into town.

"Lord have mercy, the cops," Lucy said. "Gladie, you distract them, and I'll get Harry to safety."

I rolled my eyes. "Uncle Harry looks fine, Lucy. Besides, how am I supposed to distract them?"

"Take your shirt off. Use your feminine wiles."

"I'm not going to use my feminine wiles." I wasn't sure I had any wiles, and if I did, I wasn't sure what I would do with them. Besides, wiles could be dangerous, and there was one person present who I needed to keep my wiles far away from.

Lucy jumped out of the car and ran toward the group. I followed her, wishing my suitcase had been spider-free and that I wasn't dressed like a homeless person.

Spencer Bolton, Cannes's chief of police and a womanizing, hottie hunk, turned sharply toward me as I approached. His mouth dropped open in surprise, and his chest inflated as he gulped air, making the fabric of his shirt stretch against its buttons. He made my blood pressure rise and my pulse race. I didn't want him to know how much I wanted to watch him strip naked while I ate chips, but I suspected he already knew. The familiar car was his.

"Uncle Harry, I'm here," Lucy said, stating the obvious. Gone was the sophisticated, sure-of-herself southern belle I had grown to know during the past five months, and in her place was a quivering five-foot-eight mass of Jell-O. Six feet even in her heels. Well, the unbroken heel, anyway.

Uncle Harry stood no taller than five foot four, his balding head reaching Lucy's sternum. Lucy giggled wildly when he said hello to her. I squidged my eyes, trying to see what she saw.

"Mr. Lupino, this development is an eyesore," the tall lady said to Uncle Harry. "A blot on the historic nature of our town. You are a cancer on this land. I cannot allow you to spread."

She sounded like Katharine Hepburn, with a wobble in her voice and a slight English accent. She was formidable even at her age and, I imagined, a force to be reckoned with. Even so, I took a cowardly step back in case Uncle Harry decided to shoot her or let loose his dogs.

"Mrs. Arbuthnot, would you excuse me?" Spencer asked the woman, and walked quickly toward me.

"I'm only here for moral support," I said, trying to duck behind Lucy.

He grasped my arm and pulled me away from the group. "Move!" he ordered the security guard and closed us in the guard's shack. There wasn't quite enough room in there for two. Spencer placed his hands on the wall above my shoulders and leaned in close.

"You have been avoiding me for weeks," he said. His breath was minty fresh and made me wish for Christmas so I could eat him like a candy cane.

"Have I?" I croaked.

"Yes. You know we have to talk about what happened."

"Don't worry about it, Spencer. Let's pretend nothing happened."

He leaned in closer, his lips almost touching mine. "I don't want to forget it," he said.